For Phae, who loved Cora very much.

And, as always, all that I do is for Terrence.

Moonlight Melodies
of
Copper & Pine

Alexandria V. Nolan

ISBN:0692535187
ISBN-13:978-0692535189

FIRST THOUGHTS

On Mackinac:
"It has the appearance of a fairytale island floating on the water which is so clear and transparent that you may see down to almost any depth, and the air above is as pure as the water that you may feel invigorated when you breathe it."
—Captain Frederick Maryatt, *Diary of America*, 1839

Under the greenwood tree
Who loves to lie with me,
And turn his merry note
Unto the sweet bird's throat,
Come hither, come hither, come hither:
Here shall he see
No enemy
But winter and rough weather
William Shakespeare, *As You Like It*, Act 2, Scene 5, Line 1

ACKNOWLEDGMENTS

I am grateful to the scores of people who listen to my book updates, who help to promote my work and who faithfully read my words(and pass it along to their friends!).

For the books of early Michigan that my father digs up out of archives and that lie forgotten on shelves. Tomes left in bookstores where he gathers them up, rescuing them, before sending them down to the blistering heat of Texas where I can read and research them.

A special thank you to my mother, who is my first set of eyes on a new book. Who finds the threads that don't make sense, and makes no bones about telling me so. Thank you for your honesty and criticism, even when I do not want to hear it, and scold you for telling me precisely what I need to hear.

For the dog and cats who keep me company as I type, type, type on my computer. The steadfast three that never desert me when I am busy, and are always happy to see me, even if I have been ignoring them all day.

Terrence. What can be said in acknowledgement to the man who makes my writing dreams possible? Not only supporting me in all things, but in the stalwart belief that what I write is important. Thank you.

PROLOGUE

She had heard the story of her birth so many times, that she almost felt like it was one of her own memories. The tale held a truth about her, an essential part of her being that sounded wonderful when woven out in her mother's singsong words, but didn't cling quite properly to her after the story was done. And so she had always begged for it to be recounted again and again, hoping to recapture something of the enchantment that trilled through her mother's voice.

Coralie Marguerite Ravensdale Delacroix was born two months too early. Her father, Jean-Luc, was away on a fishing boat with one of his river men, unusual for Jean, as he preferred the steady strength of the land. But as soon as the paddle of the canoe had grazed the water of the straits, his wife, Cora, had felt the stirring in her belly. She had called for Waseya, the half French-Menominee woman who had been her nurse and teacher when she was a child. The pains came too suddenly, too violently, all the joy of birth hushed in the rushed moments. The babe slipped out quickly, too quickly, an eerie silence greeting what should have been a chaotic and noisy birth. She did not breathe, did not stir, her pine-green eyes frozen in death that had never seen life.

Waseya had chanted and beat her chest, she had cursed the manitou and wailed that he had cheated his daughter, Coralie's mother Cora, out of one babe already, and that he could not keep the spirit of this new one for himself. She had kicked the doctor out, then she had built up the fire, and cut into her own flesh. This was not tribal magic nor any kind of native tradition. It was a much older enchantment, as old as the earth and older than the sky. Finally, she stuck an arrowhead into the fire and marked her wrinkled cheek with it. She had then marked Cora faintly behind the ear, and the baby's arm with the searing flint. All three women connected by fire and blood and flesh. The manitou spirit had been pleased by the offering, for all of the women contained the power of the island within them, and they had offered a fitting sacrifice.

Coralie had lived, but was marked forever. Not only by the arrow burned into her arm, but her sandy blonde curls had turned black. And as she grew older, one of her eyes had frozen into a cold, empty blue, while the other was as green as the Mackinac pine. As green as her father's.

And though her name might have been Coralie for her mother, and Marguerite after her grandmother, after that night the manitou knew her only as Raven.

The bird that straddles both worlds, the living and the dead.

:1:

Raven

It wasn't that Raven didn't love the trees as her mother did, or that the spirit of the island wasn't pulsing through her heart. It was only that the wind through the trees sang to her of other forests, other shadows beckoning for her footsteps to mark their pine-needle strewn floor. She knew, somehow, that her life was waiting for her to join it, away from these shores.

Her green eye saw the island as her father and mother did, the poetry and magic of its beauty. But her blue eye, so light as to be almost white, just the the softest periwinkle of a baby's veins through pearly skin, this eye saw differently.

This eye saw the secrets of the world that no living being should glimpse. Looking out from the cold, blue eye, Raven could see the color of a man's character. His or her secret self was illuminated in different shades around their person.

Her father was green. The green of the pines and summertime maple leaves. He was all that was calm and peaceful, strong and steady and gentle. Her younger brother, Jacques, had always been a dreamy turquoise, a mix of water and island. But since his 15th birthday, he'd gone fiery red around the edges. Burning with the desire to be a man, flaming brightly to take his place among those who had proved themselves worthy of respect.

A gossiping housewife might be a sickly green. The green of algae on standing water, the green of envy coming off of her in waves. A drunken man might be a fuzzy grey, his life and memory kept deliberately out of focus.

Every man's character had a color, and those shades were as recognizable to Raven as the sound of their voice or the features of their face. Cora, Raven's mother, was all colors. In the morning, she was the pink of dawn, and at noon the yellow of sunshine. At gloaming she would flash as violet as a Mackinac sunset, and when darkness fell, she was the sparkle of the stars and moonlight in the northern sky. Cora *was* the island, so in time with its changes that all of the colors were necessary to see her true self.

Raven's color was a smothering black. Smoky black tendrils shot from her fingers and sprang from her feet as she stepped. She was a woman touched by death, after all, and it clung to her still. An odd bedfellow, but one she'd grown as comfortable with as her own skin. She'd never known another soul with an aura of black, the dead having no color at all, and the deathly ill simply blurred before her. Waseya, her old nurse, said it was a gift—the kiss of the manitou, but Raven had always wondered if it was perchance a curse instead.

She had tarried in the forest a long while this morning—too long. In fact, she would be late if she did not hurry. But something stayed her tread on the well-worn path. Soft as a feather of a blackbird's wing, she felt a presence. Her gaze moved up, up, up the tree before her, and the ghost smiled down mischievously.

It was the form of an Indian boy, an Ottawa by

the beading on his moccasins. She had seen him there before, or sometimes the little spirit was trailing behind her Uncle Nicholas. He would be walking soundlessly a few steps behind her uncle, a sad smile upon his face, before he realized Raven or Cora could see him, and then he would vanish. Now, he was perched in the tree, and Raven made a mental note to ask her mother who he was, who he had been. But, this time, their eyes met, and he did not vanish.

Instead, his shadowy smile grew wider, and wordlessly the boy motioned toward the straits. His arm pointed, and the wind whispered, but in a language that Raven could not understand, no matter how hard she concentrated on the syllables it uttered. She looked back to the branch his legs had been so easily looped around, and instead saw only the robin, a sacred bird, looking back at her. His head cocked to the side, before taking flight without so much as a backward glance for Raven.

By the direction of the sun, she knew she would be very tardy in arriving to the mission school. Raven assisted in the schoolhouse in the afternoons, teaching the children that were too young to help their parents out-of-doors, or the children of the tribes whose parents saw the use in the white man's knowledge. She scurried back into town, her long dress dotted with a pattern of moss roses billowing in the whipping Mackinac winds. She needn't have bothered about being late, no one ever expected her to be punctual. She was met at the door by one of the other teachers, a young woman whose father had a shop near Uncle Nicholas' in town. Not a friend, for Raven was not in the habit of keeping them, but a friendly face after her ghostly encounter.

Hours later, twilight was falling over the the little main street of Mackinac. There were more and more people living in the town, and every year it sprawled farther into the island, but it still seemed small to Raven. It remained a wild place, pine covered with the whisper of spirits and woodland animals mingling among the trees and limestone cliffs.

She walked up the steps of her house on the edge of town, the green glow of her father evident on the porch. Her parents had lived here since before she was born. It was a ways outside the hum of town and the tinkling bells of shop doors. The backyard abutted the forest, appearing to be slowly swallowed by the wilderness. She sometimes found it difficult to believe that her mother lived indoors at all. Raven would observe Cora's shoulders relax when hiking the trails, her hair wild and flowing freely. Nothing about her was restrained, and Raven couldn't imagine her mother pulling the mass of black coils into anything more restricting than a loose plait or a low bun. Flowers bloomed beneath her feet, shoots would sprout from the snow in winter when she strolled past. The boughs of the trees bent to gently caress her olive cheeks with their leaves or lowered to shade her on sunny days. Cora Delacroix could almost be mistaken for a normal human being when she wasn't immersed in the wilderness. Though, even without her ice-blue eye Raven could have seen that her mother was magic.

Her papa, Jean-Luc, was smoking a pipe, little clouds of fragrant fog floating off the end, spinning and twirling lazily into the growing dark. She paused to kiss his cheek tenderly and he glowed greener still, as if having her returned home brought him an even deeper peace. She loved the smell of his tobacco, earthy and familiar, and she spied a volume of Shakespeare's plays open on his lap. Her father, the secret romantic poet.

Her mother's voice singing in the kitchen, sweet and lilting, called her toward it. Though they were wealthy enough for a cook, Cora Delacroix preferred to prepare her family's meals herself. Simple things she grew in her own garden, or mysterious offerings of honey or sticky maple syrup would appear in the winter time—treasures that only Cora knew from whence they came.

But tonight it was the leaves of early spring lettuces and rose petals. Whitefish stewed in maple syrup and dusted with black pepper, an extravagance provided by her father's trade, for the Delacroix family were the proud owners of Cross Shipping Company. As attached as her parent's were to Mackinac, they were fortunate in the running of the shipping company, being able to import the very best of the globe to their own doorstep. Her mother paused between tasks to sip on last year's blackberry wine, her eyes twinkling with mischief. Before Raven could inquire about her mother's mood, the reason for it spoke into her ear.

"Bonjour ma belle"

Raven knew that voice, she turned and grinned, sticking her tongue out at her Uncle Philippe. He had been dead since before she was born, and she could only see him out of her blue eye. His spirit was restless, as it too had been in life according to her mother. He liked to go out with the voyageur brigades in the winter, haunting their canoes and exploring the frozen north from beyond the grave. He tugged on her ear, playfully, hummed a few notes of the voyageuring song her mother was singing, and then faded like a morning fog in the noonday sun. Cora looked at Raven and rolled her eyes, briefly stepping close, enveloping her daughter into an embrace, before quickly releasing her with a wink and turning back toward the table.

Raven sat on a stool near the fire, watching her mother's deft fingers fly over the meal, scattering spices and flipping white fish in the skillet. They often didn't speak at all, neither one of them noticing the silence. Instead, it was as if a ribbon of conversation ran between their minds and after quitting a room, Raven would feel as if she unburdened all of her thoughts, just the same as if she'd given voice to them.

But today, her mother did speak.

"All right at the mission school?" A nod from Raven prompted a satisfied smile. "*Bon.* Your brother Jacques' foot is on the path home even now. His heart is heavy today, so pray do not tease him—too much."

Her eyes twinkled again as she pulled a loose curl behind her ear, which only sprang free immediately after being detained. She bit her lip in concentration as her focus went to pushing the fragrant fish from pan to plates, the mixture of pepper and sweetness filling the small kitchen. Raven thought a moment, and then biting her lip too, a mimic of her mother that she didn't notice, her words broke through the bitten lip and into the room.

"*Maman,* I never tease him. And…his heart is always heavy now. He feels his own limitations, painfully, I think…and something is changed in him.

8

Some secret he carries but cannot speak of…"

Her mother cut her off with a reproving glance. To her, Jacques' only limitations existed in his mind. Any infirmity of his body was invisible to the spirits of the island. Raven felt differently, but would not quarrel with her mother, so she changed the subject quickly. They hadn't much time before her father and Jacques came in, stomachs rumbling, tasting her mother's cooking on their lips before it was served.

"*Maman*, do you know the ghost who follows Uncle Nicholas?"

If the strange question surprised her, she didn't show it. Cora did not turn around for a moment, instead tasting the glaze one final time before pouring it evenly over the fish and snap peas. She was a tall woman, and barely touched by her years of motherhood. Something in the rebirth of spring seemed to erase the lines from her eyes every year, and her hair still grew in bouncing black swirls. She turned back to Raven and narrowed her eyes.

"Do I know him? Or did I know him when he was alive?"

Raven shrugged, surprised by the response.

"Both or either."

"Yes…" Cora replied, and poured some lemon juice into a small clay bowl, adding another of her father's imports, oil from olives in Spain. Raven sighed and pursued the subject.

"I saw him today, in a tree in the wood. He smiled at me…and then, I think he was trying to give me a message. He...he pointed to the straits and...he vanished before I could determine what he was trying to tell me."

"Poor little mite. He is awfully mysterious, isn't he?" Cora continued humming and Raven grew exasperated.

"*Maman*! Who was he? What do you think he was trying to tell me?"

Cora placed the last of their dinner on the table in the kitchen, which pleased Raven. She preferred the cosiness of the kitchen fire to their formal dining room. Cora snapped her fingers at a coal black terrier snoozing in the corner, and gestured toward the porch.

"Turtle, fetch Jean-Luc."

Raven could almost swear the little dog nodded before trotting out in search of his quarry. Cora turned to her daughter and untied her apron, smoothing the midnight blue and white striped silk beneath it.

"His name is Beshkno. He used to be a playmate to your father, Uncle Nicholas, Aunt Isabel, Philippe and I when we were children. He died...suddenly. Quite violently. Your Uncle Nicholas was there when it happened..."
Her eyes took on a faraway look and Raven could see her mother as a child, hearing the news of a fallen friend, his childish laughter to be heard no more.

"Coralie..." And now Raven listened even closer to her mother, for she only called her by her birth name, the name she was given before the manitou tried to keep her for his own, when she was very serious.

"Coralie" she said again, "You said he was pointing toward the straits?"

"*Oui, maman.* Do you think he is telling me that I should leave? That I should make my destiny somewhere else?" Raven's eyes glimmered hopefully and she held her breath. She could feel the wide world tugging on her sleeve. Perhaps this sign was what she needed to convince her parents.

Cora's eyes were still far away. The steam from the fish coiled and twisted like ghostly fingers before her face.

She shook her head. "No." she replied with finality. Raven could hear her father's voice and her brother's step in the hall, close behind the sharp click of the terrier's nails on the floor.

"No, I think that your destiny will be here on swift waters. That your future has come to your doorstep from the straits." Her face relaxed and her eyes came back into focus. She smiled at her husband and son entering the snug kitchen, and one could almost believe she hadn't spoken the unusual words at all.

But Raven could feel them still, lightning bolts in her mind, setting off a storm of thoughts that she knew would keep her awake that night.

:2:

Jacques

Sometimes his sister unnerved him. Her eyes had followed him throughout dinner, watching his every move. Jacques wondered what she was seeing through that frosty crystal eye, what was he missing? He too, could sense his Uncle Philippe, of course, his phantom form sometimes seeming a copy of life if Jacques squeezed his eyes together just right to see him. But he never told anyone, and he doubted anyone suspected that he too could see the dead. Besides Maman…she always knew everything.

But Jacques didn't want people to know that he saw ghosts, or that he could smell change coming on the wind. He was different enough already. All Jacques longed for was to be normal. Not because he resented his otherworldly mother or sister, or disliked the wagging tongues of gossip on the island. No, he yearned to be ordinary simply because he was already enough of an outsider. He'd had proof, signs in the months past, that he could fit in. That there were some on the island who saw him for more than he seemed. But the memories of that triumph were fading, and he had little to encourage him since.

Sometimes he didn't even notice. He could almost convince himself it was in his mind. But today, in the shipping office, he'd had a spell. It left him gasping for air, clawing at his throat, desperate to capture the breath that lay just outside his ragged lungs. He had been laying on the floor of the office with his father's men surrounding him on all sides, eyes agog. How could he ever take the helm of the shipping company, if these same men would see that image when they thought of him? How could he be a man with such weakness inside him?

Back in his room, the taste of his mother's dinner still on his lips, but it couldn't be farther from his mind. He was laying prone on the bed, hoping to bury his head in his pillow, not unlike the ostrich in the natural history book on the shelf in his father's study. He could hear his father lazily draw a bow across the strings of his violin, and his mother and sister quietly speaking on the porch. His mother had clucked at him when he rose from the table and made for his room, but he plead a headache and she'd left him be. His father's frown, however, was in his room even now, hovering dejectedly at the end of the bed. He buried his face deeper to avoid facing his shame, hot tears glistened on his cheeks, and these too, he ignored.

Coralie always gave him one of her piercing stares now when they were together. A look that had always meant that she knew something was troubling him and it was high time for him to reveal his secrets. It was this look, over dinner, that had clammed him up even more.

Jacques knew that his family assumed it was the mood swings that accompanied coming of age that had changed him so, but they were wrong. If only it were something so ordinary. A usual problem for an uninteresting, normal boy.

But, no. It wasn't the gradual agonies of a boy growing older. It was the lightning realization and the constant reminder that he wasn't a true man. He would never be hearty or strong or revered for his acts of derring-do. For, like his older sister, Jacques had been born early. And like his sister, he was marked for life.

Not with the blessings or curses of the Manitou as Coralie was marked. Not with the ability to see into men's hearts, nor with his mother's sway over nature. No, Jacques was marked with lungs that never fully developed, not having enough time to do so in his mother's womb. He also had a weak heart that screamed in his chest when an activity was too strenuous. It had bothered him as a child, but nothing like the pain he felt now. Now that he should be becoming a man, taking his place among his peers. Jacques had hoped for his father's broad shoulders, and had reveled in the tales of his uncle's agility and fleetness of foot. But now, he could hardly lead his sister in a waltz without fearing collapse.

His father had laughed it off, of course. Not because he was cruel. But instead because to Jean-Luc nothing was an obstacle. He believed in good things coming. Wasn't Jacques the most educated man on the island? With the perfect mind for sums, an abacus for a brain? Didn't Jacques speak four languages and have knowledge of the classics? Literature? Botany? Anatomy? Was not Jacques able to consume an entire book in a day whilst completing the work of two men at the office? No, Jean-Luc never worried about Jacques.

All of that was true, but Jacques still felt he was lacking. He could feel it in the rattle of his lungs and the shuddering of his broken heart. Yes—broken. Shattered and staggering before it really had been given the opportunity to be damaged by love.

A soft tap on the door and Jacques sat up, smoothing one hand through his sandy blonde curls, the other down his rumpled shirtfront and trousers.

"Come in" he mumbled weakly, even more downcast to be seen so wretched.

The door opened, without the aid of the knob being turned, a trick of his mother's he was used to, and the woman herself stood in the hallway outside, both hands clasping a book. She smiled sweetly at him, her riot of black curls hastily plaited. Her golden eyes glowed like their terrier's did at night.

"Jacques, *ma petit*, why do you sentence yourself to exile? Your papa was going to come in, but you scowl at him even more than you do me, so I came in his stead."

Cora had a way of speaking that was slow and melodious, her hands rising and falling to the rhythm of her speech. The combination of sound and movement was a kind of hypnotism. Her words hummed around his seated form, seemingly adjusting his buttons and smoothing the creases in his shirt.

"I'm sorry, *Maman*. I just want to be alone right now."

"Nonsense." This one word from her mouth shooed all of those he had just spoken back under the blanket. "You always want to be alone lately. And what's more—I know your secret, so you succeed in hiding nothing."

Jacques cringed and his face grew hot with anger, and he blanched with worry. His next words exploding from his mouth before he had a chance to bite them back in, he was afraid that she would hear the terror in his voice.

"How? Did a *ghost* tell you?!" He didn't know why he lodged it like an insult, especially when he knew perfectly well that they did exist, but in the moment he wanted her to feel as though he viewed her as some of the ladies on the island viewed her. Ridiculous. But she didn't take the bait. Instead, she exhaled out her nose, calmly, and raised her eyebrows slightly.

"No, there was no need. I know your secret grief because I have two eyes and a brain in my head. One that functions considerably less well than yours. You have been spending far too much time moping about, pitying yourself."

He made to interrupt, but she raised a hand, silencing him, her other hand still clinging fast to the book.

"Do not deny or try to explain. You are sorry for your lot. Blubbering into your pillow about the unfairness of life. You have enough intelligence for three people. An aptitude for learning. Two working legs and two working arms and a family that loves you. You have a handsome face, and though your heart may be weak, it is good and full. Your lungs may struggle, but they are filled with the clear air of the pine trees and the sweet breezes from the lakes. Do not bemoan that you are not a man—you have the soul of ten men!"

Jacques' mouth hung open, and he pinched the bridge of his nose and squeezed his eyelids in disbelief. As she was speaking, her eyes had glittered and he could swear that her feet had levitated off the wooden floorboards. But now, her eyes were their usual vivid gold, with no extra glitter, and her feet rested on the ground.

She smiled sweetly again, and stepped forward to rumple his hair. She handed him the book as she did so. The title read,

Experiments and Observations on the Gastric Juice and the Physiology of Digestion, by Dr. William Beaumont.

Jacques raised a quizzical eyebrow, and his mother smirked in response.

"There was a trapper here on Mackinac, by the name of Alexis St. Martin. He met with an accident at the fur company—a shotgun wound to the stomach. All thought he would die. How can a man survive with a hole gaping through his middle? Do you know this tale, Jacques?"

She paused and Jacques sat still. He'd heard the story before, of course, but only in pieces. Gruesome details that younger boys like to dwell upon. He nodded in answer, but motioned eagerly for her to continue. He had always loved his mother's stories. Or perhaps the escape they allowed him. Her voice and words swirled and swam around him, embracing him with their warmth, drawing him in like a siren song. Jacques was thrice blessed for storytellers; his mother, his old nurse, Waseya, and his Uncle Nicholas could all trap you into the world of a story from the moment their mouths opened. He nodded again, and she continued.

"But live he did. I spent some time with the good Doctor Beaumont, who saved the man, helping to nurse the trapper to health. The man grew stronger and stronger, never thinking or worrying about his injury, as he was in too much of a hurry to get back to living. In fact, Dr. Beaumont had to leave his post as the fort doctor to follow after St. Martin, so eager was he to return to his life trapping in the wild."

She pressed the book into Jacques' hands, stooping to kiss his furrowed brow.

"There is time enough for death. Let it be. Try *mon cœur*, to fix your eyes on the shining sun rather than the storm clouds that may or may not break."

She cocked an eyebrow and stepped back into the hallway, the door closing behind her without the aid of her hand. Jacques flipped through the pages quickly before setting the tome on his desk. He wasn't convinced, not yet, but his mother was nothing if not persuasive. He listened for a moment, his mind considering carefully her words, and he heard his papa's violin singing still from below. He reached for the door, and paused, a thought shooting into his mind like a bullet. It was so easy for his mother to perceive this secret—but she was still so hopelessly in the dark about Coralie. His sister might think she'd fooled everyone, might assume the secrets of her heart were locked away, but Jacques had read them plainly in her every movement, gliding across her skin like the print in a book.

He looked back at the doorknob in his hand and was certain he had felt it turn on its own. He squinted at it, smiling. Perhaps he had more of his mother in him than he imagined.

Jacques headed toward the front of the house, where his family still sat in the twilight, soaking in the very last yawns of the day. There was nothing for it but to join them.

He took a seat amongst them, singing along quietly to the old French songs, but his mind was somewhere else. Filled with his sister's secrets, his own troubles, the one part of his secret that his mother hadn't known… and the beginnings of a plan to become the man he dreamed of being.

If he had seen himself through Raven's eyes that night, he would have seen the red around him cool, just a little, back to the turquoise she knew and loved so well.

:3:

Peregrine

He shook his head back and forth for some minutes, his eyes looking at nothing, or perhaps trying to see beyond the nothing. Could it really have happened almost a year ago? He looked again at the date on the diary entry he'd just written. The Twentieth of June, Eighteen Hundred and Forty Three. Yes, it was almost a year hence from the day that Gabrielle had closed her eyes for the last. He felt the familiar squeeze of his heart, as if someone was trying to wring all the blood from it inside his chest. The pain wasn't as sharp this time, a sensation which bothered him. He didn't like that he laughed more easily now, or that when he thought of her it didn't constrict his chest so hard that he felt he could barely inhale without breaking his frame.

He'd come to Mackinac Island the past autumn after his parents hadn't known what to do with him. He had a kind of second cousin or some such here, a family connection at any rate, and his parents had thought perhaps the change of scenery would heal him. Nothing here in this foreign place to bring back vivid reminders of Gabrielle. Ah, her name again in his mind evoked the image of her alabaster skin, small fragile bones and halo of yellow angel's hair. She'd been so small, so delicate; a prize orchid that a cruel wind might have withered. And a cruel wind did. If he was being honest with himself though, he knew it was he who was the wind that took her. His heart squeezed again, this time harder, giving him an odd satisfaction and ragged, painful breaths.

Peregrine pulled a hand ineffectually through his unruly auburn hair that blazed like burnished copper— A Rast family trait. His second cousin, Nicholas, whom he called 'Uncle' because it seemed more appropriate, had opened his home to Peregrine with no questions asked. He treated him as if he were as dear as his own children, who were only a few years younger than Peregrine. His Uncle's wife, his Aunt Isobel, was kindness itself, and he had nothing to complain of. Perhaps his mother had been correct, that this change of scene was a step toward healing. But Peregrine did not deserve to heal.

He was staring at nothing again, and his foot had begun to fall asleep under the desk. He drummed his fingers on the wood, deciding if he would leave the room just yet. At dinner the previous evening, his aunt had told his uncle of the Delacroix boy, her sister's son, having another of his attacks. Her voice was low and he could feel the worry in it. He had felt his ears perk up, eager for details to make a diagnosis. It had pricked at his fingers and the garnet ring on his pinky had grown so hot that it took everything inside of him not to tear it off and throw it across the room, certain that it was burning his flesh from the bone. Gabrielle's ring. The ring he had promised her forever with. How could forever have ended so quickly?

Almost a year ago.

Peregrine knew that his aunt would like him to examine Jacques Delacroix, but, he was all finished with medicine now. True, he had been the youngest physician to graduate from Oxford, qualifying with a degree from the Royal College of Surgeons at 20. Though some thought a man with independent fortune training as a doctor was irregular, Peregrine believed it a calling, a mark of being worthy of an angel like Gabrielle.

He'd had his own small practice, healing the sick and giving comfort to the infirm. His own tiny surgery wherein he performed minor amputations to injured workers, set bones, on occasion assisted in childbirth and bandaged wounds. He had known this to be his purpose when he met Gabrielle at the tender age of 14, and everything he'd achieved after had been done with the promise of her love before him. His guiding light, his own north star.

How is it then that with all of his training, all of his knowledge, his vows to preserve life...that his hands... his careful surgeon's hands... could kill her?

A knock on the bedroom door and Peregrine couldn't conceal the frown from stealing across his face. His uncle stepped in, wearing a broad, affable smile. Nicholas Rast was a strange man. Peregrine always felt that there must be a tragedy in his uncle's past, but he couldn't decide what it had been. He seemed to have recovered from whatever it was remarkably well. A doting wife, a booming trade and a brood of affectionate children. Yes, his uncle was a happy man—but there was still that shadow of something on his face. A dark secret that threatened to pull the edges of his continual smile downward.

But the cause of his mystery wasn't going to be revealed this morning. His uncle stepped in and sat quickly in the extra chair. He was still an attractive man, though he'd developed a little paunch in his middle that he attempted to hide under his waistcoats. Peregrine couldn't see why he bothered, he thought it gave him a greater air of content.

"Good morning, Uncle Nicholas. To what do I owe the pleasure of your company? I would have imagined you'd be in the shop by now."

Nicholas had held an important position with the fur company until it had closed in '38. According to Isobel, Nicholas had bounced back with his usual good humor and opened a dressmaker's, tailor and milliner's shops, herding his own growing children into helping with the various businesses. Peregrine hadn't realized before he'd come to stay that Nicholas had grown up in England alongside of his own father and aunts. But because he had, he was more familiar with fine European fashion and salesmanship. He also had a knack for making hardier northern fabrics look as posh as gauzy chiffon or the sleekest satin.

His uncle had not answered his question and so Peregrine waited patiently. Every doctor learns this kind of composure as one of the greatest tools in his medical bag. Though, Peregrine would admit to himself later that he never would have thought Uncle Nicholas was visiting in a medical pretext.

Without speaking, smile fallen from his face like a cast off cape, Nicholas presented his arm, and began rolling up his sleeve, never taking his eyes off Peregrine. Beneath the linen shirt were several layers of crudely wound bandage.

With no time for thought, Peregrine jumped up and began unrolling the inexpertly wrapped covering. With his tuned physician's nose, he could already smell the blood. Drawing away the last of the covering, a long jagged gash extended from the middle of his forearm to the elbow. Calm settled over Peregrine, and quickly he snatched his doctor's bag from where it had been hastily stored and ignored in the corner of the room.

A quarter of an hour later and the wound was clean, and Peregrine was placing the last stitch. Not a word had been uttered by either man.

"You've a fine skill there, Perry. It's a wonder you'd hide such a rare gift."

Peregrine's cheeks burned looking over his handiwork. He hadn't meant to pick up his medical bag again, but his mother had insisted he bring it with him, and now, almost a year later, he'd used it. He'd meant to refuse. To send his uncle to the fort doctor. But the blood in the air and the silence had called to him. His hands were doing what they were meant to do. His careful surgeon's hands. The hands that had stolen the life of his angel, Gabrielle.

For once the garnet ring did not feel over-tight on his little finger. As if in doing the work he had satisfied its need for blood and bone.

He wiped his brow, beads of sweat had gathered there due to the intensity of his focus. Without looking at his uncle, he brought his gaze and his opposite hand to the ring, turning it this way and that on his finger. It had all happened so fast, his response had come so quickly—so eager to be engaged in the work he'd tried to put away for so long. Just as the familiar feelings of guilt began to creep in, his uncle shattered the icy stillness of his reverie.

"As I said, it's a rare skill that you have. The kind of

gift that comes not only from practice, but that is bestowed to be used beyond yourself. I have never asked for the details of your tragedy, Peregrine, never inquired what sent you to these shores. And I never will. Every heart carries its blood weight in pain. But, I do know that you must find a way to use the pain."

Peregrine motioned his hand to interrupt with a protestation, but Nicholas continued on as if Peregrine's voice was silent to his ears.

"My nephew, Jacques Delacroix, is afflicted. He was…born too soon for this world. He and his sister, Coralie, well, they're different from other folks on the island, same as their parents. Beloved of the spirits, some say…"

Peregrine involuntarily rolled his eyes, but Nicholas pointed a finger in warning.

"Magic is not to be laughed at or besmirched, my boy. Especially in this family. Your eyes have been firmly closed in the blindness of your own misery since you arrived this past autumn. You would do well to look about you."

After this odd proclamation, Nicholas stood up, rolling back down his sleeve, and fixed Peregrine in place with cool grey eyes, the mirrors of Peregrine's own. Eyes the color of dawn on the lonely moors of England, a grey so hard and bleak it cut Peregrine to be pierced so.

"I'm not ordering you to do anything. But, I have the rent of a very small cabin just next to town. An old trapper's cabin that is now vacant. It has been cleaned and whitewashed and fitted out with the rudimentary elements needed for a surgery. I invite you to have a look at it. If not, it will be given to a new doctor, probably hired from down state. Someone not affiliated with the fort, or with that insufferable quack in town selling spirits as medicine. My nephew, Jacques, has been told to meet me there at 5 o'clock this evening. If you do not show, he will shrug his shoulders and head home, thinking how strange his Uncle Nicholas is."

Peregrine's face had grown hard and his palms itched as if he would hit his uncle. How dare he presume to suggest such a thing?! He was done with medicine!

Seemingly divining his thoughts, Nicholas' beaming smile appeared once again on his face, and he pointed toward his recently stitched arm.

"Something to think on at any rate. I am very much obliged to the quickness of your hands in sewing me back together. As I said, it's a rare gift you have."

He nodded his head, offered Peregrine a wink and was out the door. Peregrine's jaw still hung limply open, his brow wrinkled in frustration. He looked down to the garnet ring that his left hand was still worrying on his right hand. The stone seemed brighter, almost twinkling back at him. The dark red of the stone brought to mind the blood on his uncle's arm. He realized with a start that he hadn't even inquired how his uncle came by the jagged wound.

Standing up, he scratched the back of his head, his eyes moving to his almost unused leather riding boots and Mackinaw jacket his aunt had presented him with the past winter. It was too warm for it now, but the boots would be welcome. Perhaps his uncle was right, he should open his eyes and look about him a bit, if only for something to do. Maybe he could look into this magic spirit mumbo-jumbo that he heard his cousin's whispering about when they didn't know he was listening. All malarkey, for certain, but diverting very probably. It was early yet, he didn't even have to walk near the little cabin if he didn't like to. But a bracing walk through the forest could be just what he needed.

He tripped down the stairs, much more rapidly than was his wont, and he peeked his head into the kitchen where the family generally enjoyed a very casual repast. His aunt and cousins were just finishing their plates, their conversations still on their lips when met with the sight of their cousin, Peregrine, awake and out of his chamber before the sun had taken her throne at the highest point in the sky. He simply smiled and grabbed a piece of toast off the rack, slathering it with his aunt's black raspberry preserves, as he headed out into the bright sunshine of an almost summer day.

Yes, the very thing, a walk out of doors, a look at the world, time with his thoughts in nature. Then, perhaps, he would meet with Jacques. Maybe. Doubtful, but possible. Stepping into the sunlight, he raised a hand to his eyes so that he might squint into the sun. He brought his hand down and ran a finger over its creases and scars, the lines of his future written in the palm. He flexed his long, capable fingers and wondered if his uncle would still have asked him to attend Jacques if he knew. Would he still praise his medical skills if he knew how much death lived in these careful, surgeon's hands?

:4:

Crow

He had taken a canoe from Mackinac City, a decision which had caused the men on the shore to grant him a double take. He, dressed like any respectable white man, with his wayward chestnut curls and well-tailored waistcoat and trousers. But, one look at him was not enough. It was in the second glance that the truth became apparent; the men took in his copper skin and dark eyes, so inky dark as to be black. This was what announced that he, Henri Crow, was not what he first appeared to be. He was not a well dressed white man on his way to Mackinac, but instead a *chicot*, a half Indian.

The ship from Detroit had docked at Mackinaw City, the last stop on the route to the Isle of Mackinac. The other passengers had thought Henri mad for alighting with his small pack from the great ship and then to step onto the rocky shore. He had then searched out a smaller vessel to pilot himself. It had been three days slow passage since he had last flexed his muscles in activity. He needed to feel the sunlight reflect off the water onto his face. He had yearned to feel the dip and swing of his paddle in the sapphire blue water, glittering like so many jewels on his oar.

It was no small task to row from Mackinaw City to Mackinac Island, a distance of some seven miles. But, it was no light task that had summoned Crow to this northern isle in the first place. His duties here in the north were not to be pleasant, but they were just. And so the rhythm of the paddle and the sweat beading on his forehead and upper lip recalled memories of his people, the people he had sworn to protect and the Christian God who would help him to do it.

The smaller off-shoot tribe of Huron that he had been born into had always called Michigan home. Back, back, before it was even a territory claimed by the French, or the English, back when it was wilderness mainly ignored by the white man. They had moved with the seasons, always coming to the Great Turtle, Mackinac, in the summer months. Then the white man had raised his head and set his eyes on the beauty of the place, like the magpie, his attention always on pilfering the glimmering treasures that belong to another. His tribe had come in the summer then too, to collect the payments issued to them for the land that the white men had stolen. Never realizing that there can be no recompense for taking something that someone does not willingly give, that no one owns in the first place. Land that belongs only to the Lord, who looks on joyfully to see his children share it.

With the winter cold, the tribe would move to the territory called Ohio, or west into Wisconsin or Illinois. Now, most of the other tribes had grown if not friendly, more tolerant of one another. Not always, but often a certain accord was reached with rival or neighboring tribes, a bonding together to kindle the fires of their dwindling way of life.

And now, this white man, this Jean-Luc Delacroix would cheat them further of their dignity? Not if Crow could help it. He had a weapon sharper than an arrow, a power that gave him more ferocity than war paint. He had the white man's law and education, he had the teachings of the Christian Bible. These things he would use in the service of his people.

The island, which had begun as a speck of white and green in the midst of the tumbling lake waters, grew larger as it grew closer. Crow felt the familiar ache of rowing in his arms. The sharp pain was invigorating and his pace never slowed. He was alone on the water, the ship from Detroit not yet hoisting anchor in the city. He could just spot a few fishing boats, closer to the island, but too far to see what kind of sloop, or what type of men were in them. Being thus on the water gave him a stilling serenity, which reminded him of his first Jesuit teacher speaking to him of prayer.

He supposed, not for the first time, that he should be grateful to this black robe for pointing out his differences from the other tribal children in the mission school. The priest *was* the reason he had the white man's weapons he could now use on behalf of the tribes. But he still could not feel pure gratitude, though he was ashamed of himself for this, for the teaching of the Jesuits had given him a measure of peace.

But, the same words that had set him on the track to this life, this moment— those words had stolen the life he'd imagined for himself as a boy at his grandfather's knee.

His mother said he was born old. As if his spirit had known it would need great wisdom for the trials he would face. She had been used against her will, violently, by a French trapper who had come upon her in the woods. Her husband had been killed in a raid by another tribe, and she had painted her face black with mourning and had gone to the forest to fast. The trapper had raped her and left her for dead. But she did not die. His mother said that unbeknownst to the trapper, he had left life inside of her. Life in the form of a babe that would become Henri Crow. The flicker of his life became a flame, a fire that sustained her broken and bleeding body until she was found, five suns later.

And so, Henri Crow was a *chicot*, a half breed. He would straddle the worlds of the white man and the red man, never able to step both feet boldly into either. He had been given a French name by the Jesuits, but he only thought of himself as Crow, the name his tribe called him for the change he brought to them, for the crow totem is a symbol of change and wisdom.

Father Marchand had seen his pale hair and his Frenchman's build, different than the lithe, sinuous forms of the Indians. Instead, even as a boy, Crow had been broad of chest and heavy shouldered. Father Marchand had seen this and so took great pains to diligently teach him French, English, Arithmetic, Latin and all that he knew of the natural world. This black robe had said Henri was marked with promise, and had convinced his mother to send him to seminary. A place where these buds of education would flourish into a thriving garden. The black robe had told his mother he was an especially promising seed that needed more fertile soil from which to sprout into his destiny. He had learned much, it was true, at the seminary. Philosophy, History, and Law. But he could not take the black robe himself, not yet. He felt that his mission first lay in the service to his people. Into maintaining their dignity and pride in the face of those that would take it from them.

Besides, there was something in the idea of not performing his duties in the outside world that turned his insides cold. His Huron blood screaming for the billowing waves of the lakes and the endless green of an evergreen forest.

The ever closer shore brought him out of his reverie, and he angled his canoe toward the huts on the beach. Scrabbling children of all tribes, Potawatomi, Menominee, Huron, Ojibwa, Iroquois, all playing or fishing, their mothers indoors baking corn cakes on the hearth or cleaning the days catch that their man had brought back from a successful day's fishing.

Crow sighed. He wished sometimes that this simple life could be his own. He was still young, in his 25th summer, but there was no woman waiting in his lodge, no child bundled to her back as she worked. He was not certain if this life was made for him. He found solace in the sunlight, but also in the books of the seminary and in prayer to the Christian God. For now, the law was his companion and he found solace again in the good that could be gained by using that law against the enemies of his people.

He had been sighted and if what looked like a white man alighting on their beach was a strange sight, the children did not bother to let on. The men though, were different. He could feel their tension. A young brave, caught between the snares of youth and adulthood, waded out into the water to pull the canoe into shore. His grin was large and generous and the sight of it provoked the same expression on Crow's features. He too smiled, displaying the small gap between his teeth in the process. Crow had hoped women would find it charming, but knew that the imperfection marred the air of solemn strength he hoped to cultivate.

The young Indian had taken little enough notice of him before now, thinking perhaps he was a Frenchman who had rowed off course from the main crescent-shaped harbor. But, a glance into Crow's midnight eyes and he yelled something that Crow did not understand back to the men on the beach. Many of the tribes' languages were related, but Crow did not think he'd heard this particular exclamation before. Either he had spent too much time around white men, or this boy spoke a tribal language he did not know.

Most Indians, however, understood Ojibwe, and so Crow grasped at the words so long left unused in his mind. He asked the younger man if he had seen the Chief of the Western Huron tribes, White Arrow. His grandfather was well known amongst the tribes for his frosty white hair. It had paled from soot black to snowflake white in one night, the night his son, Crow's mother's husband, had died in battle. And although Crow was the son of another man, a man who had disgraced the tribe with the treatment of White Arrow's son's widow, the Chief had chosen to keep his son's wife and child in his lodge. An act that dared anyone in the tribe to treat Crow as if he were not White Arrow's own blood.

The youth's eyes had been at first surprised that Crow spoke the Ojibwe tongue, but his smile returned full and bright as the dawn. No, the tribe he spoke of had not yet arrived for the season.

"Please direct me to your chief." Crow spoke quietly, but directly. Not revealing his connection to the tribe, wishing instead to be judged for his own character, and not the footprints of his grandfather's moccasins.

They pulled the canoe some ways onto the beach,

and Crow followed behind the young Indian watching the sun reflect off his long black hair, envious of the ease of his movements in his deerskins. Their chief was wise to keep his people in deerskins rather than the calico cloth the white men would seek to clothe them in. It gave them a force of dignity that no fashionable jacket or shiny leather shoe could equal.

The hut they entered was larger than the others, but still small in size, and smoky within, the fire emitting grey clouds that moved as fog about the cramped space. The chief sat on the earthen floor on a woven mat. His eyes were closed and the tobacco pipe that stuck out from his lip added small puffs to the bleary room. Crow cleared his throat and coughed into his hand. It was not usual for an indian to smoke for recreation, but instead in accordance with a ceremony. But Crow saw no ritual in the chief's actions and the sight troubled him.

The younger indian spoke the same language that Crow had not recognized before and ducked out the door of the hut. He and the chief were alone.

Crow waited respectfully for the older man to speak, taking the time to make a careful inventory of the room and of the man before him. He could tell that the chief had at one time been imposing and muscular. His back was straight as the birch tree and long grey hair fell around his face like the branches of a willow. In old age his form had taken on extra weight that sat awkwardly on his frame. He looked to Crow like a bear preparing for the long winter, fattening himself up before his last sleep. There was something in the Chief's weathered features that struck Crow as wrong, incongruous. His eyes were too small, lips pressed too thinly together, pulled taut by too many expressions of displeasure. The room was mostly bare, save for a few small trinkets, store bought blankets instead of fur, glass bead bracelets that curled Crow's lip—no Indian should have such things.

Without opening his eyes, the Chief spoke in French.

"Who comes to my lodge and sits in my judgement?"

The words contained a hint of anger, but Crow felt it was more from habit than an emotion directed at him.

"Chief…"

"I am called Grey Wolf"

Crow blinked his eyes and took in the man before him once more. Grey Wolf? The fearsome warrior his grandfather had spoken of? He could hardly believe it. In his mind, Grey Wolf had been a figure much like his grandfather, as wise as the ancient oak, as mighty as the lake in a storm. This man was…ordinary.

"Grey Wolf, I have heard much of you…"

"I asked who *you* were. You are no French man, nor American. You are not of a tribe. Who are you that comes under my totem?"

Crow was taken aback. He was used to the rudeness of the white men when they saw his differences, but this was something else. The chief was genuinely hostile.

This time when Crow spoke he used Ojibwe, brandishing it as a mark of his identity.

"I am called Henri Crow, and you are right. I am a man of more than one tribe, and no tribe, and I am come to the island to fight for all tribes. I am trained in the law and I have heard of a man here who is doing wrong by the indian. I am come to remedy this."

The old chief cast a weary eye upward, lip still stubbornly stuck to the pipe, unimpressed with Crow's speaking Ojibwe and his speech.

"You speak many words, but they are wind. They trail out of your mouth and blow from one end of the island to the other. Settling back onto your fine coat and shoes to add to your own importance."

His other eye opened and suddenly, he saw something in Crow's face that he had not noticed before.

"Your eyes…those eyes I have seen…long ago…" His once bored voice grew fearful, as if he were speaking to the manitou of Mackinac himself, disguised.

Crow would not explain that his eyes were the same piercing blackness of his adopted Grandfather's. He would not give Grey Wolf the opportunity to respect him only because of his origins.

"If I say many words, it is because I have little time. I must go now, but I would ask if you could alert the tribes to my presence and my mission while I am here. Tell them to give the white men no reason to find fault with their actions until I have brought my suit against them."

"Why would I lecture any member of my tribe at the request of one who is tribeless?" The chief's former rancor returned on swift wings. He had closed his eyes again, taking a long puff on his pipe, blowing the smoke in Crow's direction.

"Because I am only come to Mackinac to repair what has been broken."

After a moment, Grey Wolf exhaled and responded, "You would not know what is broken, being a shattered man yourself."

Crow controlled his face, exasperated beyond all measure by the man's words and actions. He wondered sometimes if it was because he saw the tribes differently during his time away. Perhaps he had lost some of the understanding he imagined he had for their ways. But, then he remembered that he had his grandfather's eyes and so he could only see through the lens of a Huron. His mother said it was his magic. To be born with the chief's eyes, a grandfather that was not his blood, but had still somehow given Crow a piece of himself.

Crow turned around now, his lungs throbbing for fresh air. His hand touched the crude latch, muttering on its hinges as if it would like to leave the smoky room behind as well. He turned his head partially back, calling one last request to Grey Wolf.

"I will be staying in town. If there is any need of assistance, please send for me. As I said, I am come to this island to help the tribes."

Grey Wold let out a soft cackle from his throat, but Crow wasn't finished.

"Also, send word when White Arrow arrives…"

Crow could not contain the tug on the corner of his mouth when he heard Grey Wolf sputter on his own smoke when he realized where he had seen those eyes before.

He hitched his pack onto his shoulder and turned toward the forest, wanting to walk around the town from behind and approach from the back as if by surprise. He hoped a walk through the trees would focus his mind and steal the smoke from his clothes and hair. As he entered the cooling shade of the pines, he saw a raven fly above his head, a black bird like his namesake, but much larger. A bird that cast light into darkness. A symbol of powerful magic, a messenger that cast a shadow over Henri's face the moment before he entered the cool, pine scented wood. Involuntarily, the shadow made him shudder. He reminded himself that he no longer believed in such signs. That the God he believed in was bigger than these things.

He did not suspect that the next Raven he met would cloud his mind even further.

:5:

Raven

There were no classes today at the mission school and so she had found herself idle. Her mother did not need her in the house, though she normally assisted her when women of the town came by for her tinctures and herbals. Today, however, her mother had been quite adamant that she leave, not offering explanation or apology. She had been hurt by the rejection, as watching her mother brew and bake, prepare and administer her various potions always gave her purpose. It was a skill in healing that Raven knew would be sought after in all wild places. It was an ability that would set her apart and grant her freedom. An occupation that could enable her to be her own master —away from the island of her birth.

But today she'd been shooed out of the kitchen like a hungry cat when there's meat on the spit. She had hidden herself just up the trail from the house, shimmied up a tree like a squirrel, and soon saw her mother's reason for pushing her out of the house. She needn't have bothered though, for Raven already knew.

Rose O'Malley may have only been Jacques' age, but she was a woman in experience. Raven had seen the yellow light, the small glimmer that hovered around her own bright red shadow. It was that second ring, like a halo on the moon, that had told Raven that Rose held another life within her. She should have yelled to her as she passed by that it was much too late. She could have explained that her mother would not end the pregnancy now—she'd waited far too long. The teas and concoctions wouldn't work with a babe so late in the womb. She wanted to say that to end the birth now would take stronger physick—a potion that may end her life as well as the little golden glimmer unborn. But, Raven said nothing. Instead she wandered through the wood to Waseya's cabin, thinking to pass the day with her nurse.

But Waseya was not at home, and so Raven picked her skirts back up and wandered over to the rock they call Sugar Loaf, thinking she might meet with her nurse yet. Looking up at the towering rocky spire, she remembered that some called it the Manitou's Wigwam. She had always thought that nickname strange, as the Manitou would have no need of a wigwam. The island itself was his home, every tree branch, every cave, every shadow of every wave, his. She perched herself on an outcropping and looked about her, lost in thought of all that she had seen that morning, and all that she dreamt of for her future. It was exquisitely calming to be away from people, a repose for her eyes and her mind.

The vivid colors of their truest hearts were always displayed for Raven, bright flashes like exploding canon revealing their secret selves. Green and blue and red and dusky violet. Her mother with her ever-changing rainbow of the island. For Raven, nature was true release, away from the crush and crowd and familiar blazes of her own family. The straits were only the blue of so many polished lapis stones, the forests only their summer mixture of green boughs and golden sunlight.

A sound, soft, as soft as a deer's hoof stepping

carefully through the foliage. A minor crackle of last year's fallen leaves that had yet to feed themselves back into the earth. Not many would have heard it, mingling as it did with the sound of the twitterings of spring robins and the sharp song of the chickadee. But Raven had been taught to hear it. Her mother, such was her hold on the wood that if she was not silent enough to hear it, not still enough for it to catch her ear, the forest would have told her of it in a different way. The wind would have whispered it to Cora softly, or the leaves would whirl in the direction of a disturbance. Where Cora was brazen and bold and commanding, Raven was meek and dreamy. Not a priestess of the island like her mother, but a natural part of her landscape. And so she had learned to know its rhythms and harmonies. This sound, soft as it was, rung discordantly.

Her blue eye, expecting perhaps to see the bright orange of a Menominee trapper or the deep rose of a Potawatomi woman, for surely only an Indian could be so quiet, found instead only shadows. There was no color to behold but a smoky black, almost fog-like tendrils of dark-grayish night, snaking and coiling out like a great monster of the deep. She took a step back and realized where the darkness was coming from.

She wasn't afraid, merely interested. The dark was not a bad omen or a warning, she regarded it as an old friend. Nothing covers you so completely as the blanket of night, after all.

Cresting the hill, not more than a good stone's throw away, was the bringer of the shadows. One man, who moved with the confidence of many men, almost carried aloft by the dark tendrils of his aura toward Raven. His well-tailored clothing, beautifully made and expertly fitted to his wide shoulders and slim waist. His brown curls tumbled over his eyes, and even as a large hand came to tuck them away, he did not see her. It was a trick Raven had; to be so still that she was almost indiscernible. No well-dressed society man would be looking for a girl in these woods, nor would he see what was right before him. She was dressed in pale yellow, a simple cotton dress that somehow blended in with the sun filtering through the boughs.

Hidden thus, she studied him freely.

Raven, to her dismay, could not understand the darkness surrounding him. It was as if the shadows hid his character from her, she could not pierce the dark to read the man beneath. It reminded her, for whatever reason, of an Ottawa legend, wherein a man's spirit becomes trapped inside the fur of a wolf. No one in the tribe saw the man behind the eyes, until they shot an arrow into his heart, and his human form was again revealed. Yes, this man too was hidden beneath the skin. But, why?

His eyes flicked over to her own, as if hearing the questions in her mind that she hadn't given voice to. She should have known he would see her, for all that he dressed like any other white man, there was something…different in him. Her jaw opened a fraction and her brow creased; she was not so invisible after all.

His eyes were intense as they tried to conceal the shifting, writhing movements of his thoughts. Raven was relieved that he appeared as surprised to see her strange eyes, as she was to glimpse his.

Deep, deep black pools, so dark as to be hardly human at all, a thought that again reminded Raven of the wolf in the legend. Except reversed. The whites of his eyes stood in stark relief to the darkness of the pupils within. If she concentrated, she could make out just the faintest twinge of another color around the black, so thin that she couldn't tell what it was. His skin too, had been a shock. It revealed immediately that he was not of European ancestry. Not wholly anyway, for the the dusky copper of his skin and the elegance of his cheekbones gave proof of his tribal roots.

Shaking his head as though waking from a dream, the man stepped forward. Raven stayed seated on the outcropping, she had been lazing on. She felt like a deer when it sees that the hunter is too close to run from. She was held in place by the dark smoke of his soul which mingled with the dark fog that followed her steps always. Her blue eye strained to see what was hiding beneath that blackness, and she realized that to find his secrets would mean losing her own.

"I'm sorry, have I disturbed you?" The man asked first in French and then quickly in English.

Raven blinked finally, studying the figure in front of her before she trusted to herself to answer.

"No, monsieur. That is, the forest does not belong to me, so it is no one's place to disturb. You would do better to ask the trees." She spoke quietly, but couldn't help the small curve overtaking her lips on these last words.

He smiled at the answer, a crinkle came to his eyes as he did so, an action obviously not familiar enough to his features to have left a permanent trace. Raven again was drawn to his darkness, the familiarity of it to her own rolling over her like storm clouds, but not menacingly. A storm she could dance in, a storm that she felt would wash her clean of her disappointments and doubts. Her eye, her exhausted blue eye that was bombarded by the colors of everyone's heart, here it could rest, on him. He, who was a song as familiar as the waves of the straits on the rocky beach or the tune of the wind through the pine needles. He stepped closer to where she was seated, a puzzled look on his face, and she realized he was only a few years older than she. The quiet stillness, the mystery of his person and his air of authority had added the gravitas she associated with her father.

Finally, he finished whatever assessment he had been making of her and replied to her words.

"An odd sentiment. I did not think an American would speak in such a way of the land they live on."

In his voice was a challenge. She tore her eyes from him, feeling as if he was casting a spell with his even, deep voice, the flickering smoke of his character and his handsome face. Something in the closeness of his body unnerved her.

"My father had always said we are islanders first, Michiganders second, and lastly we are citizens of this new America. And so, as an islander, I believe that this forest belongs to anyone whose step does trod the path, be they moccasins or buckled shoes." She pointedly looked down to his own shiny pair.

"Your father seems like a remarkable man." His eyes burned into hers, and she could feel the heat of his gaze all the way to the back of her neck and on her palms. He was so close to her. No man save her father and brother had been so close to her. She did not think he stood so achingly near to her to be overly forward. No, it seemed instead that he hardly noticed it. That he was like a trapper in winter, and she was his fire in the snow. His body reaching closer and closer to the flames.

He was so close that the shadows around him seemed to envelop her within them, until she closed her white-blue eye, just so that she could gather her fluttering thoughts.

"Your eyes…" he began but something in her face snipped the thought off early. The mood had shifted.

"Yes, as you said, my father *is* remarkable. He is the greatest man on the island, and I would be surprised to find a better in the whole of the world." Raven spoke the words proudly, but also wondered why she spoke them. Was she warning this man? She couldn't think straight. He was so, so close to her.

"Ah, I do not doubt it. But have you seen much of the world, little bird?"

She realized too late that his tone had held no teasing or judgement. She had already adopted an angry scowl, and her words shot out like thorns.

"No, my world is this island. I would imagine that even had I combed the world over, though, that I would find that people are much the same everywhere. I would find that in every place there is someone who seeks to make those with less experience feel small and unimportant…" She paused just as she was warming to her argument. A look of horror stealing over her features. "Oh, I *am* sorry. I apologize. Sincerely. That was not correct, nor how I truly feel. You must forgive me."

"Nothing to forgive, we all have a raw spot that, like a house cat, unleashes our claws the moment it is prodded…"

She jumped up suddenly, the skirt of her gown fanning about her in the hurry of her flight. What was she doing? Insulting a man she didn't know, and then almost confessing the secret desires of her soul in the next breath? Perhaps she had been too long out of doors today. But before she could flee, she felt a hand grasp on her arm, lightly but securely.

"I truly take no offense. So, pray do not fly away just yet, little bird."

Raven looked up to see his brow crease and his mouth draw downwards, as if his words had confused him as much as they confused her. Who *was* this strange man?

"Please, I beg you, stay a moment. I do not even know your name." His words were quieter now, and they stood even closer than they had before.

She looked down at his hand on her arm, an action he copied, and ashamed of his forwardness, he snatched it away as quickly as he had clasped it onto her. She laughed, involuntarily, even though naught had happened that was humorous. Strange? Yes. Intense? Most assuredly. This was one of the more unusual encounters she'd had in her almost eighteen years—and she was a woman who saw ghosts!

He looked at her strangely again, both of them aware of the many odd glances and strange feelings unspoken between the two of them. He slowly moved his hand instinctively back to her arm, before remembering himself and taking it away again. She spoke.

"I laugh because you must be a kind of mixed-up mystic, or perhaps have a knack for games of guesswork. You called me "Little Bird", and all who know me well call me Raven. A raven is a large and rather ominous creature—not an endearing little sparrow at all."

His eyes bulged, and he chewed his lip, something she had said had affected him, she knew not why. She hastily added, "But my given name is Coralie. Coralie Delacroix."

She extended a hand and he took it, shaking his head quickly and offering her a reassuring smile before bowing over her fingers and bestowing the most perfectly rehearsed courtly kiss on her fingertips. Fingertips which she knew were slightly sticky-sweet from the spring sap of the trees. He then gave her a deep bow, his composure regained, and introduced himself.

"Henri Corneille Crow, lately of William and Mary as a student of law and before that of St. Charles Borromeo Seminary in Pennsylvania. But to those who know me, I am Crow."

They both smiled at one another now, the intensity of their closeness, the sharp smell of the sap and the pine trees surrounding them adding a raw, unguarded air to the introductions. He was still holding her fingers within his hand, and though she knew she should snatch hers away, she could not for the world disconnect her body from his. They smiled still, two black birds who both felt oddly unsteady on the downy, dark wings of their inner thoughts.

"Raven", he said, kissing her fingers once again.

"Crow", she whispered, though she did not know why, there was only the two of them. She wondered fleetingly about her mother's words, how prophetic, to say that her destiny was winging its way to her...

And then, like a crack of thunder, her hand was dropped, and the warm lights around his eyes faded away, leaving the inky blackness. The shadows around him swirled before her vision, covering him in a cloak that obscured him and his thoughts from her more deeply. The bud of whatever that had been blooming between them was nipped.

She took a step back, wondering if she'd imagined the past few minutes. Her eyes darted back and forth, searching for a reason for his sudden coldness.

"Delacroix? Did you say, *Delacroix*?"

Her eyes narrowed, confused at the harsh tone of his voice.

"*Oui*, Coralie Delacroix."

"And your father, this prince among men..." he said with a sneer, "what is his name?"

"My father? Jean-Luc Delacroix, owner of Mackinac's Cross Shipping."

He cursed under his breath, and looked at Raven as if she'd stolen something from him. For some reason, she put her hands up, blocking the blows of his sudden angry mood. The anger that coiled around him and seemed to hammer at her with the ferocity of his feelings.

"What is it? What have I said?" She cried, though

she could not account for her emotions with this man she had only met moments before. She was wounded. Raven had glimpsed something behind those bottomless black eyes, something familiar in the darkness of his soul, and he had snatched it away, hidden it from her.

He turned his back on her and spoke. His voice was tight and controlled, but she could not tell what emotion he was concealing now.

"It is your name that gives me offense. And so, it is best that we see no more of one another. Adieu, Little Bird."

He took one step after another, straight on, never looking back, as if it would make him weak to meet her eyes again. Raven was hurt, and confused, and oddly hollow. Bewilderment settled like a cloak over her.

A few minutes before, she was Raven Delacroix, dreaming of adventures beyond the shores of Mackinac. And then an adventure, in the form of a handsome stranger and mystery had all entered the clearing—and then just as suddenly had left. Taking part of her along with it.

She sat stunned, still collecting herself, gathering her runaway thoughts like so many leaves in the wind.

"Henri Corneille Crow" she said aloud to herself, as if saying the name aloud would break the enchantment of their meeting. She repeated the name again, like a spell, and the corners of her mouth turned upward, her cheeks flushing without permission.

Gone were the shadows of his character, so like her own, that trailed after him. The absence caused the forest to look somehow more subdued and ordinary. The golden sun had lost its luster, the green of the trees less brilliant. She frowned. So unexpected and heady a meeting—and so strangely ended! Torn away just as she felt the prickings of a new beginning in her fingertips. He must have been jesting, surely. To run so hot and cold so quickly, why, not even the chill of night overtook the warmth of the daytime sun so fast.

Raven shook her head and realized it was growing late. She had sat with her thoughts too long. As she walked beneath the boughs of the trees, some evergreen, unchanging with the seasons, others softly flowering, she laughed under her breath. She felt she had stumbled into one of her father's favorite plays. Which one was it, something Shakespearean surely. Papa often said that every story can be found in Shakespeare. As she walked, she puzzled, all ideas of hurrying home forgotten. Perhaps *A Midsummer Night's Dream*, as the forest on the island did seem a fairytale place, especially when her mother passed through its paths. Or mayhap it was *As You Like It* that she was thinking of. She, like Rosalind, should have adopted a disguise when meeting her Orlando, this Henri Crow. Though, she could not have known her true identity would be so oddly hateful to him.

Raven felt sorry for herself, and her stomach hurt terribly, like bats were flying around inside. She felt the warmth of his skin, so close to her own, could see the sun reflecting off one of his wayward curls—she might have reached out and twined her own fingers in it. His lips on her hand, and then gone. She didn't know why it upset her so, or why her thoughts insisted on lingering on the bizarre meeting, but it was there. Haunting her as she stepped over knotty roots and hopped over fallen branches, stooping here and there so as to not disrupt the intricate weavings of a spider's web, or accidentally tear a new leaf from a tree.

And then, on the edge of the wood, merely steps away from the grass at the end of her father's house, she was haunted again. But this time, a true phantom, not the vision of Henri Crow that had assailed her moments before, but Beshkno, the indian boy. He was sitting comfortably cradled in the branches of a beech tree. His foot had been kicking lazily back and forth, to the rhythm of a song she would never know. She was reminded again of *A Midsummer Night's Dream,* this copper-skinned Puck, this ghost-story sprite had just the sort of mischievous look she would have expected to leap from Shakespeare's pen. He was staring at her now, intently. The last ray's of the day glancing off his straight black hair. There was a wistfulness to this spirit's expression, a hidden sadness that was familiar. It was the same sadness that she carried within her own heart, a grief that had been lifted briefly today, and then replaced fresh. A despair she had recognized in Henri Crow, even as his lips burned the coolness from her fingers.

The boy, the ghost, scowled at her, and she made to speak, though what she would say she did not know. But putting a finger to his lips, he silenced her. He opened his arms wide, as though he were capturing the whole of the forest within them, and then he pointed back, back to the clearing near Sugar Loaf where she had met Crow. He gestured again toward the straits, and vanished from the branch.

Raven exhaled, and mumbled to herself. "It is not always so wondrous to dwell in this place of spirits. In face, it is tiresome." Passing by the kitchen window she saw Philippe, her long-dead uncle perched near the hearth singing a voyageuring song to her mother. Raven stuck her tongue out at him, weary of ghosts and fairies, of the flutterings near her heart and the mysteries of the straits and colors of the characters of the people on the island. "Damn you, Henri Crow." Raven mumbled, "I don't need your closeness or your midnight eyes. I *need to leave this island,* and that is all!"

But her gloomy thoughts scurried away at the sight of her father reading poetry on the porch. Jean-Luc Delacroix was wild for words and poetry, insisting that his own fool lips and rough hands could never write a verse so well as Blake, Byron or Keats. He sat quietly, sipping something thick and ruby colored, his eyes drinking the words down like physick. The green glow of calm surrounding him returned all of her smiles. Raven thought perhaps she should tell her Papa of her meeting in the woods. He would know which of Shakespeare's plays it resembled most.

:6:
Jacques

Even after all this time, he still could not think of this space as his own office. It had been his father's when he was a young man, and had been given over to Jacques when his grandfather had left the running of Cross Shipping to Jean-Luc.

The very next day it was, though he had been still a very young man, much younger than now—not yet ten years of age—Jean-Luc had brought Jacques and his tutor to the little space. He had said it was the perfect place to learn his histories, geography, arithmetic and all other fields of study Jacques could consume. It had succeeded in making study a vocation instead of a chore. But still, though he had come to this office for almost six years, he felt his father in every part of the room. As if every emotion, success or tribulation had been left behind, soaked into the walls like the worn white paint. Or hiding between the ledgers on the shelf.

He had paused in his work—it being truly shipping company business he labored on now. Jacques had quickly exhausted his tutor and his knowledge, and after that every book he had gotten his hands on. A feat that did cause Jacques to wonder if the weaknesses in his body had led to a stronger vigor of his mind. He had paused to relish the repast his mother had lovingly sent him off with that morning. Corn cakes, as usual, with wild strawberry jam so sweet and red that he felt he was swallowing sticky-soft rubies. His mother's preserves had a little enchantment in them, he was certain. But whether it was from the tune she hummed as she stirred the boiling pot, like a good witch from a fairytale, or the way her hands harvested the berries so gently from the hillside, he had no idea. But each mouthful of jewels conjured visions of her smile, of downy soft kisses on his cheeks when he was small, and warm summer days wading in the frigid lake waters. Happiness and his mother in every bite.

Jacques was not alone in the office, but it wasn't only his father's memories that lingered alongside him as he toiled over ledgers. But also, his Uncle Philippe. It was strange to think of this spirit as his uncle, when he was only five or so years older in appearance to Jacques. His parents did not speak of him often, but Jacques knew he had been a voyageur, a brigade leader. He had been a man of adventure, apparently—as he had died so young, and in a fight in a tavern. The ghost divided his time between wintering with the brigade or amongst the members of his family. The ghost seemed to haunt Jacques' mother the most, and he assumed it was because his uncle had been in love with her in life, and perhaps still was. Or a memory of him was—though it mattered little now. Sometimes he wondered what exactly had happened between all of them, his parents and their friends when they were blooming into adulthood, just as Jacques and Coralie were now. But, he didn't think on it too hard. His mother was the moon, how could anyone keep their eyes from her when all the rest of the world was a cold, dark sky?

But Philippe was with Jacques now, though he did not let on to anyone else that he could see him. The spirit paced the office, or rather floated, skipping sometimes and kicking his feet together in the air, an impromptu dance, and he sang. Other times he told Jacques stories, legends of the island that he often garbled up and then laughed himself hoarse—a whispery spider's web laugh—afterward. But today he simply sang his sad voyageur songs and gave Jacques a dramatic bow before vanishing. Probably off to haunt some of the pretty girls on the island, or flirt with Jacques' mother.

Jacques licked the last candy red strawberry smudges from his fingertips and looked back at the account book on the desk before him. He'd gotten a stray crumb or two on the pages, but no preserves, thank goodness.

Cross Shipping was still afloat, but they were making less money than the year previously. They had ships here in Mackinac, and in Mackinaw City, St. Ignace, Quebec, Detroit, Chicago and two ships that made runs as far as Boston. His father had recently hired on teams of natives as sailors, dockworkers or fishermen, any indian that wanted to work had a position. His father had been dismayed at the treatment they were subjected to in this young United States, especially after the Treaty of Washington in 1836. True, it had provided a huge economic boost to Michigan to have the payments to the tribes here on the island, but they had lost their lands, and for many, their way of life. In his father's mind, circumstances had only grown more appalling when the Michigan territory had achieved statehood, only a few years past. His parents respected and admired the tribes, had played alongside the natives as children, even as Jacques and Coralie had. Jean-Luc had decided to employ any native, from any tribe, and for the same wages as the American, British or French sailors that worked his ships. It was not ideal, for many young braves would have preferred the United States government to leave them in peace, to live their lives as they always had, but Jean-Luc and Cora could see that the world was changing. And so they would offer succor where they could, to help the tribes find a fragment of independence and restore some of their pride, in a very small way.

But it was this fair wage and influx of workers that had begun to drain their profits. Every column, every row of numbers showed chips and weak spots, and it gnawed on Jacques. Reminding him of Turtle, the little black terrie, with a bone—an incessant grating and grinding of his teeth against it, until the bone crumbled and dissolved away.

Jacques sighed and turned away from the dour, decaying numbers before him. This too, was another symbol of his powerlessness. His body, that was failing him with every gasp and wheeze, and now the figures that he couldn't make right. Sometimes he wondered what the point was. It was clear that he would die young. His mother may not want to believe it with her inspiring books from famous doctors and grand speeches, but it was true for all that. No sense in training him up to be the next master of Cross Shipping. He'd never marry, never have children of his own. He'd even been happy with a mysterious, mournful creature like himself. But, no. It had been made clear that no girl on the island would look on him as a suitor. No woman his parents would approve of anyway. All of the books he'd consumed, all of the hours spent learning all there was to know, and loving his family, all of the corn cakes slathered in strawberry preserves, none of these could alter his fate.

Then there was the trouble with George Wells. A lumberman from downstate, he was visited the island often, ostensibly to establish good relations, but Jacques didn't like it. The man seemed to always want something. His father's ships, his father's business, his father's contacts. And the fact that Cross Shipping wouldn't sell, wouldn't re-negotiate their contracts to pass by Mr. Wells logging activities, this caused a ribbon of tension. A rope pulled so taut that Jacques felt as though he was continually looking through the accounts to find the fray. But, Cross would endure. Jacques had to believe it.

He sighed, filing away the issue of lumber interests back into the part of his mind he'd had to revisit later. His uncle reappeared, as slowly as he'd vanished before. There was something more unsettling about the sight of him against the dusty white paint. In the light of day the spirit seemed another part of the mysteries of the wild northern island, but within the walls of the office, his paleness, his shimmering gauzy movements appeared as a vulgar imitation of life. But still, Jacques liked the company. It kept him from digging too much deeper into his burrow of self-pity. Besides, he had seen Peregrine yesterday afternoon, and though the young doctor had given him no reason to hope, it had been a relief to finally cast his own fears away from himself like a kite on a string. Though those same fears would too soon be twisted back in, seeing them floating aloft of himself was freeing.

He had agreed to meet Peregrine, (Jacques still unable to think of him properly as Dr. Rast), again this evening at the small cabin outside of town. He couldn't imagine what the lugubrious and trembling doctor could do for him, if anything Peregrine appeared more ill than Jacques. But there was a kind of quickening in his person, a fire in his eyes when he had begun the examination, like Turtle when he was on the trail of a rabbit. Something almost...animal about the change in his manner. Peregrine had quite altered, his hands steady, his voice confident, questions flying from his mouth in a steady, calming cadence that seemed to know the answers Jacques would give before the question was uttered. It was for this reason alone that Jacques had agreed to meet again. Well, that, and because he knew his Uncle Nicholas was trying to help.

A knock on the door to his office and Jacques looked up, startled out of the bobbing waves of his thoughts.

"Come in", his voice came out deeper than normal, a slightly false sound to his own ears. A dry cough and the grating sound of a man clearing his throat preceded the entrance of the same Peregrine Rast that had just occupied his thoughts. He had dressed with more care than Jacques was used to seeing, his usual air of careless indifference somehow smoothed out and straightened into something resembling poise. The man's eyes too, generally shifty and unwilling to meet anyone else's, took on a new appearance of authority. Peregrine was every inch the dauntless medical man that he had claimed he wasn't when examining Jacques the day before.

"Good afternoon, Monsieur Delacroix."

"Please, Dr. Rast, call me Jacques, we are relations, after all."

"Quite. Yes, indeed. Then you'd better leave off calling me, Dr. Rast as well, Jack. Can I call you Jack? Jacques is a trifle more difficult for my Britannic brain.

Capital."

Peregrine's eyes were almost feverish, his speech was rapid and punctuated by a quick laugh every few words. Jacques tried to fit this image of his cousin with the one he'd seen in glimpses this past winter. He'd been a skittering rat, sticking to the comfort of dark shadows, and now...well, now the man must be drunk. But, even if that was so, Jacques had to admit it was a marked improvement.

"Call me what you will, Perry. I am glad to see you in better spirits." Probably *due* to drinking spirits, Jacques couldn't help but add silently to himself. The comment, made in earnest, seemed to somehow offend Peregrine, whose smile folded down in the corners. It was as if he did not know he was wearing it. His whole face then fell, whatever invisible force that had taken the weight from it, slackening. Jacques was more puzzled than ever.

"Right. Well. Spirits, yes. Hum, you see, I hm, I came to your office...incidentally, I'm quite sorry, I didn't realize that you would be occupied. That is, I should have known that you would have your attention on business, as these are business hours. But, I hm, well, I suppose I didn't think, and dreadfully sorry Jack, I'll...I'll be off then."

Turning around he made to step back the way he'd come. Jacques called his name loudly, much deeper than he'd planned, his voice coming out like his father's. The Peregrine Rast who had seemed competent and self-possessed only a moment before had melted into a spluttering puddle of unnecessary apologies.

"Peregrine?" The man stopped, one hand was holding a black leather bag, and Jacques could see the hand was trembling. A muscle in Peregrine's face moved and his body swung around. In three long strides he was standing over Jacques' desk, dropping his black bag gingerly on the floor. Jacques took a deep breath in, steeling himself for some kind of bad news. The only thing that seemed to fit with the young surgeon's flighty, strange behavior. Had Peregrine discovered something horrible about his condition? He could see that Peregrine, too, was mastering something within himself before his face relaxed, and he spoke, his voice regaining its calm.

"I came here today because I have some ideas. I couldn't wait until our rendezvous later" He spoke the first words tentatively, testing out his thoughts before he launched into the meat of his mission.

"Though I cannot heal what is broken within you, I think I may know how to strengthen you. I have been looking over some of my medical texts, and…well, that doesn't matter now. Just know that I think I can…help you. If you are…amenable."

For a moment, Jacques couldn't breathe, and he worried he was on the verge of an attack. His heart fluttered and raced, but from excitement not exhaustion.

"Yes! A thousand times, yes. When do we begin?"

A phantom smile played over Peregrine's features, vanished almost before it appeared.

"Meet me after supper tonight…about seven? At my quarters in the cabin just away from town, same as yesterday evening. We will have an hour or two of light left with which to begin. Be sure to bring your boots."

Jacques was beaming. "Thank you, Doctor…" Peregrine winced as if the word cut him, "Erm, thank you, Perry."

"Don't thank me yet, I've done nothing." He smiled though his words did not, and he walked quickly to the door.

There was something changed in the man. His character was in transition, inscrutable. Jacques was reminded of his sister, Coralie, and how secrets seemed to hover about her like a black cloud. Peregrine Rast had his own secret sins, Jacques was certain. But the man was wrong, he *had* done something for Jacques. He'd given him a glimmer of hope. A light to grasp at, a star to follow.

He sat unmoving in his chair, looked over the crumbs fallen on his ledger. His mind was on the book his mother had given him, and on these ideas of strength borrowed from Peregrine. Hope, a new feeling for Jacques. The word appeared in his mind, a floating cool, refreshing wind soothing his fevered worries.

In the corner Philippe's ghost, pointed at Jacques' smile and matched it with his own, and his strange breathy voice sang, "*Il y a longtemps que je t'aime, Jamais je ne t'oublirai…*"

Jacques translated the words as the specter crooned. "For a long time I have loved you, never will I forget you…" and his anticipation froze into foreboding. Jacques remembered that he was surrounded on all sides by secrets, even those his failing body kept from him. And the secret sin that he was guilty of, a secret that he could not forget, and he worried would not be kept long.

:7:

Crow

He had heard once that crows remember the faces of those who have wronged them, and that they were known to bring in other crows to attack if they saw that same face again. A murder of crows. A menacing name for a group of black birds. Birds that deal in vengeance and grudge.

Crow did not know if this was true, but he thought it likely. The way the birds turned to look at you, fixing their beady black eyes almost down to your soul.

Perhaps ravens did the same. At least, he knew one Raven that had feasted on his heart, with her strange eyes and glossy black hair like a veil of night sky cascading down her back. He had most certainly memorized the details of her face, the image branded on his eyes. But, it could not be—a cruel joke of fate. She was not for him, nor he for her; her father was an enemy to Crow's people.

He had run away from Raven Delacroix, near the rock they call Sugar Loaf—but she had been with him ever since. He wiped a hand over his eyes, pulling it roughly over his cheeks, attempting to wipe her memory from himself. He shook his head to clear it, and was angry. Disappointed in his weakness, enraged at his distraction. He had come to make a difference, to bring about changes for the tribes, to prove the worth of his half Huron blood, to serve God, who would grant his people justice. And one face, one bird of his same feathers had sent him off course.

Still, something about the meeting stayed with him, no matter how he pushed it aside. The love in her voice when she had spoken of her father, the heat of her hands in his own. Not gentle, tender hands, but instead strong and capable, willing to be used in activity or work. She had his mother's hands in fact, fingers that itched to be in motion, in preparation and readiness for tasks yet to come. He shook his head again. For all that she had an indian woman's hands, she was no native. Nor was she a friend to his people if her father's conduct was an indication of her own feelings. No, Raven Delacroix was no indian—but then Crow remembered, neither was he.

He had meant to walk toward the town, but somehow he had gotten hopelessly turned around in his agitation. He stopped, and the Huron side of him could not help but look up and around, adapting himself to his surroundings, finding peace in the natural world. Here, he was stillness. His ears heard a doe with her fawn, their hooves lightly crushing last autumn's remaining leaves. He heard the cry of the whippoorwill and the hoot of an early owl, addled by the semi-darkness of the trees into thinking it was nearing night.

Softly, he heard something else. A sound that had at first felt a natural part of the forest, as much as the wind on the treetops or the flight of a robin or thrush. But his ears drank in this new sound, and without thought, his feet followed the lilting rhythm. He had no thought, but like a ship steered blindly toward a lighthouse, he did not pause to contemplate if there may be jagged rocks or snares ahead.

His feet and ears led him to a small cabin, no larger than one room, very simply constructed from the woods surrounding him. It existed there so harmoniously that Crow could easily believe that the forest itself had volunteered the wood that made up its construction. The singing stopped. It had been something akin to Ojibwe, but somehow more musical. The small door opened, and a tiny woman with braids of black and silver stood in the entryway, beckoning him in.

In the days that followed, Crow would struggle to remember his journey from outside the cabin, into the small cozy room within. The steps themselves seemed vanished from his memory. It was as if as soon as he decided he was curious enough to look in, that he was already inside. He didn't recall choosing his seat before the small fire, or how he had come by the cup of steaming liquid in his palms, but here she was, sitting near him, singing again the song that had called him.

Without speaking, Crow turned his head to look about him. There was a small desk with pages of papers bound together on top, a few leather bound books whose titles he could not see. A painting hung on one wall, a recognizable depiction of Arch Rock, with two figures standing hand in hand atop it. There was a black pot on the fire, not unlike a witch's cauldron, and a few implements near the hearth. Drying herbs of various kinds hung suspended near the fire, the heat passing through them adding the fragrance of rose petals, wintergreen and dandelion root to the small cabin. Taking a cautious sip from the mug in his hands, he tasted the sharp coolness of fresh peppermint tea, and his eyes came back to the painting on the wall. His eyes studied the color and line and love that had rendered the lovers atop the rock, the joy of the moment was palpable in the paint. He decided that the artist had a special connection to this moment, and wondered what it could be.

Following the direction of his gaze, the old woman smiled, and quit her song.

"*Oui,* you admire my painting. You have good eyes, though sometimes you are blind. And I think a good heart, though you understand little of loving."

Crow stared back at the small woman. She was advanced in years, it was plain, though her face did not have the time etched onto it as so many scored marks. She could have been fifty or one-hundred for all the answers her face gave. But her eyes, her eyes told another story. In her eyes, Crow saw the experience of many years, the bitter bite of more heartbreak than he'd ever know, and the warmth of more sunshine than he'd ever feel on his light copper skin.

"Do you know me?" he whispered, "Who…who are you?" His voice trembled a little and he felt as he had as a boy in his grandfather's lodge. Loved and warm, but also under a cape of deep respect and fear.

To his surprise, she laughed, hard and long. Her laughter came out like ripples in a stream, and then she sat back, regarding him thoughtfully.

"I am Waseya of the Menominee, though my people are long gone. Their children return every summer in their canoes. Some of them, they remember and they come to me for the stories. Others, they have already forgotten, and so their moccasin never treads the path near this cabin, could not see it if they were looking through the trees, could not hear the tales of our people if they listened all through the night. I am like you, Henri Crow, a *chicot,* a half blood caught between dawn and sunset, never beginning or ending, but caught somewhere between and within. I have known you from the first, have felt your coming for many years, and I have waited for your foot on the path. Your step called to me just as my song called for you."

Crow blinked rapidly and shook his head. He was, of course, used to legends, and the tribal elders that had a special connection to the natural world, the weavings of the tapestry of life. But he was also a learned man. A man of biological understanding and mathematical formulas. A man who respected law and the order of numbers and the puzzle of ancient and modern languages. He had learned the love of the true God from the priests in the mission and at the seminary. Had felt the words of the savior cleanse his soul. Waseya seemed like a very old and wise woman, but her words fell like pebbles on the sand in his ears. No meaning resonated from them. And yet. Yet, there was something true in them, no matter how his reasonable mind pushed against them.

He fixed his eye on the painting again, avoiding the openness of Waseya's gaze. She spoke again.

"You do not believe the words your heart sings, though I repeat them back to you. It is no matter, all in time. Your eyes keep finding their way back to the painting on the wall, so I will explain why you are so drawn to it. In the painting, is a memory of a memory. Painted by one who was not fully there to witness the event, but wished to capture the image for her own heart."

"What was the event?" Crow asked, unable to

swallow back his curiosity. "And why am I drawn to it?"

Her eyes crinkled in happiness. I will allow you to work out for yourself why it holds meaning for you. But in the painting is the moment that two lives became one, and one life became three."

Crow's eyes narrowed, and an eyebrow creased in befuddlement. "You speak in riddles, then."

"No, there is no riddle to a moment such as that one. There is nothing more simple or natural. It was the moment the woman told her man that she was with child." She sat back into her chair and closed her eyes, humming softly. The firelight caught the silver in her hair in its dancing flames.

Crow's brow cleared, and he breathed out heavily, his shoulders relaxing and his body too settling more deeply into his chair. There was something in her voice that covered him in a blanket of comfort, and also kept his guard up. A warring conflict of feelings—but the blanket was winning.

"I see. The lovers became one, united with love for their child. And the one life they shared became three separate souls."

She inclined her head toward him in approval, but did not speak. The fire crackled and jumped, and Crow stood to add another log to the top, stirring the venison stew bubbling contentedly in the pot, before returning to his seat and drinking his tea. She did not have to ask him to do these things, he knew to do them. He had done the same for his own mother and grandfather, so many times before.

His eyes fell to looking from the painting to the fire, and then back again. His mind conjured the image of

Raven in the flames, her peculiar blue eye, the warmth of the green in the other. The flush of her cheeks, hair as black as her namesake. He was shaken from his traitor thoughts by Waseya's voice, which had grown stronger and vibrated with heat and youth. He looked at her carefully, as she spoke, searching for proof that she had not, in fact, grown younger.

"You have come for a story, then. Although, now that we meet, I think maybe the story is not for you. That maybe it is meant for another."

Crow shook his head, once again confused. "No, Waseya, I came only because I heard your voice, I followed the song here." His first thought was how strange those words sounded to his own hears, and his second thought was to be surprised to be speaking Ojibwe. The language that had been thick and awkward on his tongue when he arrived on the island, was now as fluid, as waves on the shore. This whole experience was like a fever dream of a madman, or a conjuring of his imagination. He felt the heat of the fire in the room, the scent of the herbs, the pinch of his toes in his fine shoes. It was real, but still undeniably strange.

"*Oui,*" She said, as if convincing herself, "if you heard the song, you came for a story. If you hadn't heard the song, you could not have come."

Crow's forehead creased again, and he moved to speak, but her gaze fell full upon him, and he found he could not.

"Which story do you need? Let me see, look at me, son of the Huron, show me your eyes, Henri Crow."

She sat up and leaned forward, searching his eyes and his face, her eyes undressing him to his barest soul. He blinked and looked away, uncertain what power she had over him. Finally, she smiled and reclined once again, evidently satisfied with what she had found.

"Yes, I see. You are not the one. But it is the story you are meant to hear nonetheless. And now, you've come. You have need of many of the tales of the island, Henri Crow. But this one is the first one I will tell you. Whenever you think on the words, you will remember them as if they had been etched onto your chest, or scrawled behind your eyelids. Though, it is a warning... for all of its beauty."

She stood up, slowly, and stepped over to the pot bubbling on the hearth and stirred it rhythmically, her whole body swaying with the movement. She tasted the stew, nodded, and then returning to her seat, her eyes opened wide, wider, and a strong, unearthly voice sounded from her lungs.

"A beautiful daughter of the Ojibwe tribe, Ownee, sat high upon the island on a solitary rock. Below her perch was the expanse of jewel blue waters that are home to the walleye, perch and sturgeon. But Ownee's mind was far away from these things. Instead her gentle, dark eyes scanned for distant dots on the horizon. Shapes no larger than a grain of sand in the distance that would announce the return of Gen-gwon, the brave who held her heart. Many moons had passed since he had departed from the island, hoping to gather more eagle feathers in a battle with an enemy. If he was successful, he would demonstrate himself worthy of Ownee; her father would think him a mighty warrior and a fair match for his beautiful and kindhearted daughter.

Suddenly, a shape bobbed on the horizon. Tiny specks that became a great group of canoes. As the canoes grew closer, she heard the voices of warriors raised in song. Ownee leapt joyfully to her feet, and began to race toward her returning beloved. But then, a freezing finger of ice gripped her. The song the warriors sang was the death song! Hey eyes searched the canoes below desperately for signs of her true love, Gen-gwon. And seeing her distress, the Gitchi Manitou took pity and whispered to her that Gen-gwon had gone to the spirit land. It was true, a feathered arrow had pierced his heart, and his last words had been of love for Ownee.

For seven moons, Ownee slept upon the great lonely rock over the straits, and seven times her ghost lover appeared to her as a shining black crow. At last she knew it was time for her too to join Gen-gwon. Her father found her broken body at the base of the rock, near to the slow Mackinac water's shores. Ownee had taken the trip of souls to join her beloved. Since that time, two black birds can be seen, always together, in the moonlight. They perch together on the top of the rock where Ownee waited, the rock we now call, 'Lover's Leap'".

A small look of satisfaction crept over her features, and she relaxed into her chair, humming softly again the song that had brought Crow to her.

Henri widened his eyes and looked back to the painting on the wall.

"Truly a beautiful and heartbreaking tale—though I do not know, besides the mention of birds— why you have assigned it to me."

He stood up again to stir the stew, his mind conjuring the broken body of the indian maiden in the legend. Waseya waved her hand in his direction languidly, dismissing his words as nonsense, whispers lost in the wind.

"Because it is a warning, young Crow. And as I said, it is not for you. Love is not guaranteed in this life, especially for one that will push the gift of it away when it is given. Love is to be grasped where it is found before its time is ended, which is always too soon for those in love."

He started to speak, but her eyes silenced him.

"But, also, it is a lesson. Love is a leap into the unknown. It is to be bravely endeavored, or not attempted at all." She studied him for a moment, and spoke again.

"There is a different ending to the story, it was told to me by the shaman of my tribe, when I was very young. Would you like to hear it?"

Crow nodded, still not understanding the purpose of these stories.

"In the shaman's story, Ownee jumps to her death, risks all to reunite with her beloved. But she is saved. Gen-gwon had waited in his crow body, and had carried her back to the place that she jumped. Ownee knew that Gen-gwon did not wish her to join him on the path of souls. And in time, she fell in love with another warrior, who loved her and gave her back the life she had lost when Gen-gwon had left the world. For the rest of her days, whenever she spied a Crow, she looked on with gratitude, knowing it was her lost beloved, Gen-gwon, who had given her another chance to find happiness when her world had been darkness."

Crow breathed out heavily, puzzling through her words and metaphors. This old woman did not even know him! Yes, yet…his childhood had taught him to listen closely to his elders. To consider carefully their messages.

Breaking his thoughts off half-contemplated, she waved her hand before his eyes again.

"Enough for today. You will stay for dinner and then you will go and stay with Mrs. Alberts in town. I have already told her that she would have a lodger for the season. Your room will be prepared."

Crow sputtered and started. He was taken by surprise, once again, for the day, an unusual occurrence for him. "How did you…? That is, how could you have known I was coming?"

The old woman shrugged and stood up, busying herself with wooden bowls and setting the table, shooing him with her eyes. All the while, humming the same melody that had become familiar and calming to Crow, a lullaby he remembered down to his bones, but knew he'd never heard before.

Sitting down over the simple meal, she spoke without looking at him, every silent word uttered as if the questions coming from him were as puzzling to her as her answers were for him.

"There are those who can read the secrets of the island as easily as you study your books of law. The spirits mutter, 'visitor', the trees sing, 'a chicot'. The waves breathe 'sadness', and the wind says, 'destiny'. I listen, and I watch, and I remember."

Later, Crow walked to the center of town and knocked on Mrs. Alberts' door, shuffled up the stair, expected as he had been foretold. His belongings from the ship delivered when it had docked an hour or two before. His worldly goods knowing their destination before even Crow had.

His mind reached back to Waseya and the tale of Lover's Leap, to her warnings and his meeting with the Chief Grey Wolf. Finally as he slipped beneath the blankets and blew out the candle, the wisps of smoke curled around the black of the room and his mind settled. He thought of Raven Delacroix, the sweetness of the sap on her hands, and the painting in Waseya's cabin. The two figures atop Arch Rock taking on the faces of Gen-gwon and Ownee, then his own visage and Raven's strange unforgettable eyes.

That night he dreamt of maple sweet kisses and falling, falling, but he wasn't sure if his body would break, or his heart would soar.

:8:
Philippe

Many imagine that they can guess what happens to a soul when the body dies. But they are wrong. It is beyond the bounds of mortal imagination.

Mais, pour moi? Rien. For me, nothing. I had never thought of death at all. My arms were vigorous and strong, rowing the canoes filled with the men of my brigade. I had no time for such thoughts as my fingers nimbly set the traps for beaver, stoat, and ermine. I was distracted with making love to beautiful girls, and pleasing myself to break their hearts, and those of my family. I did not even think of these hearts, truth be told. The heart, they say is a great strong muscle itself, I dismissed the notion that it could break, or stop beating. I treated it as I did all the other muscles and sinews and bones of my being, a thing to be used fully, and often. I will not say I took it for granted, I simply...never thought of anything at all.

But now, thought works differently. It no longer moves in the straight lines of time, because my time, as it were, is finished. Instead my presence and my intentions move in coils, circling around like smoke signals, attempting to attach themselves onto the moment as it is happening in order to leave a mark proving I still exist.

Now I spend my moments haunting the family I gave no thought to, and lingering over the woman I chased away. I wish I could say that I found solace in seeing the love between two people I hurt, my brother Jean-Luc, and the love I lost, Cora. But, I cannot. Not because I despise happiness that can never be mine, but because I am somehow…distant from these feelings. Instead, I go to the places where my spirit finds rest and warmth and calm. These are the only sensations I experience now, and so I pursue them relentlessly.

I float through the world that I used to call my own, seeing everything and doing nothing. I can change nothing, but see the changes coming as they sail into the shores of the island like so many ships into the harbor. I can be near my family, those I should have loved in life, but I cannot love them. Not truly. Love is for the living.

A shadow cannot love for all that it follows you. The mist cannot embrace you for all that it surrounds you.

Mon dieu, il est vrai, so I wait and I watch and I sing my songs.

Youpe! Youpe! Sur la rivière
Vous ne m'entendez quère
Youpe! Youpe! Sur la rivière
Vous ne m'ententendez pas

Huzzah! Huzzah! On the river
You can hardly hear me,
Huzzah! Huzzah! On the river,
You don't hear me at all…

:9:

Peregrine

He had arrived back to the small white-washed cabin after speaking with Jacques, still unsure if dabbling in physick was a wise decision. Sometimes he would look down at his hands and they were covered in the fresh crimson of life-blood and he would pause in horror before realizing it was his mind playing tricks. He felt a veritable Lady Macbeth in these moments, and for good reason.

He had murdered his wife, after all. Double, double, toil and trouble, indeed. And stepping through the door, he sensed another presence before he saw it.

Looking up, he beheld a man of middling height nervously wringing a handkerchief in his ruddy paws. The man's appearance seemed to echo the health and vigor of those same strong, squirming hands, which made their anxiousness that much more perplexing. His cheeks were red, flushed with his walk there, which told Peregrine he hadn't been waiting long. The man's eyes were a forgettable cornflower blue, set atop high cheekbones that at one time would have been handsome, but were now somewhere between angled and puffed out. The most glorious part of him was the stark whiteness of his hair and thick, whipped cream eyebrows, like two dove feathers on his red face. He looked so much like a burning ember, white ash at the top and glowing red beneath that Peregrine could almost think him hot to the touch.

Neither man had spoken yet, Peregrine because he

was confused and dismayed at the man's being there, having hoped to have time alone in the surgery to peruse medical texts and prepare himself for Jacques' arrival.

The man before him though, barely seemed to notice Peregrine's arrival and subsequent study of his trembling person at all. His own private thoughts and worries so absorbing that he seemed to have forgotten his errand completely. Finally, Peregrine was forced to break the silence when the peculiar man had unnerved him thoroughly.

"Sir, may I assist you? Perhaps you are arrived by mistake…"

Roused from his attitude of mesmerized disquiet, the dim blue eyes found Peregrine's. Smiling weakly, he shoved the handkerchief into his pocket, and then patted it three times, like a ritual.

"My apologies, my apologies, I'm sure, Mr. ah-hem, *Doctor* Rast."

"There is nothing to forgive, sir. Though I find that I am at a disadvantage, not knowing your name."

"Ah, quite right. Quite right! Yes, my apologies, I… well, I came here after I saw your inimitable uncle had purchased the cottage for use as a doctor's quarters or some such."

Peregrine forced a smile. The man had still not revealed his name.

"Well, feel free to look about the space."

The man nodded, his bushy eyebrows bobbing about comically in the midst of his aggressive head-nodding. He started to turn around, when suddenly, his head whipped back to the front, as if remembering something he had momentarily forgotten.

"Stevens! Mason T. Stevens, Mayor of this great Isle of Mackinac, the great turtle of the straits."

Peregrine extended a hand, his smile again automatic, though his brow was etched deeply with lines of worry. It had occurred to him that the man could be quite deranged. As if sensing his doubts, Mr. Stevens pulled the handkerchief out and blotted his face—cheek, forehead, cheek, and then replaced it into his pocket, patting it three more times.

"Mr....ah...Doctor Rast, it did come to my attention that you were, that is, *are* a man of medicine with training from the Royal College of Surgeons, no less."

Peregrine offered him a small bow, and Stevens paused in his affable, casual speech and squinted both eyes, nodding his head slowly, as if they were sharing a great trust between them. Though, Peregrine could not imagine what it was or could be.

"This is true, Mayor Stevens. But, I am no longer practicing. I have come to your fair Mackinac to live quietly among my uncle's family."

Peregrine made a gesture that would signal the end of the discussion, his eyes leaping toward the volumes of medical texts he was eager to look through. But when he looked back at the mayor, the man was still standing in the same attitude, not taking the clear hint to leave. Mason Stevens' arms came to rest on the top of his great belly, like a small natural arm rest that had formed of necessity for his tired limbs over time. Peregrine saw the way Stevens held his hands together, tightly clasped, and realized that if he were to release them they would no doubt fly back to his pocket to worry at the handkerchief.

And all at once, Peregrine understood the man's odd behavior and speech.

"You are come for medical aid, Mr. Stevens?"

And though a large part of him wanted to push the round man out the door, like rolling a boulder, that secret part of Peregrine had already overruled him. His hands had already begun rolling his sleeves to his elbows, his eyes traveling over Mr. Stevens' person, searching out causes of dis-ease on his robust figure.

Leading Stevens to a chair, Peregrine opened up his black leather doctor's bag for the third time in the last two days. He quickly examined, observed and asked questions of his new patient. His ears taking in every nuance of the man's speech, every hesitation in his answers.

Peregrine turned around and walked over to the work table, looking through the stores of plants and herbs his uncle had procured. He hadn't yet made an exhaustive inventory, but he noted with pleasure the thoroughness and variety of the plants. His uncle must have consulted with a midwife, and probably a native healer. Before he could remind himself that these few patients he was helping were exceptions to his vow to no longer practice, he had already made a note to find the healer who had advised on these herbs. He would be eager to learn. And this time, he didn't catch himself thinking that treacherous thought.

A guttural throat clearing and the sound of a rumbling stomach brought Peregrine's focus sharply back to Stevens. He couldn't help but roll his eyes as he turned back around. Stevens' dull blue eyes were narrowed again, but now with worry, and one hand was hidden behind his protruding belly, no doubt making its way to the handkerchief.

"Well? What is it, Doctor? I suspect it is a cancer of some kind? Or perhaps typhus? I had a cousin who was taken by typhus. Rotten luck. But that's my kind of luck, truth be told. Tell me true, Doctor Rast, the mayor of Mackinac's term in life and in office has come to an abrupt end." Without waiting for a response of any kind, Stevens hung his head and stood up stoically, making to leave. "I'll have to break the news to my wife. But I will carry on, Doctor, I assure you. I thank you for your diagnosis."

The words were spoken with such a dramatic finality that it was all Peregrine could do not to laugh. Instead he adopted an expression of earnest solemnity, adding his own theatrics to the scene and called for the man to take a seat.

Mr. Stevens sat back down, nodding with a grim expression across his plump features, which rather robbed him of the respectability his manner was calling for. Peregrine swallowed a smile and spoke.

"I'm afraid, Mayor Stevens, that the diagnosis is indeed dire."

Stevens' chin bobbed up and down, soberly, obviously satisfied that his own feelings on his condition had been confirmed.

"Go on, Doctor. You needn't fear my reaction, I'm not faint of heart."

Peregrine did not understand the element of drama that Mayor Stevens was insisting on, but he realized that he rather liked the man. For all of his oddities, he was resolutely genuine in the face of his invented calamity.

"You are suffering, sir, from an intestinal upset. That is, a disquiet in the bowels."

Mr. Stevens nodded gravely once again, as if he had been given a death sentence rather than a common ailment, that although uncomfortable and potentially embarrassing, was in no way dangerous.

With the same attitude of seriousness, Peregrine continued, "I will prepare an elixir, to be steeped in hot water and drank after meals. Which, I should not need to tell you, must have heavy creams and butters removed and no game meats or excess sugar."

Mayor Stevens stood again, exhaling heavily, and shook Dr. Rast's hand heartily.
"It will be a trial, Doctor, but we all must soldier on. I can't thank you enough. I have high hopes that with your good physick, my determination and the good Lord above, we may beat this thing yet. I'm back to the office, now. Time stops for no man, no matter his affliction, you know."

Peregrine suppressed a smirk and swallowed another laugh, his stomach filling with hilarity.
"I have heard something of the sort. I have every hope as well, Mayor. I will send the tincture to your home this evening."

"Bless you, pray send the bill along as well."

Before Peregrine could protest, for to accept payment would mean he was truly a doctor once more,

Mr. Stevens had rolled himself out the door. He was now bustling back into town, his great belly proceeding before him, a herald of his presence.

Though silence was what Peregrine had hoped for on his return, the sudden departure left too much space for his own thoughts to crowd the room. It seemed that only when he was focused on a remedy for an illness that his mind could grow quiet. His greatest solace was keeping his mind on the present moment, never allowing it to stray down the path of his tortured past, maintaining a blessed distance from the memories of his dear, sweet Gabrielle. And then, inevitably, his thoughts would find her. He would be lost once again, the image of her consuming him as he fought his way back to the experience of *now*, a place where he was free of her.

He turned the garnet ring around and around on his hand, the red stone seeming to glow with intensity. He would never be free of her. He never wanted to be. He didn't deserve to be.

Shaking his head, he made a mental catalogue of the surgery. First, the tools; a trepanning set, for draining blood on the brain. A spring lancet, for bloodletting; a practice Peregrine had little faith in, his patients always seeming weaker rather than healthier afterward. A tourniquet, scalpel, Hey Saw, bone saw—for limbs, and a metacarpal saw for fingers and toes. Peregrine had done a fair amount of amputations with rather more success than many other doctors. Though, he attributed this to chance rather than medical art. He stared at the metacarpal saw, recalling a small boy, a farrier's son, who'd had his tiny wrist stepped on by a horse's hoof. And though Peregrine had set the bone correctly, the damage was too great, and blood poisoning had set in.

His small face had been bloodless and white, but he had been eerily quiet as Peregrine sawed the little bone off. He remembered it had felt barbaric to use the capital saw—the bone saw, so large it had seemed next to the boy's arm. The child had worn the face of death, though he had lived. But no longer as an apprentice to his father, for a farrier needs both hands to shoe a horse. Instead, the boy would live a half life, a burden on his family, and so, it *had* been a kind of death. The boy, laying on the table, with his arm dead beside him, and with it, his future.

Peregrine exhaled heavily, choking back a strong emotion he hadn't realized was still connected to the event, and turned his attention to the herbs. Ginger for nausea, peppermint for indigestion, comfrey for bedsores and healing broken limbs, aloe for burns, arnica for pain, chamomile for heartburn, upset stomach or colic. Then, his eyes found a few herbs that he did not recognize, probably local flora that did not exist in England. Some of the herbs in the collection had come from the island, but others were surely imported in. Which led his mind to Jean-Luc Delacroix, and his family. He had heard that his wife was a kind of healer, perhaps it was she that had helped stock the surgery. But, if she was so learned in healing, why did she not help her son herself?

He continued his catalogue, shooing his mind away from questions he could not answer. Mullein for chest congestion, garlic for colds. He reached into a few different jars, sniffing the contents. Reaching into a few of the containers he measured out a bit of this, and a few spoonfuls of that, beginning the tincture for Mr. Stevens. Rhubarb, magnesia and laudanum, adding a touch of wormwood before he placed it into a small packet.

His mind was fully occupied on the herbs when he heard Jacques' voice outside the door, the sound reminding him that he had quite missed supper. He turned his body and his mind to the door, and to the case of the boy about to come through it. There were a few different elixirs he could concoct as physick, but to begin with, he decided he had a different kind of medicine for the young man. As Jacques stepped in, face open and expectant, Peregrine took a good look at his young relation, no longer a boy, but with the same desperation of the young farrier on his operating table. He would not allow this boy to feel a burden to his family. Jacques would have a full life, for Peregrine would do nothing else in halves.

He turned his ring, twice—thrice upon his finger and resolved to make this boy whole again.

:10:
Sarah

She watched from the window as her husband trotted up the lane to their house. His hand came to his pocket and patted it three times, then to his mouth, which he also patted lightly three times. Sarah signaled to the maid, Rose, to tell cook that it was finally time for supper, late again, as usual.

Mason came in through the door, and she approached him, both of them pressing their foreheads together for some time, before he squeezed her hand—thrice—and waddled into his study. Sarah smoothed the top of her hair, relieving some of the pull from the severity of the pins, and looked lovingly at the study door, which stood ajar.

Mason had been elected mayor twice now, and though the office gave him an air of respectability, she knew her husband was thought ridiculous. A competent and hardworking mayor, but absurd nonetheless. His strange behaviors and rituals, three pats, three knocks, three kisses goodnight. This did not trouble *her* though, because she was thought idiotic as well.

They hadn't always been thus, two people who found themselves the objects of kind-hearted derision by their neighbors. It was a consequence of their shared past tragedies that had made them so. And she was glad of it—for if the choice was between buffoonery or maudlin eternal melancholy, she knew which she'd rather.

The Stevens' had three stillborn daughters in three years, though this was many years ago now. Then, a son, who was bonny and bright and blooming. But, he'd wandered away from his nanny in the wood one day when he was but three years of age, and they'd not found him for three heartbreaking days. When they did finally, it was his cold body, his lips the same light blue of his father's eyes.

It was that day that Sarah had stopped talking, all of the thoughts of her mind dying on her lips, her words caught in the snare of her throat, blocked by the screams she'd bottled and stored there that day.

She'd taken to only wearing light blue herself. All of her shawls, scarves, gowns, stockings, all pale, frosty blue.

But for all of this, Sarah adored Mason. And so their daily forehead kiss had begun, a way of pressing her thoughts and words into his mind every day when his feet brought him back home.

From her windows she saw much. She'd seen Rose leave and head in the direction of the Delacroix house, as if Sarah hadn't already guessed what sort of medicine the girl would be asking for. She'd seen Peregrine Rast, Mr. Nicholas' nephew, wandering through the forest with Jacques. The man supporting the boy, evidently showing him how to breathe when his face pinked too warmly. She'd seen the chestnut haired stranger, his own sorrows laying as thickly on his brow as they did Sarah's, walking toward town, probably seeking lodging for the night.

All these things she observed, and they became a narrative in her mind. A story she would draw for cook and Rose later, and they would give her thoughts voice in a way she could no longer.

Sarah sighed and turned toward the kitchen. She liked to be around cook and the little maid, they chattered enough between them that her silence went unnoticed. Even if Rose had been melancholy about her troubles, not trusting cook or Sarah with her sorrows—sorrows that both older women had known of for some time—she was still sunshine in Sarah's life. The girl hadn't any real family, all of them dying of smallpox when she was small. Rose had been unwillingly taken in by a neighbor. Sarah had offered for the girl to live with her and Mason, she felt motherly affection for her anyway, but Rose had declined. Probably unwilling to give up the relative freedom she had in living in town.

Footsteps outside, coming swift. She pressed her face nearer to the window, searching for the author of those steps. A skill of those who do not often speak is the talent of intense listening. The run itself sounded native, like wind through leaves, but the tread was harsher, a white man's shoes.

Stepping quickly to the door, she opened it, before the man outside even had time to knock. It was the same curly-haired stranger she'd seen earlier, though now she noted the copper of his skin.

He was flushed, and his features were consumed with fear. "Madam, is there a man within? Just there…" he pointed in the direction of the Delacroix house, which lay some few hundreds of yards beyond their own, and through swarm of trees, "…I have found a boy, his lips are blue…I…"

Sarah's hand went to her head and she felt a swoon, which she fought. No more boys with dead lips, this one she would save. She tried her voice, clutching at her throat desperately, but all that came out was a humming "Mmmm" sound.

Mason had come out of his study and left quickly with the stranger, and before she could realize what was happening, she called out,

"It is Jacques!" and her husband nodded following the other man more swiftly. She watched them both hurry to Jacques, whom she'd seen walk that way some time before, a while after seeing him with Mr. Nicholas' nephew.

She walked to the kitchen, grabbed the blackberry brandy and headed out herself to assist however she could. It was not until she stepped into the green of the leaves that she realized she had spoken, though now, again, the words would no longer come.

:11:

Raven

Raven's eyes stayed closed for much of the walk. She had felt it was a kind of betrayal to be leaving the house at all, and felt guilty admiring the beauty of the summer day when Jacques could not.

She thought of him now, her heart aching for her little brother, thought of the bright turquoise light of his character, hushed now. Raven almost turned back around, running to his supine form, pale and unmoving.

But, her mother had shooed her out. She had spent too much time lying next to his bed, her hand clasped in his, a cold cloth or a sip of water to cool him when he awoke from his fevered dreams. If it had been her choice, she would have remained in the sick room, reading to him though he could not hear her, singing to him, telling the stories of their childhood to him and to herself. But, instead of returning, she embraced him with her mind, sending back loving thoughts with each step.

It had been an entire week since she had been out of doors, the longest she'd ever gone in the whole of her life. She was on her way to the cabin of her old nurse, Waseya, accompanied by the steady step of Turtle. His small, black paws hardly leaving a print in the trail. A kind of mournful ghost, padding silently alongside her. The poor terrier had been shooed out as well, too many days spent sleeping on his master's chest, and his feet, anywhere that was close to the boy he loved so much.

Waseya had been at their house the night of the accident, practicing medicine alongside her mother and her cousin Peregrine. Raven was surprised that he was doctoring again—there had been a kind of finality about him when he first came to the island, as if his life was ending and Mackinac was to be his purgatory. She was glad he had changed his mind, the change did something to brighten his eyes and brought a glow to his handsome face. His decision had probably saved her brother's life.

Jacques could not recall what had occurred. Upon waking he had been overjoyed— apparently he and Peregrine had been engaged in a breathing exercise earlier that day. The young doctor had spent time with her brother on that last day, brisk walking, jumping, gamboling around the forest working to strengthen Jacques' weak lungs. To her brother's mind, all he could remember upon waking was the feeling of triumph, and of hope. Hope for the future he might have now that he could grasp onto the edges of his own health.

And somehow the snake bite had been forgotten, or blocked out.

It was shocking—unheard of—for the massasauga rattler to be found on the island. No one had ever seen or heard of such a bite happening on Mackinac, even in legends. The snake was barely found in lower Michigan. The doctor had labored, drawing the venom out bit by bit, until red-faced and spent, he claimed it was all he could do. An act that was incredible enough to all present to warrant their approbation. He'd learned the skill of it from a doctor who had served in India he'd said, and he had added to that some ideas he'd gleaned from books. To Raven and her family, to simply have said it was magic would have been sufficient.

Cora and Waseya had then sang and brewed up teas to strengthen the blood and chanted to shoo away malevolent spirits. And somehow, in and out of consciousness, he had lived.

Waseya said that it was a good omen. That the snake had died in the biting, its body laying still and silent near Jacques when Henri Crow found him. Waseya said that it was a blessing from the Manitou, Jacques had lived through the trial and was now reborn stronger.

Without warning, Henri Crow himself flashed into her mind, illuminated in detail behind her closed eyelids. Tall and broad, his strong arms carrying her brother home as if he weighed nothing at all, Mayor Stevens trailing behind. He had handled Jacques gently, most gently, but swiftly. She had caught a few glimpses of him throughout the ordeal, watched him obey all of Peregrine's commands the moment they were given. Her eyes had met his a number of times, but fleetingly, neither able to keep the fire from them before looking away. There was a kind of magic between them for all of his strange behavior, but when she had looked for him as dawn broke, announcing that Jacques survived the first night—Crow was gone. And as joyful as she was to see Jacques rallying, as much as her heart brimmed with relief, a few tears of sorrow had fallen to have missed his leaving.

Her mind lingered on the memory of his strange eyes, so bright and warm in the firelight. Forgotten was her pain and confusion in the wood forgotten, just the memory of his lips, those lips that had kissed her hand so ardently...

"Coralie! Come in, child."

Raven broke from her reverie, blushing, and opened her eyes. Her feet had known the way without her sight to guide her. She was just outside Waseya's cabin, and Turtle was impatiently scratching at the door.

The door opened into the room, and Raven stepped neatly into her old nurse's outstretched arms, kissing both of her cheeks fondly, just as she had as a child. Waseya folded her into an embrace, and for a moment, she *was* a child, retreating into her nurse's arms after a scraped elbow or a bee sting. The past few days, the worry, the fretting, the tears she would not allow to fall, willing herself to remain strong for Jacques who needed her to keep her courage. All of the trials of the past few days melted from her body and out her arms into the small indian woman she loved so much. Waseya said it was her gift, to absorb sorrow. It did not sink into her, weighing her down, instead it bobbed on the surface of her, like a ship through the waves. Easily sailing from one part of her to another, not a hindrance, but a shot of silver in her hair, or an extra gleam in her eye.

Inhaling from the embrace, she took a few sure steps across the wooden floorboards of the oft-trod cabin. She heard the scratch of pen and paper, and casting her eye to the chair by the fire, she found the source was her Aunt Isobel, her Uncle Nicholas' wife, who was furiously writing. Raven stepped closer, and her aunt, sensing her presence, looked up, startled, as if she had forgotten where she was. Isobel was her mother's younger sister, though no one would have guessed it. Where Cora was tall and dark, Isobel was small and fair. Raven's mother had much the same figure she'd had in youth, kept trim with long rambles through the wood and daybreak swims with her daughter. Isobel was softer, rounder, her sweetness drifting from her eyes, out of the ends of her hair and borne aloft to whomever she was speaking with. There was always the color of the palest pink surrounding her, like early spring roses.

Isobel had taken up recording the legends of the island. Sometimes from her husband, Nicholas, or from Cora and Waseya. She documented the ways the stories changed from storyteller to storyteller. Isobel hoped to publish a volume recounting the legends to preserve the history of the island. To keep alive the folklore of the varied tribes who called it home, even those tribes that only came for their summer payments.

But now, her brow was creased with concern, her eyes focused on Raven. She extended a hand out, gently pulling her niece in with an attitude of beseeching worry.

"Coralie, darling, you look drawn and weary. How is dear Jacques since I last saw him?"

Aunt Isobel had come with her three daughters the day before and had sat with Jacques. She had hummed to him in her soft voice, sometimes singing a nursery song whilst he slept. Kindness seemed to come to Isobel as easily as breathing, a trait that Raven admired but could not master in herself.

"Jacques is weak, Aunt, but mending."

Waseya crossed in front of the hearth, hanging a kettle on the fire. She was muttering something about the signs of the Manitou's favor and that they were only bestowed after great trials of spirit. Raven remained silent. If her nurse was resolved to see a blessing in the hardship, so be it.

"My mother has sent me. She said that when I left, I would take some of Jacques' pain with me, sprinkling it piece by piece onto the trail behind me. And when I return I will bring the renewal of the forest to his room."

Both women nodded, obviously agreeing with her mother's logic, though Raven had to hide the the roll of her own eyes. She did not shy away from the mystic or enchantment, but she did think it odd how easily both women accepted whatever strange things her mother said. Most other women on the island, or in Michigan, would think her soft in the head after making such a statement.

Clearing her throat, she changed the topic, slipping into gossip. Not something her family generally engaged in, but an easy turn of discussion for minds wishing to think of something other than sorrow.

Raven sat comfortably on a stool near the fire, Turtle curling into a black ball at her feet. She smoothed her bottle green dress over her knees, thankfully the gown was made from a light cotton else the fire would have smothered her.

"The day that Jacques took ill, Rose O'Malley came to my mother's house."

No one spoke. Her aunt picked up her pen once again, and looked as though she would continue writing. Waseya's lively fingers formed corn cakes and the light from the window shone in to catch the silver in her braids.

"Oh?" Isobel finally said, smiling slightly. "How nice."

Raven looked down at the dog beneath her feet, it certainly was *not* nice. She wanted to speak to these women, to get their thoughts, only she wasn't sure how to broach the subject.

"She is with child." She blurted. The words were out. She was certain it had been the wrong way to go about it, but if she'd waited until her aunt and nurse asked the right questions she'd have as much grey in her hair as Waseya.

"How do you know this?" Waseya was speaking but not looking at her, intent on the cakes. "And if this is true, your mother will assist her in growing a healthy child, or to release the spirit back into the island. It is not your place to stand on another's path."

Raven felt the rebuke sharply, but Waseya did not understand. She looked back down at Turtle, the flames of the fire shedding gleaming light onto his glossy fur. She looked up and met her aunt's eyes, her pen resting gently on the open page.

"What is it, Coralie?" Her aunt had no gifts like those of her mother, no deeper understanding of the world, no magical connection to ghosts or spirits. Her gifts were more ordinary. The ability to see into the hearts of others, and to believe the best of her fellow men. It was a gift of great empathy. Raven couldn't help but wonder which sister had the greater strengths. She straightened up, and looking from one face to the other, spoke.

"I know because…because though she has taken out her stays, the large growing belly is very easily seen under her dress. And I have seen the second glow around Rose. And when that is seen, it means that she is too far along for a choice. It means that my mother will only offer physick to make a child strong and healthy. But, I am afraid that this is not what Rose did want to hear."

Isobel's face flashed with fresh concern.

"What do you think she will do if your mother has refused her?"

Raven opened her mouth to speak, but it was Waseya who answered.

"If Cora does not give her what she wants, she will go to the beaches. There are always those that are wicked in some of the tribes—those that will sell the herbs and charms that rid the mother of her lifeblood along with the life of an unborn child. But if she is desperate and the tribe is desperate…" She spread her arms apart, fingers still coated with sticky ground corn, in a gesture that was something between a sigh and surrender.

Isobel finished the thought, "And if the government payments are anything like they have been in past years, then Rose O'Malley may not be the only in danger."

Raven darted a look at both women and mouthed the word, "salt".

In that one word was a warning. A memory not her own from the year of her birth. That summer the government had sent salt as payment to the tribes, to be doled out to them according to the size of their lodge. The difficulty and eventual uproar had rested on one simple fact, a truth that the government had been too ignorant or too shortsighted to see. Though many in the new United States considered salt valuable, but the red man did not use salt. Most could not abide the taste of food prepared with it. There had almost been a rebellion, as many tribes depended on the metal coins and yards of calico to survive the coming winter. All this, even as the government chipped away at their territories and hunting grounds giving their lands to the ever increasing influx of white settlers.

The women's eyes all traveled to the fire, the ghost of unresolved difficulties sitting too close for all of them to find comfort. Many of those problems had crept into the room with them, stowed in their secret hearts, even though the women had not voiced their fears aloud. But, there was a kind of solidarity born of the nearness of the others. So even if each woman's concern was not spoken, the ache that it put on her soul seemed less.

For Raven, the conflicting behavior of Mr. Henri Crow, coupled with her concern for her brother now mingled with the larger, looming problem of Rose and the possible unrest on the island. She looked over to her Aunt Isobel, and saw the glimmer of one solitary tear drop down her cheek. She wondered what secret sadness her aunt contained within her breast, and was moved to ask what was troubling her. But Waseya bustled between them, placing her corn cakes on the griddle gingerly, as if sensing the room had grown too maudlin.

"No more gloom. I was to begin a tale for your aunt

to record. One that you have never heard, little bird."

Raven laughed, "I doubt that very much. I think I have heard all of your legends. At least three times each."

"Humph!" Waseya teased, "Not this one." The lightness in her voice twisted into a firm line on her face. She took a seat in a high-backed chair that had been cut exactly to her form. Raven's father had carved it himself out of maple.

"I have only told this tale once before. To Nicholas and Cora. Jean-Luc was out playing boy's games with Philippe, and Edward, Nicholas' older brother, may his soul be safe with the Manitou. And you, Isobel, were in the other room embroidering."

Isobel's cheeks reddened, feeling a scolding that hadn't been in the old woman's words. "It took me some time to see the importance of the stories."

Waseya did not acknowledge the comment, but instead was slipping into the other part of herself. The core of her being, where the stories lived. A place where she was neither young nor old, ugly or beautiful, but instead *was* only the story on her lips.

"An old man had a son of whom he was very proud. When the time of fasting came, that his son might become a man, the father was determined on his son receiving a greater guardian spirit of any in the tribe. And so as the boy prepared, his father bade him to not only fast for the seven days, as was custom, but for twelve. Not wishing to disobey his father, the young man agreed. His fasting lodge was built, he lay down on his mat, and began his vigil. Each morning the father returned, urging his son to continue so that he might bring honor to the tribe. Urging his son to become a warrior or a hunter. Thus it continued for nine days."

Waseya paused, and licked her lips, leaning forward to flip the corn cakes.

"On the tenth day, the son spoke. 'Father, my guiding dreams whisper of evil to come. May I leave off my fast?' The father answered that all of the son's glory would be lost if he did so and bade him wait two more days. The next morning, the son asked his father again, warning of the sorrow in his dreams. The father refused again. On the twelfth day, the father came to the fasting lodge, bearing food. At the door, he paused, for he heard his son speaking. He peered through the door to see his son painting his body black. His chest and his arms and his back, even his eyes took on the blackness of night.

'My father has ignored my pleas, and so my guardian spirit, the crow, shall take me as his own. Up into the skies and the branches, and he will be as a father to me now that my man's body is lost to the earth.'
The father ran to his son, who was now black from the hair on his head to the bottom of his heel. 'Do not leave me, my son!' But the young man had taken on a new shape and flew to the top of the lodge. 'Now I am called Crow. Regret not the chance you see, for I shall be close to my guardian, and to Mackinac, near to the people in times of woe."

Waseya had finished, and was now lifting the cakes gently from the fire, offering one to Turtle, who licked his nose over and again after swallowing, searching for a stray crumb. The women were silent for a few moments, the only sound the steady scratch-scratch of Isobel's pen. Finally, Raven whispered.

"I had not heard that before. It is…very sad. What does it mean? And why did you tell it now?"

Waseya's eyes returned to normal, her breathing easy and her features relaxing, gathering her spirit back from the world of legends.

"It is tale of knowing when to listen to warnings, about forgetting pride and acting with courage before it is too late. A little of your revelations this morning called it into my mind, little bird. As for why I did tell it…" Her eyes went far away again and Raven and Isabel exchanged a puzzled look.

"I met a man a few days past, the day of your brother's blessing in fact. He came here and sat…just there." She motioned absently toward Isobel's chair. "He was a man called Crow…and I wondered if he was sent from the Manitou. So much sorrow hung to him, like feathers on wings. Then, at your father's house, I saw him again and knew it was so. A Crow, sent by the Manitou, to usher the island into the coming sorrows, and perhaps to fly away from his own and back to the manitou…"

The sun dimmed, and Raven almost grasped her throat the way Jacques did when he could not breathe. What was this strange wind of unrest blowing across the island? All the more did her heart beat in a rhythm of footsteps, her own, she thought, fleeing these shores as she had always dreamed.

:12:
Crow

Crow drank deeply from the cold draft of cider that Mrs. Alberts had solicitously brought into his chamber some minutes before. Every day since he had arrived had been much the same. Mrs. Alberts finding excuses to fuss about the room, treating his shirts as though they belonged to a king, tut-tutting over the state of his boots after a morning's trample through the woods, or adding another portion of dinner on the plate when she thought he wouldn't notice. She was a woman who had spent the whole of her life waiting to care for her husband, a Delacroix Shipping captain, only to have him taken from her too soon. He had passed on three winters earlier, too soon for her to have realized her plans to spoil and coddle him in his advancing years. She had been a good mother, teaching her son and daughter well. Now, they were grown with families of their own, and though she was loved, she was no longer needed.

All this she told Crow as she plumped pillows and folded blankets, straightened and pressed, mended and scrubbed. Crow felt at home, though it was not like any home he'd ever had. She made him feel what home often was in novels, a place of warmth and comfort. He was looked after, cared for, worried about. Welcome. Mrs. Alberts might prattle on until her voice was hoarse with use, but she never pried into his business. He could almost pretend that the aim of his sojourn on Mackinac was a visit with her, a long lost relation or widowed aunt. But, he continued to remind himself that he had come on important business, the Lord's own justice—even if it seemed that he was the only one who cared to right the wrong.

During the weeks that he had been on the island, Grey Wolf had sent no messengers and no indian had come to see him at all. He had word that his grandfather and his tribe were coming later in the summer, but this information was from Mrs. Alberts, who had a finger in as many slices as there were pies. He thought perhaps to go himself and see Jean-Luc Delacroix, to waste no more time in laying the case before the man, except…except there was the matter of the boy's accident. Crow found it increasingly difficult to think of M. Delacroix as an enemy. His genuine kindness when Crow had carried the young man, barely breathing, into their home, laying him tenderly on the table. Delacroix's obvious respect for Waseya's medicine, treating her with equal regard to Dr. Rast—a licensed medical man! M. Delacroix has chosen a wife with something wild about her, as if the island itself was a part of her spirit. Tinctures that mixed themselves and herbs that seemed to appear without being gathered as if the forest was working on her behalf. And those eyes, those glittering cat's eyes… peculiar.

And then Raven. It was she too that made it difficult for Crow to hate M. Delacroix. When she entered a room, everyone breathed easier, as though she had brought a refreshing breeze with her steps. The worry lines would lessen from every face, and Jacques' color warmed from a sickening white to the pink of health. Dr. Rast had been more precise in his dressing of the wound and more confident in his abilities when Raven stood at his elbow, assisting him. She had a power over others that she seemed completely unaware of. A power over him most assuredly. Their eyes had met a few times that night, and inexplicably, Crow had wanted to take her into his arms. To hold her to him, selfishly, to keep some of that calm for himself. He did not understand what the force was exactly, what power it was that drew him to her, but when he was with her, he felt that he needed her like he needed air to breathe.

And so he had left their home without saying farewell to anyone. He couldn't bear to be around her a moment longer, he feared he'd lose himself completely. How easy it would be to be drawn into their world, how happily he would melt into it. But no, that was not his purpose here.

He just had to continue telling himself this.

But, he could not stay away. He left Mrs. Alberts every morning and plodded through the wood trying to convince himself that he wasn't seeking Raven, but then feeling forlorn when he did not spy her. He had not seen her emerge until today, eyes closed with her little black terrier on her way to Waseya's cabin. He wanted to follow her there, it took everything inside of him to keep himself rooted to the spot he was in, observing her from afar. He wished somehow he knew what to do with his wasted heart, that pulled against his will to join with her's.

And so he had returned, reminding himself of the hardships and indignities suffered by the indians he had met with in Detroit. Of the trust they had put into the promises of Cross Shipping, only to be stripped further of their honor. His mind ran over the many varied insults and betrayals the tribes suffered by the white man, each half of him warring against the other. He thought of the other successful campaigns that had been waged against corrupt men and dishonorable companies to give independence and honor back to his mother's people. He thought of his part in them, and how through his singular upbringing, his education and his knowledge of the tribes, he could be used as God's instrument to right all wrongs for them. Yes, he was resolved to make M. Delacroix answer for his conduct, to ruin him if need be; but, not yet. Not yet. He could not bring more sorrow to the Delacroix. The timing was not quite right.

Crow sat, thinking, his body turned toward the fire, watching the jump and dance of the flames, taking sips of the cider—glad that it wasn't strong enough to cloud his mind. Mrs. Alberts was sitting across from him in the small room, telling him another tale of her life on the island. She was old, with small spectacles perched on her nose. She appeared very much the kind of woman who had spent her whole life waiting to be old, her body finally able to plump and fill out into her wide skirts and her grey hair almost sighing in relief after a lifetime of brown. All of her years waiting for a comfortable retirement, golden years to spend with her husband that had never been realized. But her laughter was quick, and her gnarled hands moved faster than any young woman's he had seen. They flew through embroidery and could snatch his sock from his shoe almost before he took it off if she happened to notice it needed darning. She broke about every rule of propriety coming in on him in various stages of undress, but because of her years she seemed to think she didn't have time for rules of behavior. Crow, at first scandalized, merely shrugged now. If she did not care, neither did he.

"Henri, do you hear?"

"Of course, madam, every word."

She smiled and rolled her eyes toward the door. "Yes, I can see you are entertained. So engrossed in fact that you did not hear the banging on the door."

Crow sputtered over all of his apologies and explanations for his inattentions, but she waved him off as she walked out into the hall and toward the front door. Crow heard her speaking to whomever had knocked, but could not make out the words beyond that it was a man's voice mingled with hers, and that her usual bubbling friendliness had turned apprehensive. Quietly, he heard Mrs. Alberts call his name from the door, a note of confusion and hesitation coming through her strained voice.

"Henri, you have…a visitor."

Crow stood up, his knees popping from sitting too long in one attitude. His mind ran over the possibilities of whom it might be, cursing himself when he realized that because it wasn't a female voice soft as a summer stream, that it couldn't be Raven. And then cursing himself again for wanting it to be her in the first place. Stepping into the foyer, he saw that the voice belonged to the same smiling brave who had assisted him in bringing his canoe ashore the day he had arrived.

Mrs. Alberts looked from the indian to Crow, and Crow nodded to her, communicating that everything was fine. Uncertainty and fear seemed to lend an acidic taste to the air in the hallway, pushing down the corners of mouths and forcing hard swallows in dry throats. Mrs. Alberts smiled weakly, finally, uncomfortably, and left them together. Her sensible black shoes sounding soft clicks under the swish of her skirts.

Crow studied the boy again, and wondered where his easy grin had disappeared to. It had hung so naturally on his features on their first meeting, that he almost seemed a different man entirely without it. His shiny black hair was tangled and it appeared that he had rushed to arrive, his eyes wide and his deerskins hanging lopsided on his lanky frame. The brave too, was studying Henri. Crow looked down and felt an odd sense of shame for his finely tailored clothes. His high collar suddenly felt uncomfortably suffocating, and his fine white shirt seemed too pristinely bright under the low cut vest. He could not see his own hair, but he felt, not for the first time, wrong to have such curling chestnut coils around his temple, as if he had somehow purposely chosen them to mask the copper of his skin.

The indian was eyeing his oversized buttons with interest and Crow finally cleared his throat loudly to curtail the strange silence that had fallen between them. The young man raised his gaze, lazily, and looked into Crow's eyes. It was only then that his air of bored nonchalance turned to respect. It was always Crow's eyes that commanded attention, the darkness of them hitting a memory within the tribes. A memory that they could not quite grasp but captured their attention nonetheless.

"So you have come. Am I right to assume Grey Wolf sent you?" Crow spoke in Ojibwe, the language coming much easier after his meeting with Waseya. The boy nodded.

"I am called Ogima." The young man spoke quietly, turning large liquid brown eyes on Crow, brown as the spring earth after a storm. Crow thought a moment. "Ogima…this is the Ojibwe word for 'chief'."

The boy nodded again, and unsuccessfully swallowed his frown as if he were drinking pebbles.

"Yes, this is so. My tribe fights Grey Wolf and his Iroquois. We are but a small tribe, and the Iroquois, they are fierce fighters. Our war drums fall silent, and I am given to the Iroquois. I was very young, I do not remember."

Ogima spoke the words with a shrug, but Crow can see his true feelings by his expression, can see the memories he claims he does not have in the boy's eyes. "I am sorry for the loss of your tribe, Ogima." Crow spoke the words softly, but with sincerity.

"And I am sorry for yours, too." The boy replied even more quietly.

Silence descended upon them again, both men feeling awkward at the exchange. Ogima turned his gaze back to the ground and spoke.

"Grey Wolf says there is trouble among some of our people. Some that have gone to labor for the Delacroix—they are angry. From his mouth comes kind words and pretty promises, but from his hands come only lies and broken agreements. It was not always so. The change has come gradually. He is known as a friend to the red man, but his actions are that of the fox. Sneaking and untrustworthy. And so it has come that many are full of anger—but many do not wish to move against him."

"Why not?" Crow asked, his eyes narrowing in confusion.

"Because a friend that you cannot trust is still better than a violent enemy." Ogima shrugged again, communicating that everything he had spoken was the extent of his knowledge on the topic.

Crow exhaled, "I think I understand. And I can

help, or at least, I think I can. It is the reason I have come, after all…" His words drifted away from him for a moment, and Ogima raised his eyes to Crow, who quickly reigned in the scattered leaves of his thoughts. "Tell your chief that I will come tomorrow when the sun is at its highest."

The boy nodded, his features relaxing as he realized he was free to leave, his discomfort at being within the walls of the house was palpable. Crow felt another jolt of shame for not experiencing the same feelings. Without another word the boy had gone, and Crow breathed a sigh of relief. Finally, he was making progress on his errand here on the island. With any luck, soon it would be dealt with and he could leave this strange place that awakened within him so many emotions that he could not understand.

He turned around, thinking to walk back to the sitting room where he would, no doubt, be bombarded with the motherly attentions of Mrs. Alberts once again. But, a second knock sounded on the heavy oak door. Crow turned back, imagining that it was Ogima again, some piece of information forgotten in their first meeting. He opened the door expecting to see the same young face, but instead he was met with the pine-green eyes of M. Delacroix, and despite himself, Crow smiled.

It was not consciously done, he could barely help himself. He knew that the man before him was his enemy in his self-appointed mission, the foe of his mother's people, but there was something so indescribably affable about him. Jean-Luc Delacroix seemed to radiate a kind of calming kindness that tugged on the edges of Crow's mouth and involuntarily brought out his fonder feelings. He was the kind of person that drew others to him, and who filled the room with an indefinable warmth, lightening the air surrounding him. However pleasant it was, it was a mood that Crow hastened to eradicate. He could not allow the man's personality to trick him into forgetting the man that lay beneath it.

"Bonsoir, M. Crow, I hope that you will pardon my unexpected visit. I pray that I am not disturbing you." His speech was sincere, and he held Crow's gaze so earnestly that he almost felt himself flinch. Henri was careful to keep his own voice polite, but stiff. He should not like to be accused later of being less than candid in his behavior toward the family. Although, it was probably too late.

"Good evening, M. Delacroix. There is no disturbance. How may I be of service?"

Jean-Luc laughed incredulously. "You? How could you possibly lend me more service than you already have? I owe you a very great debt, monsieur. There is no treasure in this world more precious than those I love. You have preserved one of my greatest jewels, when else it may have been lost like a pebble in the bottom of a lake. No, pray, do not mention service to me. I could live a thousand years and never repay you."

Crow was shocked and moved to see that M. Delacroix was shedding tears.

"My apologies. I do not mean to blubber like a mewling calf. But, my family, M. Crow, is my whole life. Without them…" His voice trailed off as his hands traveled apart leaving a black space.

Henri was truly amazed. The accounts he'd had of the man were night and day to what he had observed.

How was it possible? Was this man really capable of the deeds he had been accused? Crow couldn't credit it, and yet…yet too often men can twist maple sugared words around dastardly thoughts and actions. All the same, he felt his whole body lose some of its rigidity and his speech softened toward him.

"Do not mention it. Any man would have done the same. There is no debt. I am only glad that I happened to be by in time to have lent assistance."

"You are modest, M. Crow. But if you are amenable, my son, Jacques, would very much like to thank you himself. He is a lad of 15, you understand, and feels the debt of gratitude keenly. I feel I must prepare you for a zealous display of hero-worship."

Crow was confused and waved away the words as if they were smoke clouding his vision. M. Delacroix shook his head, and chuckled.

"No, M. Crow, you do not understand. And ordinarily, to any other man, I would never speak of it. But because you have safeguarded my son's life, I will be frank. Jacques is …unwell. He suffers from a… weakness. Born too soon, you understand. This is why, more than most, it was imperative that whomever find him needed to act swiftly. Though I do not see my son's infirmities as obstacles, I am keenly aware that life's dangers do prey on him more menacingly…" He trailed off again, but Crow understood. He was not entirely certain why M. Delacroix felt that he deserved to hear an account of his son's sorrows. But again, Crow found that he was deeply touched by the confidence. Why was the man so difficult to hate? Before he could stop himself, he heard himself voice the thoughts in his mind.

"What of Raven?"

M. Delacroix's head jerked back, as if reeling from a slap. "Coralie?"

Reddening from the question, Crow nodded, "Yes, your daughter…"

"She is well, thank you. I did not know that you were acquainted." M. Delacroix's face contained only curiosity, not anger. But Crow felt strangely anxious, as though his thoughts were floating in script about his person.

"Only a little." Crow kept his response light.

"Of course, at the house during the melee. You would be glad to know her better I think. She is a remarkable woman. Everywhere that Coralie goes…is magic." One corner of his mouth lifted and Crow felt no improper suggestion in his urging for Crow to seek out his daughter. Rather, he found only genuine pride. As if he knew his daughter was singular and her father believed that all would benefit from an acquaintance with her.

Both men were silent for a moment, Crow lost in his own thoughts. He turned his gaze back to M. Delacroix and was greeted again by the startling leaf-green eyes and an expression of expectation.

"Will you come then?"

Crow was puzzled, "Come where?"

"To our home. My son speaks of nothing else now that he has awakened. He claims he cannot go another day without thanking the mysterious M. Crow."

Crow smiled sincerely this time, and grabbing his hat, agreed to go. He called out to Mrs. Alberts and matched M. Delacroix's stride toward the house on the edge of town. He braced himself for the questions he knew must come, questions he'd rather not answer. All the while, every footstep bringing him closer to the strange, soul-searching glass-blue eye of Raven Delacroix. The girl whose face seemed tattooed on his eyes, as her image had been burned onto them them the moment they'd met in the wood.

It was immediately evident that M. Delacroix would not be asking any intrusive questions—he was in too much haste to return to his son. So much so that Crow was forced to quicken his own pace to hear the stray bits of conversation that did fall from the older man's lips. Something about his company, and the changes in shipping. He mentioned that once fish had ruled the day, and that Cross Shipping had been one of the first companies to ship as far away as England. It seemed that while the freshwater fish was still a staple export, other companies had grown wise to the profits that could be made, Cross Shipping had turned its attentions to varied other enterprises. It was evident from his conversation that M. Delacroix loved his company, but it was also obvious that his priority was his wife and children. His knowledge of the other aspects of his business were vague, and Crow couldn't help but wonder about this, filing the information into his mind for a time he might need it to piece together the puzzle of Cross Shipping and its owner.

Along the way, M. Delacroix had paused to point out landmarks, but his steps never slackened. Finally, he turned to Crow, and with a smile, asked the question he had been dreading.

"So, M. Crow, what brings you to our fair Mackinac shores?"

He did not want to lie, and he did not seek the man's enmity, yet. Crow chose his response carefully.

"As you may have noted, I am of partial Huron

heritage. I have studied the law in hopes to aid my mother's people in circumstances of injustice."

This pronouncement stilled M. Delacroix's steady steps, "Truly? That is marvelous. *Mon Dieu*! If only more young men were so inclined. Have you had any success in any other territories with this noble mission?"

Again, Crow was taken aback by the man's response. Could there be a mistake? The tribes downstate had been so certain...and Ogima's words, spoken only a few minutes before...

"You consider yourself a friend to the tribes, Monsieur Delacroix?" Crow asked, testing his reaction.

"*Mais oui*! But, of course! I am a Mackinac man above anything. And to be a man of the island is to admire the tribes."

He spoke so easily, the words rolling off his tongue like tumbles of waves in the lake. Crow had no time to consider before they had tripped up the steps to the front door of the Delacroix home. He saw the bouncing black curls and the bright olive skin he remembered so well, but then, his heart resumed its regular rhythm—for the eyes were as golden as a cat's, and there were smile lines faintly around the eyes. This was Cora Delacroix then. He had seen her before, but faced with her now, he could hardly believe he hadn't noticed how unusual she was.

Crow had to blink to be sure, but it almost appeared as though sparks flew from her fingers and her skin emitted a strange hypnotizing glow. He'd heard from Mrs. Alberts that she was a healer, a cunning woman, and Crow could see why people believed this was so. He had but glimpsed her and knew it was. He had to restrain his hands from making the sign of the cross on seeing her.

She did not speak, just squeezed his hand and widened her eyes meaningfully, as if she knew his mind without him having said a word. M. and Mme. Delacroix embraced, and though it was quick and chaste, Crow felt embarrassed. The bond between them was a strong one, and filled the house, every room cozier and brighter for it.

M. Delacroix lead him through the hall and up the stair, bringing him into Jacques' room. Then, offering him a small bow from the neck, and a quick tousle of his son's hair, he left him alone with Jacques Delacroix.

The moment he entered the room, he noted again how different Jacques was to his sister. There was nothing in their appearance that gave away their relationship, and yet no one could mistake the connection. Her presence hummed within the room, a suggestion of her person hovering even in her absence. It was something in their shared attitude, a guileless innocence that they both approached the world with. It was not a trait Crow had often seen, even amongst the tribe or the priests he had been raised amongst.

The young man was hurriedly attempting to prop himself up on the pillows, eager not to appear at a disadvantage before Crow. The thought filled Crow with an unexplainable feeling; he realized that he had never met anyone so keen to make a favorable impression on him. All at once, he was filled with shame. What was he doing here? Given his aims on the island, he did not belong here, with this family. Yet, something tender pulled on his heart, and his feet only moved him forward into the room.

"Please, do not trouble yourself on my account.

Wouldn't want you to re-injure yourself somehow."

Though he had meant the words kindly, Crow saw it had the opposite effect than he had intended. Instead of putting Jacques at ease, the boy was now caught between sitting up as an equal, to give respect to the man who had saved him, or settling himself back into laying down so as not to appear ungrateful for the life he felt Crow had restored. The result was neither propped up with a straight back, nor lying supine, but instead somewhere uncomfortably in the middle.

The young man cleared his throat and looked with shining eyes to Crow, "Monsieur, Thank you for coming to see me. I am…honored to have you in my chamber, and honored to be in your debt, sir. I owe you my life, monsieur. A thing I did not know to be precious to me before I felt it slip from my fingers."

Crow had made to wave off his gratitude and overly formal speech, as frankly it had grown increasingly irksome to be showered with this show of indebtedness. Crow had found him, yes, but it was Dr. Rast, surely, that deserved the praise. But, before he could shoo away the words of appreciation, he was pulled in by something in Jacques Delacroix's face when he had spoken his last sentence. Something that had nearly cleaved Crow in two. A pleading desperation that spoke of real suffering, an emotion that Crow knew too well. What lead this boy, who lead such a life of love and comfort, to think that his life was so unimportant? He did not strike Crow as being someone prone to displays of dramatics.

"If I may ask, M. Jacques, why did you hold your life to be of such little value?"

Jacques fingers played with the fringe on the edge of his coverlet. His face was white and his golden curls tumbled over his forehead messily. He turned his startling green eyes to Crow, he chewed on his lip, his brow furrowed, the wrestle of his inner thoughts playing on his face. His face cleared, a decision reached, and he spoke.

"My father, M. Crow, is a great man. You could search the world over and not find a man of his kindness or temperament. He is loyal and good and sees the potential in every man—even when a man cannot see it himself. In short, he is a leader of men. It is his desire that I will take over Cross Shipping one day…"

Crow interrupted, "Ah, but you do not wish the same?" It was a common enough scenario, and though unfortunate, not something a man should value himself less for, in Crow's thinking.

"…No, sir. It is not that at all. I love the shipping company. It is that I do not think I am equipped to lead. I…I have a weak heart, sir. And lungs that tire with the smallest exertion. What men could find strength or be confident serving under someone such as me?"

His face had turned pitiful, but, remembering himself, he looked back to Crow and continued, "But, whatever my failings, I am glad to be alive. To use the talents and intelligence I have in the service of others for as many days as the manitou, or the Lord above, has allotted me." He smiled, and for some reason it broke Crow's heart.

"I am delighted that through my action, however insignificant, that your hope has been restored. And though I do not think myself worthy, as I believe it was the Lord's will that I found you. But, I will gladly accept your thanks. In return, you must accept the terms of the repayment of your debt to me."

The idea had only just occurred to Crow, but it was the perfect way to end this talk of debts owed, and would hopefully change the boy's mind about a few things. In response, Jacques forced himself up straighter, wincing when he moved his leg. He gazed at Crow with such a look of readiness that he had to restrain his grin. He fully believed that if he had demanded the boy run a lap around the island he would have attempted to do so.

"Yes. Anything. Please tell me what I can do."

His earnestness tugged on the corners of Crow's mouth even further. He believed he could have demanded the boy give over his best shoes or tell him to swim to Mackinac City and back and the boy would attempt it. Could this pale, golden little man truly believe that there was something lacking in his character? Could he not see the strength within himself that all men admire and follow? Jacques might see his own goodness as weakness, but Crow had seen enough of the world to know that it did him naught but credit.

"Well, my request is this: when the Huron tribe comes to Mackinac for the season, you will be on the shore to meet their chief. And…you would do well to ponder the other strengths important to a leader."

"Done and done, sir."

Crow gave Jacques a quick bow and clapped his hand on the knob of the door, already kicking himself for getting involved further with the Delacroix's.

"Stay, sir, might I make one further request of you?" The boy's voice was small, but hopeful.

Crow spun around, wondering what Jacques Delacroix would say. "Yes, of course."

"Will you meet with me again—next week? I am determined to be back in the office by then. I could even have Maman pack two lunches."

The words were spoken so kindly that Crow could not think to refuse, though this continued intimacy with the family was growing alarming. He bowed again, and as he grabbed the knob again, the same image that was now imprinted on his mind sprang to his eyes, and he wondered if he'd glimpse Raven on his way out. A thought that gave him cause to curse himself, yet again. As he stepped through the door, Jacques Delacroix seemed to have divined his thoughts. A quiet voice, almost a whisper, from the bed said,

"My sister, Monsieur Crow, is now in the woods." And Crow felt his cheeks pink in the darkness of the hallway.

:13:

Raven

No matter how bright and caressing the sun, the forest was always cool. A safe haven for thoughts, a silent place filled with only the sounds that belonged. The rustling of the wind in the leaves, a small brown squirrel leaping from branch to trunk. The chattering tweets of birds calling on one another, speaking in a tongue only her mother and some of the natives could still speak. Raven could only hear their music, and within it, their content to live in this wild northern place.

She stepped into a pool of sunshine, bright against the shadows on the forest floor. A root stuck stubbornly out from the earth on the path, and last year's leaves softly crunched underfoot. Jacques himself had sent her from his bedside, telling her with a forced scowl that he was tired of seeing her face every time he opened his eyes. They both knew it was said in jest, but the siblings understood one another, and so she'd left as soon as she'd plumped his feather pillows and bestowed a kiss on his cool brow. The ragged rattle in his lungs worried her to distraction, but she knew better than to comment on it.

He'd always known her secrets as well as she knew his without either of them speaking them aloud. She hadn't wanted her concern to be met with one of his barbed observations. As they grew older, their awareness of one another hadn't faded, but they had learned to step lightly around each other's confidences. A dance that neither confidently waltzed to, only picking the tune up as they went, hoping not to blunder.

She was glad in her heart that he'd sent her away. Now that she was in the wood she felt that she could not gulp enough of the sweet pine summer air into her lungs. And here, with only the trees and flickering of sunlight, her thoughts could roam more freely.

Though she felt traitorous to do so, especially with Jacques' near death experience and all that should capture her thoughts, Raven still caught her eyes drifting out onto the straits. Beyond the waves, beyond the glittering blue of the lake, out there just beyond her extended grasp, lay her future. She was certain of it, though she worried that the the longer she waited to seize it, the more it became like a stick in a stream, caught so swiftly in the current that it might pass her by if she did not grasp it in time.

Henri Crow's arrival had loosed an urgency, a gnawing desire to take hold of this future now. Deep inside of her she wanted the possibilities that his life held. Adventure, risk, not belonging to any place. Raven sensed that the not belonging troubled him, but to her, it was the very thing she yearned for. To no longer be defined by the place she came from. Her mother and father, *they* belonged to Mackinac. But Raven dreamed of flying like her namesake, making her home everywhere and nowhere. To live on the winds and travel wherever they might blow. This is what Henri Crow could not see. He had this great gift, this freedom to wander. Perhaps what they both were missing was a fellow wanderer to explore the world alongside, their wings ready to unfurl in flight together.

She had sat long in the same attitude, thoughts passing through her mind like the breeze blowing through the branches overhead. Afternoon had turned to evening and still she was mesmerized by the sight below the trees, looking down onto the pebbled beach below, until she heard footsteps behind her.

She knew it was Henri Crow without turning, her ears identifying the familiar soft scuff of his leather riding boots. She felt him, his presence bonding to her own, the darkness of him growing deeper when joined with hers. Although they had only been in one another's company twice before this moment, she felt that she should always know when he was near. The hairs on the back of her neck stood on end and a shiver ran down her spine. The moment stretched on, neither speaking, nor acknowledging the presence of the other. As if in that acknowledgement a crack would split them in two, separating this moment from all the ones that came before it, changing them both. She felt the shift as it was happening, just like the first time they had met, she knew she would walk away from this encounter altered, though she could not predict in what way she would be changed.

Finally, he cleared his throat to announce his presence, and came to stand alongside of her. She thought he would now speak, but still he did not.

Then, his hand gently, so gently, sought out hers, and he held it lightly, like a bird he was afraid to crush within his large palms, testing the feel of her hand within his.

"Forgive me", he whispered, though he did not release her fingers.

"Forgiven" she whispered back, a trifle louder. They stood thus for some moments, both of their eyes soaking in the same darkening scene below, though it meant different things to their eyes. The longer they stood, hand in hand, the more she considered how she should feel, how she was taught to feel if an unknown man would dare touch her hand with such familiarity. But it did not feel wrong. Raven could hardly credit it, but instead it felt...like home. Which was a place Raven had never considered she would find, for she'd never felt it on this island. She still wondered about his strange behavior when they had met, and then remembering the circumstances of their second meeting, she gasped. Dropping his hand, she pressed both of her hands to her mouth. He turned to look at her, surprised, his chestnut waves concealing his soulful dark eyes, though in the shadows his cheekbones stood out more sharply, giving away his Huron blood.

"What is it, Raven? As I said, please forgive me, I was too bold." She saw him blush with shame, and in response she shook her head and closed her eyes, shutting out the combined blackness that surrounded the two of them, blackness that coiled and undulated holding them both in a kind of embrace that was suddenly too much for her, overwhelming her thoughts.

"No, you mistake me, Mr. Crow. I reacted so strongly because I have realized that I have never thanked you for the service you provided my brother, his very breath..." He waved a hand, cutting her words short.

"If I am thanked yet again today for the very small service of carrying Jacques to his home in order that Dr. Rast could aid him, I shall drown in gratitude. Please, the greatest way to thank me is to speak no more about it."

She smiled at him uncertainly, and nodded her head,

turning back toward the straits. Crow cleared his throat and spoke again.

"I have only just now been to your home. Your brother told me where to find you—though I did not ask him where you were."

The corners of Raven's mouth strained a little upwards. "Jacques is skilled in divining the wishes of others. It makes him an accomplished businessman and a pest for a brother. He reads my secret desires like a book. It is his own magic, but do not even think to tell him it is a gift. He will scoff at you and claim that any man can read what is clearly written on someone's face."

Crow laughed, a deep throaty thing that rang joyfully to the beach below. Conversation with Henri Crow came easily, Raven thought. She felt that he would understand her words even before she brought herself to speak them.

"I hear…" Crow began, but then looked around uncertainly, as if he feared the trees were listening. "I have heard that…there are others in your family with such gifts."

It was now Raven's turn to laugh, and she nodded. This was no secret on the island. "Yes, we have all been given different ways of seeing the world."

His expression was rapt, but a smile spilled over his features in spite of himself. "That sounds a very tame and vague way to answer the charge." Once again, she noticed that he nervously swallowed and cleared his throat. "provided that what I have heard is true." His eyes met hers, finally, and then they moved to her lips. Her throat grew dry for a moment, and her heart beat so loudly that she wondered that he did not hear it. She forced her voice to take on a lightness she did not feel.

"I suppose that very much depends on what it is that they say." She tried her best to offer what she thought was a coquettish grin, but his eyes were impenetrable, and his face was overcome with strong emotion.

"They say that you see into men's hearts. In town, they say that you see the color of a man's soul with that crystal eye of yours."

Involuntarily, she blinked the eye shut, feeling suddenly vulnerable that it stared out of her face. He breathed in, shakily, and then in one motion drew her into his arms, so close to his lips that she could feel the warmth of his breath. "If it is true, then you must now see the torment in mine."

"Only that it mirrors my own." she replied breathlessly, and then she tilted her head up and kissed him. She felt his hands on her back and in her hair, and her own body flattening to his. She could not get close enough to him.

Everything else surrounding them was forgotten. The trees, the spots of sunshine on the forest floor, even all thoughts of Jacques and plans to leave the island. The only thing that existed was the moment, the taste of his mouth, and the heat of his body.

Slowly, slowly, the urge of *now* drifted, slipping from her like an ill-tied shawl. Something was wrong. A sensation of feeling about her ankles forced her to end the kiss, and looking down, Raven was not surprised by what she saw.

To his credit, Henri Crow only laughed, which broke the frozen moment. Turtle, his black fur wild and glossy, was nudging her legs, his little paws brushing her skirts, and cautiously sniffing Henri Crow's boots. He tested his teeth on the leather, attempting to determine if they posed any threat to his beloved mistress.

Raven stooped to scoop the little dog into her arms, where he easily balanced on her hip like a toddler might. The dog placed one paw behind her back, and gingerly settled his chin onto her shoulder, provoking a hearty guffaw from Crow. Raven thought how much she liked hearing the sound, and at the same time realized she'd only seen him laugh or smile in her own company but a few times. Instead of feeling self conscious about their stolen kiss and intimacy in the prior moment, she only wished she knew how to make him laugh again.

He reached a cautious hand toward the terrier's head, who, sighingly, submitted to be pet.

"Your dog is horribly spoilt. I believe you've quite ruined him."

Raven rolled her eyes, "On the contrary, papa says we've done him a great service. He is well on his way to becoming human himself." She had thought he would laugh, because he had seemed so merry, and judging by the dog's behavior, it was almost indisputably true. But, instead, he only bristled when she mentioned her father. After what had happened between them, the force of attraction, the draw of their bodies toward one another, how was it possible for him to grow cold so quickly? Even a fire's embers will stay warm for a time after the flames are doused by a sudden storm.

He said nothing, but she felt rather than saw him fold back into himself. What was it about her family that affected him so? She felt her own face grow hot with anger. She suddenly felt extremely foolish. And wanton. And she didn't know which was worse.

"What is the matter with you, sir? I cannot begin to make you out! Burning fire and then bitter ice! Your moods are so rapid as to make me dizzy!"

His emotions at her outburst caused the clouds about him to spin, growing even darker and she knew she had struck a chord. Sensitive to her mood, the dog seemed to cling to her even more tightly with his paws, and a low growl sounded from his tiny throat. His little pink tongue then began covering her in very undignified kisses.

Crow looked down, as if avoiding her frost blue eye, afraid of what she was seeing when she looked at him. Worried at what he might glimpse if he saw himself reflected back. He swayed side to side, putting his weight in one boot then the other, weighing his words before they escaped from his mind.

"Even had I not heard you were an enchantress of some kind, I should have known it anyway. You are a witch, because you have me even now under your spell. You have bewitched my thoughts, for they are always on you, and my eyes, because I see only your face."

Those same eyes were strangely black again, all traces of the soft earth browning around his pupils disappeared, leaving only shiny black mirrors that frightened Raven. Instinctively she pulled Turtle a little closer.

"Every time I close my eyes. Every night as I try to sleep, it is you. Haunting me like a spirit. When I wake it is you, appearing before me like a fairy from a children's story. How did you take over my senses so quickly? I barely know you, yet I would know you anywhere. I...I..."

A low growl escaped his throat, and his face twisted in torment. The response flew from Raven's mouth like so many arrows.

"Why is this so terrible? Is it not... a beautiful thing, this bond between us?" Her own voice was foreign to her, high-pitched and near hysterical. The dog whined in sympathy.

His eyes no longer met hers. "It would be. For another man, maybe. But for me? No. Not for the both of us. You distract me. Your eyes, your voice, they throw me off course. You seek to confound me, to muddle me and twist me into a man I do not recognize. Every moment with you I lose a little of myself."

With that, his shoulders, which had risen up as he spoke, shuddered down all at once into a great shrug. The darkness around him buzzing with energy. Giving her a small bow, he loped off, not running, but walking as quickly as he could without breaking into the indignity of racing away from her.

And yet, the sweetness of his kiss lingered on her lips and on her arms. She walked home, among the trees, drawing on the sympathy of the forest for consolation. The little black dog happily remaining on her hip, bouncing along as she walked. There was something about her family, about her, that drew Henri away, kept his walls up. But what, precisely? The elements that might have drawn him away, the rumors of magic, their strange connection with the island, these seemed to bother him not at all. It was something else, something personal, something that his mind wrestled with behind those enigmatic midnight eyes.

Her thoughts were broken by the sounds of a young woman's sob, incongruous with the stillness of the wood around her. The birds had shushed in response to the discordant wails of this crying woman. Turtle began fidgeting in Raven's arms, he'd always been sensitive to humans in distress. Setting the fluffy black dog on the forest floor, Raven followed him to the source of the sobbing. Sitting red-eyed and streaky-cheeked at the base of a pine was Rose O'Malley, and Raven did not wonder what her tears were shed for. When Rose realized she was discovered, she shrank against the grey bark of the tree. She attempted to disappear into the shadows of the growing evening, as if she could press against the wood and somehow be encased within it. But then, meeting Raven's gaze, her look of shame became defiance.

The girl's strawberry blonde hair was wild and fell around her face becomingly, even tear-stained and blotched as it was. For a moment, Raven felt a pulse of envy in spite of herself. This girl was rosy and fresh with skin like new milk and sunlight in her hair. Not a creature of shadows with char-black hair and mis-matched eyes. Raven's beauty was the beauty of sunset, and Rose's the promise of spring. But as soon as the jealous thought entered her mind, Raven cast it out. Not only was it unworthy of her, but Rose's looks made her prey to the very situation she found herself in now. It was Raven's place to console, not to judge.

With a sigh, Raven bent down and took an uncomfortable seat next to the sorrowful girl. She hoped she was not dirtying the pale-pink muslin of her skirt, she didn't need any further dramatic scenes for the day, especially with her mother.

"Come to mock me in my shame?" Rose sniffled with a withering sneer. Raven recalled that this was a habit of Rose's, a proneness to be unkind to other women, and overly friendly to men. Raven could hardly blame her, if she'd grown up the same as Rose, she'd probably be similar. After all, it wasn't as though the women of the island had gathered about to help when her father had been caught stealing, and then sent downstate to be locked away. Or when the rest of her family had died of the pox. Her grandmother had said it was bad blood, but Raven didn't believe in bad blood, only bad choices.

"No, Rose. I have come to offer you any succor that I might have in my power to give."

"A very pretty speech Mlle. Coralie Delacroix. How *kind* of you to swoop down from your high perch and deign to speak with the likes of me." She sneered again, and Raven noticed how the expression marred her looks.

"We both know that I'm with child. I know that you find a way to know everyone's secrets. Although I do not know whether it is done with that devil's mark on your arm, your witchcraft or that evil eye."

Raven flattened her mouth into a hard line, holding in the army of words that were rushing to the battle for her character. No matter what arrows shot at Raven, she could not be hit if she urged her wings to fly above the flint-tipped missiles of Rose's own unhappiness.

"Yes, I have known that you are in a struggle that I cannot begin to imagine." Raven paused, and then gathering strength, continued. "I know it is not my concern, but what of the father? Is there no hope of him doing right by you?" The words fell heavy from her mouth and she cursed herself for speaking them. It was not her place, and yet she was curious. The memory of Henri Crow's kiss suddenly seemed dangerous, the way her body had burned for his made her dizzy. The girl before her was proof of where passion like that could lead.

Rose's eyes narrowed to slits and a sharp smile played upon her lips. The color that surrounded her swirled and changed, growing darker. "What if I was to tell you that it was Jacques? That he did me violence, forcing himself on me?"

Raven's head jerked backward in surprise. She did not, for a moment, believe it. But they were of an age, Jacques and Rose, and she could see where the wagging tongues of the island would credit the possibility. Not that Raven could ever believe Jacques capable of violence.

"Is that a threat? None would believe it. It is an impossibility." Raven spoke quietly, immediately wishing she had not thought to comfort this snake. This viper that would try to bite and poison Jacques and the rest of her family with her venom. It seemed that both she *and* Jacques had encountered a snake in the wood, but Raven did not have Henri Crow close by to rescue her.

Rose grinned wider, "It might be. Your mother would not give aid when I asked it. That's no way to heal a body, is it now? Come to her in good faith, but she turned me away with excuses and pretty words. Must be where you learned all your pretty, empty speeches, now that I think of it." Rose looked sidelong at Raven. "But you, Ms. Coralie, you know her craft as well as she does, I'll warrant. She probably taught you a little of that along with those empty words. You wouldn't want your family's name dragged through the mud *again,* would you? And what if I *do* speak true? It would probably stop Jacques' tired little heart to shame his family so. Tsk-tsk. We can't have that, can we?"

Raven couldn't pretend to understand what Rose was referring to, nor could she understand the mocking tone the threat was delivered with. It made her cold, gooseflesh appearing on her arms and on her legs beneath her heavy skirt, to realize that you could know someone the whole of your life, and never know them at all.

She knew that there had been rumors, once upon a time, long before she was born. Something to do with her mother and father and her Uncle Philippe. So, so long ago now…almost 20 years. But she could see in Rose's eyes that the girl knew she had found her soft spot in mentioning Jacques.

"If my mother turned you away, it is because it is too late. Your child has already quickened and is grown too large— is growing even now within you. Any tincture she could offer you may kill you as well as the babe."

"Lies!" Rose said the word with a desperate fury and Raven's eyes grew wide. Rose stood up, pushing Turtle aside as she did so. She began to walk away, acting as though Raven no longer existed. Shaken, Raven got to her feet and stared after her very pregnant retreating form. Turtle jumped on his hind-legs, pawing to be picked up. Before Raven could bend over to place him on her hip, Rose spun around, her eyes glowing with hatred. Raven could feel her own smoke that trailed her, become a wall, protecting her from the waves of malice Rose projected.

"In a fortnight, it will be a full moon. I am told that such a thing is good fortune for spell-casting or whatever it is your family does. You would be wise to meet me back in this spot at an hour to midnight. If you do not, your brother's name and the name of Delacroix will be ruined on this island. I know your secrets and I will tell all— I swear it!"

Spinning back around, she skipped away, leaving Raven open-mouthed. Turtle nudged and licked at his mistress' fingers, picking up on her unease as though he could smell it.

She felt a coldness in her palm, like a breath of winter air. Closing her green eye, she saw her Uncle Philippe beside her, holding but not quite holding her hand, mouth moving in words of soundless sympathy and fear. He nodded gravely, and vanished.

Raven took a deep breath, squared her shoulders and made a decision. Two people had stalked away from her this evening, taking the last word as though it were their own. With a straight back and a firm resolve, she headed away from home, and instead to Mrs. Alberts' house. She had a few words for Henri Crow.

Later that night, lying in bed, Turtle having finally quit her side to return to Jacques, whom he preferred, she could hardly believe she'd accomplished it. But she had. He was going to meet her at Sugar Loaf tomorrow noon. And though he did not know it yet, he would be meeting her every day, until he revealed his secrets. Until she might tell him hers. Until he agreed to take her with him wherever he might go. Finally to be free, to not be reminded of her legacy and duty and attachment to an island that could not be her home.

So filled with success was she that she had pushed back all thoughts of the strange threats and late night appointments with Rose O'Malley a fortnight hence. It was only when the terrors overtook her dreams that she recalled.

:14:

Peregrine

Peregrine had been very sincerely under the impression that if he did not have a proper roast beef or at least a thick cut of mutton soon, he would surely become a fish himself. The seafood and turtle soup his aunt prepared were undoubtedly delicious but there was something…unwholesome about only consuming large amounts of white fish and other lake inhabitants. Perch, walleye, sturgeon, crayfish and the occasional bass or bluegill—too spiny for his taste— were so… light. With only venison thrown in intermittently, he missed the heavy gravies and roasted meats of his home in Devon.

That was, until his aunt surprised him with a fatty, marbled side of beef, specially imported from the mainland. Joy quickly became discomfort, however, and it wasn't only he, he was glad to note. The whole family seemed incapable of digesting it. Stomachs around the table growled in protest when asked to break down the heavy meat and after a few moments of strained smiles and sweating foreheads, Peregrine, as a medical man, had insisted that they all give up the effort. It wasn't that it had been prepared incorrectly or unwholesomely, it was only that he had lost the taste for it. The fresh fish felt so much lighter on his palate and sat in his stomach easily. He supposed that like his uncle's family, perhaps he was no longer made like an Englishman. That something in the air here had already changed him. Apparently, from the inside out.

This didn't signify that Peregrine was content here in this new life, nor that he had found peace in using his skills to heal and tend to those in need of his surgeon's hands. On the contrary, the only part of him that had found any measure of equanimity were those same hands. Those vile surgeon's hands that deserved no absolution for their past wickedness. But Peregrine couldn't seem to stop them—they flew to each task of their own volition. Mixing physick, preparing poultices, stitching wounds, setting bones, they worked without his consent. Searching out illness in an expectant patient before his mind could refuse. Gabrielle's ring burned a lusty wine-red on his little finger, brighter than he'd ever seen it. It was as if each patient, each task he performed intensified it vivd blood-like sheen by constant transfusions of the gory polish.

The stone was mocking him, he supposed. Sometimes he was almost certain it would speak, perhaps the spirit of his darling Gabrielle would emerge, her milky white face, her large sparkling eyes staring blankly back, seeing all, seeing nothing.

Peregrine almost wished she would appear. He wanted to glimpse her again, one look, even if it was that last horrifying memory of death. He wished she would announce that he was a murderer. A charlatan , a sham, a surgeon who had taken his wife's life, who had looked on as her spirit fled her twisted body.

But it was all fancy. She never did appear, though the ring glimmered bolder and brighter at the end of every day in the small cabin.

When he was first called to attend Jacques, his initial thought was that the fault was his. Perhaps he'd overstrained his lungs, kept the boy out of doors too long or had overestimated the abilities of his young heart. To discover it was the bite of a snake...well, Peregrine would not have admitted it to anyone, but his relief exploded into the sweetest excitement. He hadn't even considered the he might not be able to save him, much less restore him to even greater health. Instead, a score of different techniques he'd read, anti-venom researches and demonstrations he'd witnessed or had been told of—they all fit together in his mind like a chain. Each link soldering itself to the one next to it. It had been...exhilarating! Intoxicating! To test these theories and procedures on his own. His old desire to use his hands to heal and ease suffering had come alive.

Yet, Peregrine shuddered at himself now. His glee for surgery seemed sometimes to be ghoulish—after all, the boy could have died! He knew he had been the only chance Jacques had, but he had vowed to give up the practice. Now, it was almost a monomania—injuries, illness or the sound of a dry cough, these made his hands itch to be of service. To work and move and fix and cure. Unsettling, disturbing...and potentially dangerous. What would they all think if they knew? What would they *do*?

Shaking his head, he pressed his face into his palms and yawned. Guilt throbbed at his temples. He wasn't certain when he had paused in his writing and instead jumped wholeheartedly onto this wild stallion of thought. The light outside the small window dimming into that hazy dusk time of day, which told him it was about time to finish writing out the log of cases he'd seen that afternoon. He dipped his pen and carefully noted his observations and plans for the treatment of each.

It was a task in itself to keep his mind to the business at hand. Without careful reigning in of his thoughts, they would gallop off without him.

Sighing, he cracked his knuckles, and arched his back where it had become stiff from sitting too long. He knew he should visit Jacques, should check in on his progress, perhaps blend together another packet of herbs to aid in healing. Though, no doubt the boy's mother had already done that and more. Coralie Delacroix had been by in the morning, having brought him a replenishment of his herbal stores that he had been correct in assuming her mother had gathered in the first place. He was glad when she had stayed a while, telling him what her mother knew of plants and their uses. There was a calm in her, a salve that made him feel warm and clean. She wasn't like young women he'd known in England—Coralie Delacroix seemed to delight in being useful and sharing her warmth with others. The cabin had been colder, and seemed to sigh when she left it.

From what he had gathered from Coralie, and his own observations, her mother possessed rudimentary healing skills, much like those that a country doctor might teach the lady of any out-of-the-way estate, but no more than that. Though her knowledge of nature was formidable, and her skills precise and sure, he now understood why she had never worked to heal her son herself. It was not in her power, and Peregrine had to admit to himself, feeling foolish that he did so, that it seemed that Jacques was somehow resistant to her healing arts. A circumstance that puzzled Peregrine no end.

Truly, however, Cora was a marvel to behold when in her element. The plants would appear and disappear from her hands as quick as thought, practically tying themselves up for drying, arranging themselves, leaves separating from stems in a blink of an eye or a tilt of her curly black head. Her daughter didn't seem to charm plants to her bidding as her mother, but seemed no less skillful or adept than her mother.

It had been enough to convince Peregrine that his uncle had been right—magic on this island was nothing to be laughed at or trifled with.

With an audible sigh, realizing that once again he had set his pen aside to be jostled about by his thoughts, he brought the heel of his hand to his forehead. His fingers moved through his untidy copper hair, mussed continually throughout the day by this repeated action. He slammed the journal shut, expecting a loud crack, but the sound from the book was muffled by the creak of the door opening behind him.

He turned slowly, his hands already anticipating movement that they might be called to perform. The other part of him was less than enthused. He needed no more patients today, no more observations to add to his notebook. Raising his gaze to see whomever was entering the small surgery, his ring caught the light, sending a glint of blood red onto the face of the woman entering tip-toe timidly in through the door.

She was very small, almost child-like with small hips and long thin bones. On one bony hip she carried a large child, roly-poly baby fat and cheeks like a chipmunk. They had the same dusky black hair and shining copper cheeks. But where the child was glowing and robust, the mother was, though still young, drawn and her skin was thin as parchment. Her hair was lank and she moved as if every effort was through water. Peregrine couldn't help thinking that it looked as though she'd given over her life force to the babe in her arms, until she herself was an empty husk, shucked off and withering.

It was not usual to see a native in his office, in fact, this woman was the first he'd encountered. From what he had observed, each tribe had their own medicine man or trusted healer, or if cases were especially troublesome they found their way to Waseya's cabin. But this young woman and her child, this was a sight Peregrine would never have predicted.

He ushered in and bade her take a seat. The baby she placed on the wooden floorboards, the child happily babbling and crawling about, oblivious to his mother's malaise. She and Peregrine sat, regarding one another for a moment, as two partners about to execute an unfamiliar dance step. Finally, she sighed and spoke to him in a broken, monosyllabic English.

"Ill"

Peregrine nodded, and considering what an examination might include, he asked:

"Where is your husband? I shouldn't want to examine you without your man present."

"Dead." She spoke the word with finality. "Many moons."

Peregrine shook his head up and down, as if in the nodding an idea might fly in.

"You say you are ill. Can you show me where?" He knew his face had adopted an expression of doubt, but he could not help it, he was out of his depth. She looked weak, but that could simply be the exhaustion of a baby mixed with the loss of her man. Or, she should be dying. Without words, illnesses like this were difficult to determine. He also retained his reservations about a thorough examination. His notions of propriety were warring against his passion for medical experience and knowledge. In Peregrine's experience, passion would beat propriety any day of the week.

But there was something else. His last female patient had....but, he couldn't think on that now. And he could never stop thinking on it.

He stood up, having decided, and gestured for her to sit back and relax. His mind tumbled about as he checked her pulse and felt her skin, memories of words in textbooks whirring through his mind, bat-like, the black winged letters flitting before his mind's eye, each ailment and symptom regarded and then flying away according to its feasibility.

The girl was silent throughout his examination, hardly moving as his hands fluttered to her neck, her cheeks, as he gently pulled open her mouth and peered into her ears. Stoic and regal, Peregrine thought, even in distress.

Abruptly, he stopped and walked over to his notebook. After jotting down a few notes, his thumb and forefinger squeezed at his chin, before plucking a medical text from his shelf. He thumbed through a few pages, and exhaling heavily, sat back down in his chair. Peregrine followed the gaze of the young woman, watching her baby, a small smile lifting the corners of her lips ever so slightly. After a moment, she brought her gaze to meet his, and Peregrine was shocked to see such resignation there. This was a woman who knew how seriously ill she was, and seemed to only want the fact confirmed.

He had a few questions before he would pound the first nail into that coffin.

"What is your name?" Peregrine was ashamed that he had not asked her forthwith. But, he reminded himself again, this was not England, and etiquette had no place here in situations such as this. She hadn't come to chat, she'd come for answers.

"Naneda." She said quietly, her eyes never leaving her baby.

"Naneda, I'm Dr. Rast. I must ask you a few questions."
She nodded, her eyes did not raise to meet his.
"I trust you have already seen your tribe's healer, yes? And perhaps Waseya as well?"

She nodded again. "Waseya. Yes. She sends me here. Says maybe white doctor can help. Maybe no." She again spoke quietly, just a breath above a whisper. But the tone was one that held no hope, and something in her attitude pulled Peregrine's heart out of his body and onto the floor with the baby—alongside of the woman's own.
"Where do you *feel* ill?" He had noted her reactions during the examination, but sometimes the patient's own words gave a story that the body would not yield, and vice versa.
Her small, thin fingers came up to rest on her bright copper cheeks and she made a gesture with her hands that Peregrine did not understand. At the expression of confusion on his face, she pointed to his face, then the baby's and back to her own. Peregrine nodded, with comprehension.
"You are flushed, darker than is usual."
She imitated a swoon, and then spread her fingers

down her cheeks as a patter of raindrops might appear.

"You are...melancholy?"

She nodded and clutched her arms, legs and back, making a wincing expression.

"You are in pain, then."

Again, she nodded. and made a mimic of eating and then crossed her hands in front of her mouth. She exhaled and brought her hands to her lap, indicating she was finished.

Peregrine's eyes found the rafters of the cabin, and he considered an ill-painted spot on the wall near the corner. It was as he expected then. No wonder the healers had been mystified. Her coloring would make her seem healthy, and the rest of her symptoms would be written off as general melancholia. But, Peregrine knew better. He reflected briefly that as much as his hands loved their grim work, it never seemed to make him feel triumphant to find a diagnosis or solution that would bring no happiness. Facts were not beautiful, truth holds no comfort. The farrier's son and his dead arm flashed into Peregrine's mind, and Gabrielle's lifeless doll's eyes, and then mercifully, vanished.

There was no name for it, specifically, and the only time he'd seen it written about was in a brief medical journal account back in England. Informally it was called Browned Skin Disease, the very color of her skin giving the woman the illusion of the health she was losing. Most of the very few patients he had ever seen with the disease also had consumption, and her lack of cough had given him hope. But the other symptoms gave her away.

He had no hope for her, no kind word to give her strength. She had not come for encouragement, though. She had not walked into his office expecting anything besides corroboration on what she had already known. She had wanted only a taper to light with her own torch, so that she might have two beacons by which to see the truth by. He hated her for a moment for sharing her hopelessness, but after meeting her inquiring glance, and nodding, he understood and his anger melted. With his validation of her own fears, it was as if the weight of them slipped like leaves from the branches of a tree in autumn. Suddenly the burden of them was relieved, and though she was now bare, she seemed lighter and freer for it.

She smiled, a real smile now, though Peregrine could only imagine the strength that would make a dying woman smile. She came over to him and extended her hand awkwardly, a sign of respect that she knew existed in his world.

She said only, "How long?" with no expectation, as she bent to swiftly replace her roly-poly baby into her thin, bird-like arms.

Peregrine smiled a small smile though the effort almost made him choke. "Not long."

She smiled again, mysteriously, and thanked him, leaving as quietly as she'd come.

Peregrine took his seat and before he could check them, the tears came hard and fast, racking his body. Why did God take such women back to himself? Did he need angels in heaven so badly? Who would raise the baby when his mother had gone? And his father already left the lodge to travel on their infernal path of souls…

Peregrine wept until he could hardly draw breath. He thought of the bitter smile that had come to Gabrielle's face when she had left the world, the struggle, the blood, but then a smile, the same small one that Naneda wore. It was death himself, Peregrine knew. That smile that mocked him, that tore at his heart, that thin curved line that stood between him and heaven. Or hell.

Pulling his handkerchief violently from his pocket. He pulled it savagely across his cheeks, ashamed of himself. He did not know whether to grieve in perpetuity for his crimes, or if he should be not be allowed to grieve at all.

Snatching his hat from the stand, he resolved to stop in to visit Jacques before dinner. Perhaps the preservation of one life could help atone for some of the harm he'd done. Perhaps guarding one life could take the sting out of the loss of another.

Not thirty steps from his surgery, his Uncle Nicholas met him as he was about to step into the wood.

"Three dead, Perry! Murdered!"

And then falling where he stood, he began convulsing so riotously that Peregrine thought his neck would break.

:15:
Sarah

It was as though the moment she had stopped speaking, she had become invisible as well. That's how it felt, at any rate. She could slip from room to room in her home without anyone taking notice. She walked from the general store to the shoemaker's and over to Mason's cooperage without so much as a glance from a passer-by.

She wondered sometimes if it wasn't only her voice, but also the pieces of her soul her children had taken with them when they flew back to God, or to haunt the islands as spirits, as the natives believed. She, for one, didn't know what she believed anymore. Or if she believed in anything at all. The preacher's words were hollow of a Sunday. As barren and empty to her ears as her womb had been of life. How fitting, she often mused, that her husband was a cooper. That his shop and his workers hummed and clanked and hammered all the day long, creating vessels to be filled. And yet, his own wife, she, Sarah, was empty and now, perhaps fading from existence entirely.

It was not surprising, therefore, that Coralie Delacroix or her own sweet little maid, Rose, had neither seen nor heard Sarah in the wood. In the time Rose had worked for the Stevens', Sarah had come to care for the girl. Even though she was forward and brassy. She had thought of her as a kind of niece or something of that ilk. It was this regard that made her ugly words all the more painful. The venomous taste of them had been thick in the air, so that even Sarah had choked on the flavor, concealed as she was behind a group of scraggly young pines, clinging together in the shadow of the wood. The disappointing saplings stunted in growth because they huddled too close to one another, none daring to extend a branch brazenly toward the sun.

She'd heard the threats, and wondered why Coralie did not answer back the thunder of Rose's insults with her own lightning. After all, it was no secret about the women in that family. Witches or cunning women, healers or faeries, whatever one believed, it was all the same. They were touched, somehow, by northern charms and enchantments.

But, Coralie only sounded worried. Concerned that Rose might have a thorn to prick her family with, and though she hadn't agreed to do what Rose asked, she hadn't disagreed, either.

Sarah had stayed hidden for a long while afterward. She crouched uncomfortably, past dark, unmoving, unseeing in the drifting blackness. She thought of her own desires for a child, hers and Mason's. And Rose's difficulty. To Rose…it was as much of a misfortune to be carrying as it was for Sarah to no longer have the chance of a life within her. Curious what a difference a marriage can make. Or a few years, or even just an altered perspective.

Sarah was surprised to find that she wasn't angry with Rose. On the contrary, somehow, she understood her. In both of their cases, their body was a prison, acting opposite to their separate wishes, paying no mind to their desires of prayers. No, Sarah would as soon force a baby on a woman as she would snatch one away from herself.

But still, she sat, unperturbed by the gnawing cold that bit harder and deeper as the night turned blacker. She paid no heed to the fact that tonight was one of the very few of their marriage that she had not met Mason with a kiss, or a press of their foreheads. She paid no attention to anything, besides the sounds of the forest in the night, strangely cold after the heat of the day. The shrieks of the owl and some courageous twittering of intrepid birds who would not be quieted by the darkness. Rustling leaves and a soft, chilly wind that glided through her hair like swirling snowflakes. If she listened carefully, so carefully, she could hear the gentle lapping of the lake, like the pages of a book being turned.

Then, soundlessly, the presence beside her. She did not need light to know who it was, or words to greet him. It was just as well, because she had no words to command. Her hand sought out his in the dark, and she could feel his smile rather than see it.

"I knew you were out here, sweeting. As soon as my foot left the door of the office. I knew. And even then I knew it wouldn't do. Wouldn't do at all to have my girl shivering in the woods. But, I came home and accomplished some of the work required of a mayor, appraised the ledger for barrel orders and the cooperage's finances, and then could wait no more. I followed my feet straight to you, my bonny girl."

He squeezed her hand lovingly. They were no longer young, no more the sweet love of sugared youth between them. But, Sarah forgot sometimes. Forgot that they'd had so much bitter sadness between them that sometimes they had forgotten that sweet still existed. She forgot all this because his soul felt the same. Especially in the dark. His odd eccentricities not visible, the creases and lines of their faces erased by the hand of night. Beneath it all, she had no pity for herself, no right to have a lack for something she thought missing. Mason and his steady presence, their clasped hands, and the conversation of their deepest hearts—this was as filled as she ever need be.

He squeezed her hand a little tighter, as though he'd heard all the words she'd spoken in her mind. And mayhap he had.

They stood, together, and walked toward home, Sarah suddenly ravenous. She knew she would have to try and communicate to Mason what she knew about Rose. She understood the girl's reasons, but she had also understood Coralie's words, and Sarah was not willing to risk Rose's life. Mason would know what to do, or at least he would know how to listen. And what was this secret past Rose had hinted at? If it was local gossip, or had been any time in the last 30 years, Mason would have heard it. The angry venom taste came back into her mouth, and fear settled over Sarah, a foreboding she didn't understand.

They were almost to the house now and something in the trees to her right caught her eye. A man, but not a man. A man that looked as though he'd been draped in the gossamer of spiderwebs and sprinkled in dew. He wore an expression she couldn't quite translate, his dark curly hair falling over eyes so icy blue that Sarah went cold. Those frozen blue eyes seemed to lock on hers. And then, in a blink, he was gone.

Sarah took a firmer grip of Mason's arm and

refocused her eyes on the light radiating softly from their front porch. Trials and mysteries and truths she'd rather not know were winging their way to her, and now phantoms haunting her step.

She was not so invisible, after all.

:16:
Jacques

The unusual sense of calm that had consumed him immediately after the bite had faded into the restlessness of those too long confined to their bed. It wasn't only the inaction, Jacques felt strange, disturbing currents in the air, seemingly just softly playing outside his hearing, a piano's keys being quietly pressed in a sonata in a faraway room.

His sister still sat hours with him, reading, singing, telling him news of the town. But behind her eyes, a fire burned, but he could not divine its meaning. Then she would blink, and he would be left staring into her phantom blue eye, her ghostly, snow-filled eye that saw more than he could imagine and gave back nothing but an icy reflection of he who peered into it.

Raven was up to something. Jacques could feel it. A mood would come over her suddenly and his palms would itch and the hairs would stand on his arms. It wasn't her usual longing to leave the island, but instead something that frightened. Something that vibrated from her skin, the silent whispers of it coming unchecked from the corners of her mouth. She hadn't given up her dream of roaming outside of these shores, but there was a different desire there too. She would be with him in the room, reading and gently tending to him—but another part of her was already bidding her adieus to Mackinac. She was wiping his brow, and waving goodbye. Her voice sang soft French songs that their grandmother sang, but her eyes were focused on whatever secret dream she had found. Jacques could feel that whatever this new yearning was, it made her more restless than ever. A fluttering, a breathless excitement that was rooted in some other happiness. And for once, it was a language Jacques did not speak, an accent of events that was foreign to him, and his dear sister made no move to translate.

And then…then there was the other. The other concern. The other secret that crossed her face like a chill wind every so often, narrowing her eyes briefly, and tightening her mouth. His sister was hiding things from him. Secrets unshared, thoughts kept veiled, and so more and more restless he became as well. He could not be angry with her, he had his own crime to atone for, though he could not allow the words of that to pass his lips either.

The days could not slip by fast enough, the hours, the minutes, he impatiently counted down. Waiting, waiting for Dr. Rast to allow him to return to the office.

It would be a lie to claim that he was more accepting of himself and his limitations since the bite. He was not. He had realized that one could wish for life, and be grateful for it, without being happy with one's own lot. This type of thinking would scandalize Father Santelli, the priest over at St. Anne's, but it was common sense to the Manitou. The spirits of the island looked to nature as their guide. A fish on a line may not relish his place, may not think about his life at all—but it does not mean that the same fish won't tug, pull and squirm to get the hook from its mouth. Jacques knew that every living thing fights for its survival. No, to be glad to be alive is not the same as to be satisfied or content with one's own life.

And Jacques understood that now.

He'd not seen Dr. Rast, Perry, as Jacques liked to think of him, in two days, though his mother said the surgeon would be by in the evening. She'd delivered the news strangely, filled with secrets of her own, lines of worry darkening her features. It may have been a trick of the light, but Jacques fancied he'd seen a few more strands of grey that hadn't been there even a month ago. Between his dance with death, and whatever other calamity had befallen her, she was disturbed, and he thought, fearful. Though, he knew if it was a secret she was determined to keep, then it was as good as locked into a vault. Safer, probably.

Their secrets were then his bedfellows, worries and fears and happiness he could only guess at, but never share in. Whisperings that seemed to mock him, as he lay listlessly in his bed. Jacques was waiting for a glimmer of the words that his family left unsaid to somehow slip into his ears.

His leg was still heavily bandaged, cleaned and dressed every morning by his mother. He'd sent Raven from his room again, sensing amidst her protests that it was what she most wanted. And so, since the morning he had been mostly alone, re-reading novels he'd already dog-eared, and writing another poem he would be embarrassed for his mother to find. He'd been content to labor mostly alone at work, as his books and calculations took most of his time and energy, but being stuck in his bed was a different kind of loneliness. Even Turtle, as stubborn and loyal as she was, happily had trotted out with Coralie, glad to have a break from the tomb silence of the sick room. His hearing had become oddly keen, able to detect the slightest movement at the bottom of the staircase, picking up every shuffle of soft-shoes in the hall, always hoping they were heading his way.

A noise in the hall, then, did not go undetected. The heavy tread of boots announced the doctor's arrival. Jacques felt certain that his recent absence was related to whatever secret his mother held. Jacques then, was eager for news of his own injury, but also for the opportunity to glean some proof, snatch some stray comment, a hasty remark that might slip from the doctor's lips. Something to illuminate the dark den of conspiracies that covered him like the quilt on his bed. Jacques had come to think of Peregrine as an older brother and a friend, and wished that he could help break through the last walls of his melancholy, and win his confidence.

A brief knock, and Jacques called "Come in", with much too big a grin on his face. The opening door revealed not the bright red-gold hair and grey eyes of Peregrine Rast, but instead the bright green searching eyes of his father, Jean-Luc.

He was disappointed, and though he rushed to hide the expression from his visage, his father was too quick for him. He glimpsed the look before it could be smuggled safely away.

Jacques loved his father, but there was a wall between them sometimes. A kinder, more generous man one couldn't hope to meet, a better father one could not imagine—and that was the rub. Jean-Luc was a mirror to Jacques, holding up a reflection of all the things a man should be. Attributes that Jacques lacked. A painful reminder of all that Jacques was not. And most confounding, his father did not seem to see it.

Jacques supposed he was blinded by love for his son, his brain muddled in his vision for Jacques' future instead of the reality before him. Jean-Luc tugged the chair that Coralie was wont to sit in backward a few inches and settled his athletic frame into the seat. He wore a troubled expression, but Jacques could tell that his father was truly happy to be near him, an observation that only made him feel more guilty for the ungenerous thoughts regarding his father.

One corner of his mouth turned up, and he reached gently for Jacques' hand. Jean-Luc moved slowly, as if deciding his son was too old for such affection, his mind seeking a more manly alternative in case he was rebuffed. Jacques willingly allowed his hand to be grasped, but could not help wondering, when had this happened? When did the awkwardness between them begin, and whose doing was it? Jacques was certain it was his own doing, and that his father had taken a cue from him. All at once, he was ashamed, and tear-filled eyes came to meet his father's. Jean-Luc mistook this expression for pain, and bounced up immediately to make his son more comfortable.

"Snakes! *Mon Dieu*! Who would have thought? *Il est fou, non*?!"

Jacques grabbed his father's hand, that was hastily plumping a pillow. "No, no, father. Please, sit, sit. I'm fine, honestly. I was only thinking that I am a difficult son, and feeling a terrible brat."

Jacques colored, and looked away. Jean-Luc returned to his seat, shaking his head good-naturedly.

"*Non*, you're a fine son. Do not trouble yourself, *mon cher fils*. I need you healed, and back in the office where you belong. I am a madman without my right arm!"

As always, it was precisely the right thing to say. Jacques perked and brightened. There is much to be said for being useful, it brings more contentment than many would credit.

After a few moments of comfortable silence, Jean-Luc stirred, remembering the purpose of his visit. He cleared his throat and took turns staring at the ceiling and back to the floor, an awkward shyness that Jacques often wondered about. With his captains, and the men who worked beneath him in the office, he was confident and sure, but at other times, in other company, his confidence fell away. Jacques often mused how his father had caught his mother in his nets like the silver fish in a fairytale. Perhaps there was charm in floundering.

Finally, his father had gathered his words like so many flowers in a meadow, and Jacques whisked all other thoughts from his mind to better attend his father's message.

Fixing Jacques with an intense gaze, he began.

"*Mon fils*, as I have told you every day since the bite, there is no greater miracle than to see you heal. But, I have realized, in my happiness, that it is time to share a very unpleasant truth with you. It is not unpleasant in that it is unbearable, but in that it is painful, or can be, and it is not happily accepted. But if you carry this truth with you always, have it with you in your heart all of your days, then your life will make sense, even when days are dark."

Jacques turned incredulous eyes on his father, waiting for the jest that would surely come. His father was good and sincere, but he was not dramatic...nor did he speak in riddles. This version of a speechifying, philosophizing father was strange. Perhaps he'd been reading Shakespeare again, or some of the poetry he hid so awkwardly between the books on the shelves in the library. But no, he was in earnest. Jacques nodded at his father's pause, as if he required Jacques participation before he would move on.

"It is hardship that forms character. A life is not measured in victories won but in obstacles overcome. An existence and its meaning can be only judged by the slow trudge onward, the brief looks back at the carnage left behind, the blood spilt, the heavy sadness that hinders your steps."

Jean-Luc's voice, which had started as a whisper on the wind had grown louder like a far off storm traveling inland, until his father's voice seemed to resonate from his bones. It scared him. He'd never seen his father this way, never heard the like of the sounds that came growling from his lungs.

"What hardships, father? You and mother have a happy, blissful life."

His father's face stayed dark, but his voice shivered into quiet. Too quiet.

"*Oui*, now our life is more sun than rain, it is true. More smiles than tears. But it is only because we bled and cried and grappled for it…" His voice broke with desperation, caught in the snares of the faraway memories.

Jacques could not fight the look of confusion from settling over his features. "Papa, I don't understand, whom did you fight? What are you speaking of?"

Jean-Luc turned wild eyes on his son, his face twisted into a sneer that altered his appearance so much that Jacques did not recognize him.

"Whom? What? Whom did we *not* fight?! We fought all of *them*. We fought each other. We fought *for* each other, we fought ourselves. We battled the manitou wherever it is that he invisibly reigns. This whole island and the loose tongues that talk, talk, talk of things they do not know!"

His face was not red with anger, but instead a shade of vengeance that was different than the crimson face of a drunken man or the anger of a nagged, hen-pecked husband. It was dark, his voice calm, and this scared Jacques all the more. The room was tight like the air on the lake before a bolt of lightning crosses the sky, and the rage of coming rain breaks the air with a snap.

"But most of all, worst of all, *mon fils, mon cher fils,* we battled a memory. A memory of a man, a memory of the past—a gap of blood and anger and broken promises that separated us like the water between the island and the mainland."

"Separated who?" Jacques asked timidly, but Jean-Luc did not hear his son, so lost was he in his own mind, clouded with black thoughts. The words were for Jacques, they were a message, a warning, but they'd taken on a life of their own. They swirled about him, tumbling and ripping at him, and he could no more control them than a captain can control a ship in a gale. But his father's voice had lost its force and was quieting.

"Now we are tested, and stronger. Now we look

back on the blood behind us, and we look at our hands, and we see that because we have continued to crawl away from the past, the farther we move away from it, the cleaner we are. A baptism of pain that removes the stains of blood from our palms and our souls."

Jean-Luc turned calmer eyes back to his son, as if remembering the purpose of his outburst.

"And so, understand this. What are our ships made from at Cross Shipping?"

Jacques had thought his father was on the verge of a revelation, and then...had asked this strange question.

"What? Papa, I don't understand..."

"Answer the question."

Jacques shrugged in confusion, "Oak, of course."

"Why? Why oak?"

Jacques pondered a moment, looking around his room asking his desk and his wardrobe what had come over his father before answering.

"Because it is strong."

His father nodded, "*Oui,* and what do the tribes use for their canoes? Oak?"

Jacques offered his father an exasperated expression, "Of course not! They use birch."

"Why, why do we not use birch for our ships?"

"Papa, I don't understand; you know perfectly well why..."

But Jean-Luc had tilted his head, and speared his son with a meaningful look.

"Very well, Papa, I'll play. We use oak because it is stronger. It has had to grow strong and tall for many years before it can be used for a ship. The oak must be able to float elegantly above the waves, and carry great weight. It is a vessel made not only for a season, but for a lifetime of hauling and work and storms. Birch is flexible and softer, good for carrying men short distances, but not suitable for shipping or the battering of heavy rains or waves."

Jacques held his palms up in a shrug. "Is there anything more? Papa, I do not understand."

Jean-Luc smiled brightly and heartily slapped his knee, "*Exactement! Précisément!* You must choose *mon fils.* Are you birch? Pliable and soft? Not made for crushing waves…or are you oak? Strong and gnarled and growing despite the hardships that await you…"

A soft knock on the door revealed Peregrine, his auburn hair burning with a deeper flame than usual, suggesting much time spent in the new July sunshine. He flashed Jean-Luc an expression that revealed much, but told Jacques nothing. Jean-Luc nodded in reply and grabbed Perry by the arm briefly, whispering something, before taking his son's hand in his own and after releasing it, backed out the door.

It had all happened so suddenly that Jacques barely had the words out of his mouth before his father could close the door. "Papa! No, you were not finished!" but he was gone, and the message stayed, clinging to Jacques, even as the doctor began his examination.

Peregrine approached the bed quickly, and Jacques watched his hands move with speed and dexterity. Almost as if they existed separately from the man to whom they were attached. They exchanged the usual pleasantries, neither remarking on Jean-Luc's sudden retreat. More than ever Jacques wished he could grasp at something to earn Perry's trust. But, Peregrine had already pulled up the blanket, revealing the location of the snake's bite. Jacques had been unconscious, or otherwise in too much pain to observe the wound before, and too embarrassed to look when his mother changed the dressing. But now he found that his attention was stuck fast to the surgeon's nimble hands as they pulled away bandages and unwound the wrappings from the wound. Just before revealing it, Peregrine looked at Jacques, his eyes asking if the boy was certain he wanted to see what was beneath. If Jacques could have imagined what would be revealed, be would have closed his eyes tightly and kept his mind in darkness.

The next moment, the doctor wordlessly pulled the last bandage away, displaying the cleanest gore Jacques could have dreamed. Here, unveiled was the muscle of his leg and inner tissues he'd only encountered in an anatomy book, the sketches that had seemed so life-like on the page, were a pale and childish rendition of the full-color flesh and blood reality. Jacques was offered a peek inside his own body, see that which was supposed to be covered safely in warm, smooth skin. He felt vulnerable, and suddenly the pain increased. Seeing an injury always made it worse somehow. He remembered a time when he was small, he'd fallen out of a tree and scraped his face on the bark as he slipped. It wasn't until much later, when his horrified mother had shown him his image in the mirror, skin scraped off his cheek and blood dripping onto the linen of his collar, that he had begun to bawl.

The same feeling came over him now, and dizzy, he laid his head back onto the pillow. Peregrine's hands were never still, though Jacques could no longer see them moving about. He felt stinging and poking, and the sharp burn of a liquid falling onto the exposed flesh. Then the deft surgeon's hands were wrapping, quickly, quickly and the quilt was replaced gently.

Jacques had to marvel at a man who could look into dire wounds and bloody carnage and not shrink from them. To look into the face of pain and strike back with a lancet or a needle. A man who looks at what is broken, and does not see gashes or bloody pulp or imperfections, but instead only sees the possibility of putting it back together again. Peregrine was a man who snatched people away from death, even as it was running swiftly with them from his doctor's grasp.

"Mending well", Peregrine broke the silence and Jacques' thoughts, speaking to himself as much as he was to his patient. Jacques couldn't imagine that anything the had seen was well. As if hearing his unspoken doubts leap from his mind, Peregrine smiled and continued.

"No sign of infection. Your mother has done a perfect job in my absence. The foremost concern with a venomous bite is tissue death. I've cut away the necrotizing tissue and any other corruption, as you saw, but the bite will heal. The skin may be patchy and strange just above the knee there, but it is healing."

Peregrine's voice was pleased, but his manner was distant, his brow furrowed with faraway thoughts. It was strange to think that only a short time ago this man had been companionable with Jacques, had tried to strengthen his lungs and heart with breathing techniques and exercise. And now...now Jacques felt the man before him was a stranger, just as his father had been a moment ago. Just as Jacques was to himself.

"Are there venomous snakes in England?" Jacques

already knew the answer and had felt foolish asking it. But it was the inspiration of a moment, a desperate appeal at friendly conversation.

"Yes, the adder. Or the common viper as it is called. Draws itself into an S shape before it strikes." Peregrine replied, his voice clipped, eyes still looking off somewhere beyond the walls of the room.

"Ah, have you seen one before, then?" Jacques had seen a picture in a book, but found now he was interested despite his motives in introducing the topic.

"Yes. Loads. They don't generally attack, you understand. Last resort and all that. But, I had a school chum, name of Reynolds, he stepped on one. Got himself bit in the wrist of all places. Very painful, not much fat there. He howled enough to bring the bricks down. Lived though, as will you." Peregrine smiled, patting Jacques lower leg, well away from the bandage. Standing up, the smile vanished behind the black cloud on his brow.

"Strange, though, your bite. Much more damage done than should have been. That native woman, Waseya, had some strange ideas about it...but, well, they almost seem plausible now." He paused and was silent for moment. Then, he mumbled a few words about returning on the morrow, and grabbed hastily for his bag. Jacques sat up abruptly and snatched for Peregrine's coat as he was drawing it on.

"What is it that has happened here? I must know."

The young doctor's eyes met his, the very contact he'd been avoiding since he stepped into the sickroom, and sitting down, he covered his face with his palms.

He looked back up, cocked a copper eyebrow in Jacques' direction and abruptly burst into tears.

"Forgive me, it's the exhaustion. The bodies...so many bodies. And the mutilation...I've never seen such a thing. A terrible...horrible thing...drowning."

Jacques looked on in horror as Peregrine, the strong, competent doctor who'd been his friend was drowning before him in hopelessness that the boy could not yet understand.

:17:
Crow

Every time they met Crow vowed it would be the last, and he intended to tell her so. The harsh words he would speak were all properly arranged and waiting in his mind. He'd steel his eyes and make his great, broad shoulders rigid against any barrage of womanly wiles she might employ, not that she had any—or needed any with Crow. But then, he'd emerge into the wood and find her sweetly lazing on rocks of Sugar Loaf. She'd be humming a melody or simply sitting quietly, her face up-turned toward the sun above the towering branches. Then, she'd open those eyes, those strange and wonderful eyes and her whole face would fill with wonder. As if he, Crow, was something marvelous to behold. The whole world diminished in those moments, the lights extinguished except the small glow of glorious color and enchantment that held them within it. She made him feel like his whole being was on fire, and she was the only water that could temper him. There were words and stories and the recanting of legends shared between them, both lovers feeling like each tale was for them alone. He thought often of Waseya's message to him when he first arrived. "Love is a leap" she'd said. And he understood that now. A great leap across a sprawling chasm in the dark—falling so rapidly and for so long that one forgot the terrible crash that must be creeping ever closer.

Today was the last day, and so he pushed the image

of her from his mind, the feel of her skin—sun-kissed and such a mix of pink and gold…no. He must focus.. He had business here and for all of their conversation, all of the secrets shared between their hearts, he still guarded closely his self-appointed mission for coming to the island. And now, Cross Shipping Company men had been found drowned and slashed, tortured to death, cruelly murdered…he could pretend no longer. He could no longer live in the idyll he had constructed for himself. He could not close his eyes without seeing their bloated faces, skin slashed to ribbons, as if attacked by a madman with shears. So gruesome that he could not sleep. Wavering between feelings of needing to see her, the only breath of freshness in this rotten reality—and the necessity to close himself to her, to break irrevocably. He *would* see this through to the end, no matter how it might break him. He was a man of God and of law, of justice for the tribes and for the murdered men. These all came before his own desires.

He was walking, bending here and there beneath low branches, his feet carrying him to their meeting place, and there she was, her back to him, her face directed down toward the roots and fresh earth beneath her feet. Crow had been hoping to avoid her strange and mesmerizing eyes, but now that they were not directed toward him, he found that all he wanted was her gaze upon him.

But no, no, avoiding her eyes would make this simpler. He stepped forward and cleared his throat authoritatively. He stood straight, and spread his shoulders wide as if making himself physically larger would give him greater courage to speak the next words, the words he'd rehearsed the whole way there.

165

He tried to think of a few verses from the Bible, something to give him strength and steel his resolution. But nothing came, his mind was blank.

Blank except for her eyes, those wide open windows to her spirit were shedding tears like diamonds, falling shining and cold onto the forest floor.

In one step his arms were about her, her body filling in the spaces that he hadn't known were empty. All thoughts and plans for breaking with her, disappeared into the ripples like a pebble thrown into the waves.

"You have heard then?" He spoke quietly, this was the first time he had seen her in two days, and because she was a Delacroix, he hadn't expected her to be as haunted as he himself had been. As haunted as he still was.

"Yes. Three. Three men that were living and breathing and holding their families close—only a few days past! And now...now their arms will remain empty, their voices silenced forever." A silent sob shuddered through her body and he pulled her closer.

"My father..." She tried speaking again in between sobs, her voice souring, "My father has been keeping things from me!" Her voice was quiet, but something in the lowered volume was more menacing than a snarl. Crow placed a finger underneath her chin and directed her eyes to his. Maybe she already knew! Now that she finally discovered the truth about her father, would she leave with him? Could he take her away from this island, just the two of them with the Justice of the Lord before them?

"You finally know, then?" He couldn't help it, the sadness of the moment had been overshadowed by his own excitement of the possibilities that might stretch before him. He did not notice the change in her face, so lost was he in his own enthusiasm.

"He's come clean? I can barely believe it. He's the enemy of my brothers, sure, but I can hardly believe he'd kill those men. A monster hiding behind that kindly smile. I'm sorry, little bird, this must be terrible for you, but I am here!"

His voice had grown louder and louder, filled with righteous indignation. But when he paused to breathe, and pull her closer, he felt, rather than heard, the silence. A charged, angry silence. One look at her face told him that something he'd said was very, very wrong. He had been grievously mistaken.

Anger, black and billowing snaked around her form. No longer folded into his embrace, the force of her fury gave her a dark strength.

"What precisely is it that you accuse my father of?"

Despite himself, Crow felt his own temper rise. Her reaction had dashed his hopes for their future together, and bringing about the realization that he had spoken impulsively. Bilious anger rose in his throat, choking the tenderness from him.

"You, yourself know his crimes! Only a moment ago you revealed that he'd kept his heinous secrets from you! Unless you *condone them?!*"

"*Secrets!*" She thundered, her voice not coming from her body, but from the trees, the earth, and breeze blowing by his face. It came from the dark shadowy blackness that had entwined itself about her. "Yes, secrets! He kept from me that the men had been murdered! He never divulged the dark history of our family, my uncle, my mother…." She snapped her jaw closed and took a step away from him, her features hard as granite. "Yes, he kept secrets from me. Secrets that father's spare their children from because they do not want to bring them pain. Which I resented. Still resent. But, I ask again, what is it, *exactly*, that you believe my father to have done?"

Something had broken within her, a crack that had traveled, splitting her into pieces. But Crow would not accept the blame, nor would he shy away from his cause. Her father, *he* was the reason for all of this pain. Jean-Luc Delacroix had secrets, and if she wanted to hear them, Crow would oblige. But before he spoke, their few halcyon days blazed before his eyes. A sunrise of moments, of the depth of their kisses, her body against his own, as familiar to him as his own skin. He pushed the memories away, not allowing them to dampen his conviction, blackened his mind with the bitterness he had grown up on. He fed his scorn, though he was sickened by the taste after the brief sweetness he'd known, that had been his, with her.

"This is the true reason I am come to Mackinac. Reports all over Detroit of your father, of his treatment of my people and the other tribes. How he pays them nothing and thinks of them as dogs to fetch and carry for him. He is no man's friend and now, before the rebellion against Cross Shipping, he has arranged for the drowning deaths of these three Menominee men that you shed crocodile tears for. That is an account of his crimes—and the same blood runs through your veins, but not heart. I know this because it is impossible that either of you would possess one, I am sure!"

He had become increasingly hysterical as he spoke,

as nothing he had said had sparked a reaction. She had stood before him, as unresponsive as stone. His words falling on her like raindrops against rock, making no mark, creating no change. And then, she smiled.

At first, small, and then wider and wider until she appeared maniacal. His resolution quivered in the face of it. Unnatural woman!

The laugh came next. She laughed, quietly, tittering over his words, her chest heaving in the cotton bodice of her gown, black hair bouncing in her hilarity. She looked suddenly to him like a demon from hell, darkness and passion and wickedness surrounding him. Finally, her humor subsided and she spoke.

"As to your charges—I will answer every one. And then tomorrow, you will call on Jacques, his first day back at the office. His ledgers and accounting books will prove all that I say."

The pain in his chest had tightened. He knew to his bones that he had the right of it, but…she seemed so certain. How could one person fill him with so much loathing and so much lust in the same moment? He wanted to strike her down, and then make love to her on the forest floor. She'd made him mad, insane with longing. And had also consumed him with anger. Her spells and charms had done this. The old woman, the Menominee had warned him…

"My father, despite any rumors you may have heard is known amongst his detractors, as an "Indian-Lover". His mother was a Romani gypsy who left France to marry my grandfather. My mother is usually suspected of being an Indian or a Gypsy as well. He has, in the last year, begun hiring natives. Indian men, who, as you well know, have had their lands taken, swallowed up by the United States government. 'Removed' inch by precious inch, their heritage and culture diminished. My father is beloved by the tribes, and any man who is honored enough to call him friend. If there is unrest in the tribes, and you are truly here as their advocate, you would do well to look into those who would benefit from him losing his reputation and business. Cross Shipping does have enemies, but the Delacroix family has never numbered the natives among them."

He sat still, absorbing all of this, feeling sick to his stomach.

"What of the dead men? How do you explain that?" He was reaching, he knew, but his righteous fury had ebbed and he grabbed hold of this fact like a drowning man would fight to grasp a raft.

"The men who died? They were no longer active in their tribal council. The men, Mishimakwa, Tiwe, and Menaka...they were Cross Shipping men. Living on the island year round, working cheek by jowl alongside my father, some of his most trusted friends. As anyone knows, their deaths were obviously not an accident, they were a message. So tell me, who would want them dead? What did they know?"

She paused, took a deep breath, as if the words were knives cutting her throat.

"I thought you were a man of rare intelligence, experience, compassion; but you are a blind man, seeing only what his eyes are looking for, instead of what is clearly before him." She closed her green eye, and looked full on him with her white-blue eye, sending a shiver down his spine.

"I had thought your character was black smoke, like

mine, because the content of your soul was made up of all colors, varied and like the night itself, too magnificently made to adopt a brighter hue. I thought we were creatures cut from the same inky cloak. But now, now I think it is because you are darkness. Your character is crouched in shadow, unlit by the colors of kindness or love. You are empty. And for all of my own darkness, I am full. Adieu, Henri Crow. In time we will forget our stolen moments, as if they never existed. And perhaps, they didn't."

Raven spun on her heel, and began treading the path home. He tried to follow but a knot would appear on the the ground to trip him, or the branches would droop lower and catch his coat. Until, he could no longer hear her step on the path, and he had lost track of what path he was on.

A great animal sound pierced the air around him, a sound of desperation and sadness. The sound was as empty of hope as Raven had pronounced Crow to be. What scared Henri most was that the sound was coming from his own heart, echoing his hollow sorrows and the darkening branches. Like a dagger through his breast, he felt deeply that he was wrong. That he'd known he was wrong from the moment he'd met Raven. Had known it when speaking to Grey Wolf, had known in every word that sprang from Jean-Luc's lips, the goodness in his eyes. No man could have such a family as he had and be evil. He'd had proof all the days he'd walked the island, but as Raven had said, he'd deliberately blinded himself to the truth. He had *wanted* Jean-Luc to be capable of such meanness. Crow wanted an easy target to blame, had desired to find something missing from the perfect family portrait that the Delacroix seemed to represent. Why did he need to spread his own unhappiness around like seeds through a furrow?

Slowly, slowly, he wandered down to a lonely spot of rocky beach, and removed his shoes, rolling his trousers up to the knee. He stepped into the water, the little pebbles beneath the waves pressing into the soles of his feet. The cool sting of the water caressed away the heat of his shame. He reached down and gathered the water into his palms, splashing it onto his face. As the water washed over his eyelids, he felt as though scales were falling from his eyes. The sun setting over the water was the first sight to greet this new vision he had uncovered. He knew that this sunset was also the ending of the old Crow. The unhappy, bitter Crow who was trying so desperately to be a man that others would admire, that he had never paused to ponder what qualities that kind of man should have. The man that Raven had seen with that perfect blue eye every time she'd looked into him. She had seen something in his soul that was worthwhile, that maybe she had thought she could love...and he hadn't even known it was there.

Tomorrow he would visit Jacques, not because he didn't believe Raven, but because now that his eyes were open, he wanted to see everything he'd missed. His mission was the same, after all. And he would still seek justice, but with the assistance of those who had the same interests at heart. And maybe now, he would understand his true purpose.

Crow didn't know it then, but when he awoke the next morning, his eyes were no longer inky black pools, staring back from his shaving mirror. The lake's blue had crept in, leaving the thinnest halo of sapphire blue around the edges.

:18:
Sarah

She had thought of little else for days. Sarah was almost glad that she lacked the voice to cry out her discovery, that she was not able to verbally chastise or berate Rose about what had happened in the wood with Coralie Delacroix. She couldn't be angry with Rose for wanting to rid herself of the pregnancy, but she was furious that she would threaten another in her desperation. Rose was in a dark place, to be sure, but Sarah was disturbed that she would try to force Coralie into that same darkness.

Her mind was troubled by other events as well. The murders of the three indians had ignited a terrible fear on the island. Mackinac almost seemed adrift, floating about in the lake, waiting for a strong wind to blow it back into its rightful place. A cloud of suspicion veiled the island, and Sarah could not help but shiver beneath it.

Her ears caught the almost-silent whisperings of rebellion, quick mutterings, half-heard words and angry faces. Her usual walk among the lodges, meeting with the arriving tribes, offering to help with young ones or sick children, had been halted by Mason. It had crushed her to discontinue visiting, but he was right, it was too dangerous. The men of the tribes met her with dark looks and all along the lodges she felt she could smell blood. Blood not yet shed, blood that they demanded be repaid.

There hadn't been an uprising on Mackinac in some

time, and even the last stirring had been efficiently put down without any bloodshed. But this, this was worse. Three indian men brutally murdered. Three, that hated number that pursued her no matter where she fled. And, the government taking more and more from the red man and giving less and less in return. Mason had arrived at the cooperage yesterday morning to find a hatchet sunk deeply into the front door. Sarah could not decide if it was a warning or a promise.

Her silence was a blessing in some ways. She truly was a ghost, meandering about the town, visiting the stalls and the general store, walking over to the cobbler in Devil's Kitchen to have a pair of Mason's boots re-soled. No one noticed Sarah, she moved wraith-like here and there, hearing every snitch of gossip every unguarded fear or piece of news. But it was at the cooperage that she heard the most troubling tidbit of all.

Mason was still shaken by the hatchet, still nervous about the reception of his wife among the beach lodges. He worried for his island, his Mackinac, and how he, as mayor, could possibly keep the peace with tempers so high—and government payments still more than a month off. The lumbermen were in town, only for a few days, sailed over from Mackinaw City, along with the indomitable Mr. Wells. A dashing and polished man with ambition, though young, he was the unofficial leader of the lumber barons in the north of Michigan. There was something about George Wells that bothered her, something about the way he conducted the business of his lumber company that seemed unsavory. He relished the opportunity to ravage a woodland, like a highwaymen plucking the rings from a lady's hand, almost hoping that it would swell so he could slice off the finger as well. It had been his wont to stay in their home when he came to the island. But his presence so unsettled Rose and Mary, their cook, that Sarah finally had told Mason know this could no longer go on. She understood that her husband had to do business with this man, because his lumber went to make the barrels in Mason's cooperage. But, it did not mean she had to like him, or allow him into their home. He made her skin crawl, like the villain in a novel, or in the way the pastor at the Mission Church described the wiliness of the devil.

There was nothing about him specifically that should have put her off, merely something in his manner, the way his eyes narrowed when he was making a deal, his nervous habit of rubbing his fingers together, an act that was unobserved by most, but not Sarah. Sarah missed nothing. She was unable to take part in negotiations or discussions, so she watched life play out before her, like a reader watching events unfold on the page. Unable to change the outcomes, but fully invested in all of the minutiae and clues that gave away character and action. In this way, Sarah was doomed to understand the foreshadowing of trouble to come, but was limited by her speechlessness. She could say nothing, simply vanishing into the background.

Except to Mason. Dear, dear Mason who had still never given up on his pathetic, mute wife. And it was because of her husband's patience that she forced herself to observe, to continue coming to the meetings, to listen to the grumblings and wrath that blew across the island like a sharp wind. She was his ears, even if that was all she was.

She had watched them agree on a price, shaking hands. The white puff of her husband's hair caught the July sunlight making it glow, his head bobbed the customary three times, his barrel belly looking so much like the wares he produced that she wan't sure whether to beam or giggle. As George Wells and his less vocal, less affable companions had turned to go, Mason had wiped his palm on his trouser leg, subconsciously feeling the need to wipe the grime of the other man's hand from his own. Sarah was in the corner, waiting for Mason to finish his business. She would attempt to communicate some of the troubling things she had heard that morning, to better arm her husband against the coming storms.

The men were passing her by, and though she was plain as day, standing in the sunlight, she dipped her head to acknowledge them, they moved right past, speaking to themselves. Sarah shook her head, took a step forward and stilled herself. What had she heard the man say? Was it possible? All thoughts of Rose and her unborn child, all thoughts of her own woes and miseries flew from her mind, only the cruel words remained.

"Mayor Idiot is terrified. But Delacroix won't budge. How many more of these redskin chugs you reckon we should kill until Delacroix turns coward too?"

The door to the cooperage had already closed, and Mason was looking at her, expectantly. But her feet, like her voice in her throat was stuck, frozen in the moment that she realized that George Wells *was* as wily as the devil.

And as evil.

:19:
Raven

Raven had been agitated for the whole of the afternoon, and as it came on evening, her anger turned to fury. The smoky black haze that surrounded her seemed to fizzle and spark. She'd roamed the woods for hours, her mind tumbling and careening down the path of, "what have I done?". She thought that the heat of her anger would burn away her feelings for Henri Crow, but instead the heat only burned away in the pit of her stomach, kindling the loss of something she'd hardly had time to feel was hers to possess.

She'd thought to go to Waseya, to unburden her troubles with Rose O'Malley, and this new heartache that she owed to Henri Crow. However, she found that her feet would not take her there. She would direct herself down the path she knew to lead to Waseya's cabin, having traversed it so many times she could do so blindfolded, only to end up somewhere completely different. Her old nurse did not want to be found, or perhaps, wanted Raven to sort her own troubles.

Longing then for her mother, perhaps a spoon of honey to go with her dose of wisdom, but that path was barred as well. Barred by secrets. Her mother's secrets, Jacques' secrets, and her own.

Raven had only the pain in her chest, a pressing, stifling ache that told her much was amiss. That the island was caught in a kind of storm of sorrows, and she could not see through the rain to know where was safe to step next. Who would be out to ruin her father?

What other calamities could befall Mackinac? There must be larger matters, darker forces at play than she had considered. Raven found a large rock, made for perching, sitting in the midst of her path. She was in a part of the forest she did not often come to, the trees around the spot emanated a keening sadness, and so she avoided it, but today it matched her own mood.

She sat and arranged her skirts before she even realized she was stopping. It was growing evening and the fury within her had cooled to ice, so that she was numb. In this attitude, she could think clearly. Looking up into the slowly darkening branches, she heard a low voice, the melody of one of her uncle's voyageuring songs. This one seemed particularly bawdy by the short pauses he made in the lyrics to chuckle. Somehow, thin comfort spread over her like water in a stream. Strange, the serenity that can come from the presence of the dead among us. Reassurance that there is more to life than what can be readily seen, the idea that there are gossamer web mysteries just beyond the ordinary.

With new perspective, she pondered the facts. Three natives were dead, mutilated and drowned in the lake. Such a grisly murder would be a difficult task. The indians were natural swimmers, born to the waters of Michigan as the fish beneath the rolling blue. Who was responsible and why? If it had to do with her father's business, then they would need local help, only an islander could have accomplished such a thing, only an islander would know where to find the men, would have their trust, and would know the secret caves and quiet spots on the island where such a heinous act could be accomplished without a witness.

Besides the tangle of her feelings for him, Henri Crow genuinely believed her father responsible. And her father had always been known as friend and ally to the native tribes, yet she knew how easily they could be led to believe untruths. Perhaps already did. How many treaties had been broken, how much pretty words, false promises and empty agreements? When the government had purchased millions of acres from the tribes, Mackinac had pressed hard for the payments to be made on the island every September. But drawing tribes here to spend their coins in Mackinac shops, to trade their deerskins for calico, this only bred more trouble. Raven reached back and pulled the pins from her long dark hair, allowing it to tumble down her back, relieving some of the strain from these confusing thoughts.

Raven could see the colors of anger, suspicion and fear swirling about the island. Discord simmered and boiled, giving off flashes of crimson red and sputtering blackness. Raven feared for her family, knowing that they could become the target of the bubbling fury, whose colors warned and terrified her.

She sighed and picked a burr from the hem of her gown. Finally, the last prickly problem: Rose O'Malley. Raven didn't know how, but she felt the threat of the girl's words without understanding why. Not that it was unheard of for a young man to get a woman in the family way outside of marriage. Was Jacques capable? All at once she was angry with herself, and understood why Jacques felt his limitations so keenly. If his own family doubted his abilities to seduce or be seduced at his age, then he had every reason to think he wasn't respected. But what if Rose wasn't lying? What if Rose's accusations were true? Well, there would be gossip, moral censure. He might even have to marry the girl. But that still didn't explain the threats. She shook the thought away. There was something else, though. Something in Rose's words that implied a dark stain on the family. A connection to the past that Raven had never learned, but knew existed. Rose's threat wouldn't only blacken Jacques' reputation, but the Delacroix name. There was some reason that the islanders would easily believe it, and that reason lay in a buried part of her parent's past.

Or perhaps naught would happen. Mayhap no one would even care. But, there was a chance. A chance that morality and decorum would win the day. Her family was already singled out for their compassion and friendship with the natives—*she* could not be the reason the scales tipped. No, especially not now when a storm cloud of trouble threatened to break any moment after the death of the three men.

But, with any luck, Jacques could persuade Henri Crow of their father's innocence. Perhaps her mother would trust Raven with her secrets. She could wish for these things but had no control over them. The one thing that was in Raven's control was the decision that only she could make. Would she assist Rose in ridding her womb of the light within it? If she could save her family, then she would do it.

She stood up, smoothed her skirts, resolved. But then doubts flashed before her anew.

What if it did not work? What if the elixir, meant to douse the flicker of light in her womb, also put out the flame of Rose's life? Raven would be a murderess. Her wings would be torn off with guilt, the whole of her own life taken with the knowledge of her deed.

Her eyes looked up to meet the liquid brown eyes belonging to the same ghostly indian boy she had seen before. They gazed soulfully into her own, and her mind resolved again. She could not help Rose. Not even if it might mean ruin for her family. It was wrong in the eyes of the manitou, wrong in the eyes of the Christian God. Something in the sadness of ghost-boy's eyes shamed her for even considering it.

He broke the eye contact, leaving her colder than she had been before it had begun. He noiselessly trod the path a few feet from her. In life he would have been young. Perhaps 10 or so. No dirt stirred beneath his phantom moccasins, and having delivered whatever his message was to Raven, he seemed to have forgotten her. She watched the beading on his deerskins sway, wondering about the mother who had lovingly put them there. The mother whom he had left one day and had never returned to. Without thinking, she was reminded of Henri Crow, something in the indian's sadness reminded her of him. Something lost and vulnerable. Her eyes were still fixed to the swinging beads, though they made no sound as they moved. She followed his journey down the path, watched as he jumped onto a tree, shimmying his way up the trunk and then hopping down, seemingly testing each tree to choose the perfect one for climbing.

Raven followed him, part of her interested in where he might go, and the other part of her knowing she should make her way back home. But something urged her on. After a few minutes of climbing and jumping, they came to a great tall tree. It soared so high in the sky that Raven felt the sun must trouble itself not to be caught in the snares of its branches. Here, the boy stopped, and placed a hand on the trunk, but did not attempt to climb. The little spirit seemed to shrink, becoming even paler in the darkness of the wood.

"Did you like to climb trees?" She asked, not wanting him to vanish yet. For a moment he did not stir. Then he looked from the tree, to her and then to a great chasm near the tree. It looked as though another tree had used to stand in the spot, but had died and fallen, exposing a great hole where roots had once snaked and coiled in the soil below. He looked back at Raven, and an idea began to take hold.

"This would be a very dangerous tree to climb, if you should fall…" but she did not finish the thought. Before her eyes the little ghost began to change. Arms and legs at impossible angles, bones burst through skin, blood came from his mouth. The eyes, alone, never changed. She started to scream, but a blink later he was whole again. A shade still, but unbroken to her eye. His mouth opened and he pointed, fear coming into his face. Without another pause for thought, she turned and followed the direction of his hand.

As she walked, she puzzled. He had died falling from the tree. Why reveal this to her? For some reason, her mind flashed back to Henri Crow, again. She suddenly longed for his arms. The bulk of his warmth surrounding her, enfolding her into his embrace. She yearned for the innocent, untainted love that was denied to them. They hadn't had long, only a dozen or so clandestine rendezvous, shared words, stolen kisses that warmed her fingertips and brought a flush to her cheeks. It had felt like love. Something in her accepting his past and his flaws without him giving voice to them. But she must have been mistaken. Love could never have existed with so many secrets barring its path.

Her mind floated from Henri Crow to the pleading eyes of Beshkno, the little spirit pointing her down a path she recognized, it was the trail that led to Peregrine's surgery.

Upon reaching the door, her first thought was to return home, the little phantom had made a mistake, or she'd misunderstood. But, her feet had brought her here, so she exhaled and raised her fist to the sturdy oak door.

Without waiting for permission, she twisted the handle and emerged into a world of potions and herbs, bandages and elixirs. Mortar and pestle, jars and clean cloths stood proudly on the shelves, puffed up with their importance in curing ills and halting illness. Peregrine was sitting in a well-made chair of maple, with a Moroccan leather notebook staring nearly naked of ink from his lap, only a few lines scrawled across its vulnerable whiteness. The eyes he turned toward her looked as vacant as the page before him, as if he did not truly see her at all. Coralie felt that she could see the whir of his thoughts playing a game of chase in his mind—too busy running after ideas to notice the intruder at the door. His bronze hair was curling on his forehead, and the grey of his eyes slid into focus. He smiled out of one side of his face, but the other corner of his mouth turned down. Since the moment she had seen him disembark from the ship that had brought him from England, she thought him handsome, it was impossible not to. He had a graceful and elegant manner, a crisp and precise way of speaking and carried himself with the straight dignity of a lone pine. She had tried to make herself agreeable to him, to make him think thoughts of love when he first arrived. She thought him a melancholy but romantic figure. But he was trailed by his own shadow. His love for his dead wife followed him everywhere. Not a ghost, her spirit did not haunt him, rather he haunted himself with her memory, refusing to let her rest. Raven knew months ago that she could not make him see her. His heart had been buried with his wife.

Something stirred and she realized there was

another person in the small surgery, facing away from her in a chair, a special chair that reclined, for she could not see the figure's face at all. All at once, she was ashamed. For following the directions of a ghost. For barging in on someone else's consultation, for all of the problems that lay in her conscience, nipping and biting at her for attention.

She bobbed her head in apology, but a familiar voice startled her into turning back around.

"Coralie, poppet, what brings you here? I hope you haven't a touch of the catarrh? Often happens when the weather changes and the lilacs are in bloom."

She started and swallowed with effort. Her jolly Uncle Nicholas was gaunt and his usual russet hair, the twin of his nephew's, was dull and streaked with grey. She'd never seen him thus. Nicholas had always bounced through her life, dancing in and out of her days as one would switch partners in a Quadrille. The contrast between the two men highlighted the stage of her uncle's decline. Most worrisome of all, he'd gone blurry. The sign to Raven of one about to lose their color forever in death.

"Uncle! What ails you? *Mon Dieu*, but you are pale!" Raven ran to his side and kneeled, all of the rest of the days' difficulties rushing from her thoughts in a moment.

"Shh, shhh... there, hush, sweeting. Nothing to worry those black curls about."

Raven looked from her uncle's wan face back to Peregrine, whose face revealed nothing.

"You will make him well?" She said, more a command than a question. Peregrine licked his lips and studied the jars on his shelf. While she waited for a response, she realized there was something she did very much like about this strange new cousin. Something in his eyes that she recognized from her own looking glass. But the answer she wanted never crossed his lips. Instead, Nicholas cleared his throat and spoke himself.

"Destiny is unknown to me, poppet. Our dear Peregrine here is doing all he knows, and I am being a very cooperative patient, I promise."

Raven nodded her head and kissed her uncle on the cheek, embarrassed again that she'd stumbled on something private. A scene that was not meant for her eyes. She could see that her uncle wished for no more questions, and in response she stood, self-consciously, and said goodbye, unable to bar the tears from forming on her eyelids like dew.

Peregrine stood to accompany her to the door, and Nicholas called out one final thought.

"Why did you come here? Are you ill, Coralie? I wouldn't wish to send you from the doctor if you require him."

Raven turned slowly, avoiding Peregrine's eyes, "No, uncle, I'm quite well."

"Well then, how came you here? It's not our Jacques, is it? Or, perhaps a different errand altogether?" His voice had the faintest rosy glow of interest. And she realized he imagined she had come to the surgery hoping to find his handsome, pensive nephew alone. The thought colored her cheeks, thinking of another man she'd spent far too much time with.

She shook her head, clearing it, and responded softly. "A spirit sent me, Uncle. A boy… 'Beshkno' my mother called him."

"Ahh…I see." Nicholas said, and nothing more.

Peregrine followed her to the door, and took a step outside, before closing it and staring into her face.

"You should not have come." He said simply. Not as a rebuke but a statement of fact.

"I know it, but it couldn't be helped." Raven shrugged. "Sometimes my shoes begin walking a path and I am left to follow along until I discover where they are taking me."

He frowned at her words, but said nothing more. He made no move to return inside either. Raven took the moment to study him more closely now that he was so near, and unguarded.

The color of Peregrine's character was unusual, he emanated a bright golden light like sunshine. Even though he seemed to walk endlessly in the shadow of a darkened world. If she closed her green eye, she could almost detect the cords pulling him back toward his surgery, and yet a force within him resisted. She knew what happened to the souls of those that fight their fate, and Peregrine's was even now cleaving itself in two. Raven wondered if his soul was so bright because he healed the lives and hearts of so many. Impulsively, she grabbed his arm. "You are a blessing to Mackinac, cousin. You saved Jacques' leg and his life. You have helped many ailing on the island."

He made a motion to protest, to brush away her words as though they were snowflakes fallen on his sleeve. But she raised a hand, silencing him.

"It is true. I can see you are called to healing. But you are poisoning your own soul by living in denial of your gifts. You have swallowed misery every morning for far too long, soon your spirit will choke on it. I can see through this blue eye, this dead, glass crystal ball that I know you would love to study. I can see that you are special. But do not mistake the manitou—when death comes for each of us, there is naught that a healer can do but ease pain. After the struggle of trying to save a life, you must bow gracefully to death as he takes their spirits to the land of souls. He releases those from pain when you cannot."

She didn't know where the words came from, only that the island itself had breathed them into her when she needed them. His forehead lost its wrinkle and his mouth opened as if he would speak, but only a long sigh escaped, a mischievous demon leaving his body. She stood on tip toe to kiss his cheek, and felt a tiny tingle in her lips as she did so. The sun sent golden lights into his copper hair, his shoulders relaxed, and without another word, he stepped back into the cabin. She thought again, how easy it would be to love him. If only her own heart wasn't broken. If only he could rid himself of the sorrow that filled his.

The last rays of the summer day were painting pink and orange across the Mackinac sky, each uneven brushstroke of color dazzling to Raven. Such a sight almost made her happy, but the gloomy memories of the day drifted in with the evening gloam. Plodding in on slow feet, settling into her chest like heavy stones. She picked her way back to her parent's home, feeling the hum of her father's violin and inhaling the scent of lake perch cooking on the hearth long before the house came into view. It struck Raven as strange that there could still be so much happiness in a world crumbling in sorrow and gossip and secrets.

She had made a decision about what she would do with Rose. She would do nothing, and when Raven failed to appear under the coming full moon, she was certain her absence would have consequences. Rose would burst open a hive full of buzzing, angry venom.

Then Henri, and the trouble with the tribes. Her eyes found her father's on the porch, his arms playing the music of their own accord, the notes tattooed into his fingers, the melody branded on his palms. His smile broke across his face like the dawn and he sent her a wink. How anyone could believe him guilty of anything malicious she could not fathom.

Her foot came to the first step on their stoop and Henri Crow appeared, a vision before her eyes. She tried to shroud the image of his face in blackness, to send it back into the forgotten pools of her mind, not to be dived into again. But instead, his hands on her hips, and on her waist, and in her hair. His eyes flashing into her own and the sweetness of his mouth on hers. She had not wanted it to be him, but when they were together, there was nothing else. No other life, no other place, no other man. Just the sunlight dappling through the trees, and the intensity of the moment. She thought of the familiar space between his teeth and the endless ink black of his eyes. His eyes...but the eyes before her were green. Green as summer leaves and warm as sunshine. It was her father, Jean-Luc, standing before her, with a gentle hand on her arm.

"Coralie, *mon coeur*, I think we have much to discuss." And the warmth of his eyes dimmed, and grew cold.

:20:
Jacques

The only word for it was spooky. That's how the first day back in his office felt. As if he'd entered the realm of the spirits, haunting all of the places he'd spent his hours in life. Several times he'd brought his hand before his face, wriggling his digits back and forth to test that his corporeal body still existed.

It was partly his fault, of course. He'd arrived early, partially in excitement to resume his duties, partially to avoid the discomfort of the men's expressions when they saw him. Jacques did not think he was equal to pity, no matter how well-intentioned it was meant.

So it was that he had spent the morning in eerie silence. The only proof of his existence the rustling pages of the account book, the haphazard notes of whatever poor soul in his father's employ who'd been tasked with keeping the ledgers current. And the throbbing in his leg. His only companions in the cramped office were the white-washed walls that transformed into specters in the changing light and shadow.

He hadn't accomplished much yet—unusual for Jacques, but his mind was full of all the news and secrets that had been kept from him as he was convalescing. These admissions that had been gleaned from Peregrine on his last visit. His own uncertain future seemed more bleak as his eyes scanned over the gobbledy-gook numbers sent from the clerk in Detroit and the bookkeeper in Mackinaw City. He was perpetually distracted by their errors. *His columns*, stacked neatly side-by-side, trailing balances, additions, subtractions, goods sold, transported, spoiled. Passengers aboard, new men hired, men let go, killed on the job, dismissed for fighting, stealing or other such offenses. The ledgers might appear to be random numbers, ever-changing, dizzying rows with no meaning to those who did not understand them. But for Jacques, they were a story. A tale he read daily that told the secrets of Cross Shipping, the successes and failures of his father's company. The impact of a new export or the sad losses of hardship or storms. It was an adventure story—but today it felt as if words were missing. The story could no longer be told because the teller had forgotten the details. By noon, Jacques had realized it wasn't poor accounting on the part of the interim man who'd replaced him, but rather, something more alarming.

Jacques could no longer read the tale, because the story was wrong. The dispatches from at least two different cities were false. The numbers faked, the story they told—gibberish. The only thing he could read in these numbers was treachery. His father's business associates, men he'd hand-picked to represent Cross Shipping on other shores were purposely falsifying documents, and Jacques was certain that the only purpose could be to cheat his father. But, his mind, fogged by confusion and the splitting pain in his leg could not divine *why*. Were they bought men? Had someone turned them from the company? How? When? For what purpose?

He replaced his pen on the desk, his arm almost spilling the inkwell, an act that would have destroyed all the proof he'd spent the past few hours uncovering. He ran his hands through his hair, sure that he was putting inky-streaks in its sandy blondness, and not caring. *Why?* And how could he explain it to his father?

Jacques heard the door open, and seeing no one, assumed it was his Uncle Philippe's spirit, or the wind. It was an old door, after all. He stood up to close it, wincing as the skin on his injured leg shifted position. From this vantage, he saw it was Turtle who had come to pay him a visit. Wagging his little black tail, once, then twice, he walked over to Jacques' desk, and with a tired canine exhale, lay in a curled heap at Jacques' feet. It wasn't the first time the dog had gotten out and strolled over to Jacques, knowing where to find him in the shipping office on the harbor, but he was especially welcome today.

Leaving the door open, he resumed his seat. Turtle's black fur beneath him reminded him of the nearly-spilled ink that he'd inadvertently thumped with his hand in his exasperation. The image of the ink spreading over his desk like a swarm of locusts, recalled other thoughts. He thought of his consuming frustration before the accident. The dwindling numbers in the accounting book that had bothered him. He thought again of the reasons profits had been down. His eyes and pen flew over the columns again, but this time adding in values that were missing, parts of the equation he knew had been left out. And thought it didn't answer the why, when the door to his office opened for the second time that day, he knew the man that entered may have the answers he needed.

But by the time Henri Crow's face in the crack of the door, the stories the new numbers told was not one Jacques wanted to hear. The tale they told spoke of deceit, theft, and murder. Images flashed wildly in his mind, faces he thought he had known well, faces twisted into expressions of hate and greed that he never would have imagined. He read the numbers and the dark tale they told until his eyes burned with tears that fell unchecked down his fair cheeks.

It was this same attitude that Henri Crow found Jacques in when he stepped into the small white-washed office. Another day, Jacques might have felt ashamed to be seen weeping, but today, the only emotion that throbbed within him was anguish.

Crow was quick to notice the boy's distress, concerned that perhaps it had to do with his injury, the bite that he knew could not yet have healed. But the expression Jacques gave this strange man, signified a different kind of pain. Jacques believed in magic and legend, but he didn't believe in coincidence. And though he could not think that Crow's intentions were malevolent, he did think that the man had purposely deceived him about his presence on the island.

The room remained silent for a moment, a confrontation of feelings that neither man was anxious to begin. Jacques broke the tension with a nod, and signaled for Crow to take a seat.

"M. Crow, I owe you my life. I had planned to assault you with a demonstration of my gratitude the next we met. But, I find that as grateful as I truly am, I have some questions that I think only you can answer."

Jacques looked the man over a long moment, and added, "And I think I am not mistaken in supposing you have some questions for me as well."

Crow nodded, his eyes intense and searching. He shifted to a more comfortable position, settling his broad shoulders farther into the spare wooden chair.

He held a hand out and motioned for Jacques to continue.

"M. Crow, it has…"

"Please, simply 'Crow' is fine."

Jacques felt his own shoulder relax into his chair. There was no need to conduct an interview like a magistrate.

"*Oui*, Crow. I am glad you are come. This morning I have been going over the shipping company's accounts, and…well, that is, I am almost certain that the discrepancies within coincide with your arrival."

Henri's eyebrows furrowed quizzically, "Do you imply that you think me in some way responsible? If so, I must vehemently protest, and I will have you understand…"

"Peace." Jacques commanded, pulling back on the reins of the galloping conversation. "No, you mistake me. I think that you have come to Mackinac in response to these errors. I think that perhaps you believe you represent a people that possess a side of this puzzle that I have not yet pieced together."

Lowering his voice, Jacques continued, "I think, Crow, that you are wrong. I think that you may not have the missing pieces at all."

Crow nodded, his forehead creased, each line holding different questions. The air in the room had grown tight. Jacques felt as though a bolt of lightning was going to crackle through the tension. And he was certain it would. He knew for certain that they both held a revelation of such force in their arsenal.

Crow cleared his throat, and pressed his fingers together pragmatically. He studied his hands, as though the words he would speak were written somewhere between his fingers.

"M. Delacroix...Jacques..." he amended, after a meaningful glance, "I am a man of two worlds. A man of the Huron, the wisdom and bravery of my tribe creating within me the responsibility to protect that heritage, that culture and the pride of my people. But I am also the bastard son of an unknown white father. I have a fine American education, and am a student of law and I think, a Godly man. I walk in the white man's world in a way that I could not if I were fully Huron. My copper skin and dark eyes are shaded by this nut-brown hair and the European set of my jaw. I am of two worlds and no world." He paused, collecting his thoughts. "I, too, have only recently realized that our purposes are aligned. I confess that when I first arrived on these shores my only thought was to ruin your father and his company, to make him pay for the injustices I was told were done to my people..." His voice grew loud with passion, and he paused again, mastering his own voice. "But as I said, I have been recently told, by one whose words I cannot doubt, that I have been misled. So, today, I am come, not for answers, but to offer my aid in finding our common enemy. And to warn you—the natives are under the same delusions from which I suffered. I fear...I fear they will rise against Cross Shipping."

Jacques stood slowly and walked painfully to a small cupboard in the corner, and took out some applejack his father had procured down state. The idea of someone wishing harm on Cross Shipping was not a new one. But nevertheless, harm to his family, combined with an indian uprising made for thirsty conversation. He offered a glass to Crow, and coming back around the desk he sat heavily and rolled his shoulders before he spoke.

"So, I was correct." He drummed his fingers on the desk, still thinking. "Cross Shipping has always had enemies. Just as any profitable business will. There are those that wish to take our prosperity for themselves. The other shipping companies that vie for our accounts, the government, the lumbermen, all have reason to be jealous of our status." Jacques brought his hand down flat on the table, and looked into Crow's dark eyes. "I am sorry that you grew up believing that you are a man of two different worlds. I pray that you look about you on Mackinac and note that in these wild places, it is the men who have knowledge of the different cultures that fill the land that are the most respected. I will not say you've come to this island for naught, misled by the scheming of a company or the tribes themselves. I, for one, am overjoyed that you've come, for my own selfish reasons" He nodded to his leg, "But my father has always been a great friend to the tribes. Last year, in response to some of the new unfair indian legislation, we began employing any native that wanted the work, and for the same wages."

Henri's eyes narrowed, "You are not pressing them into service against their will?"

Jacques was taken aback, "Surely, you are jesting? Cross Shipping would never…we would never have need or desire to do such a thing!"

"And you say they are paid…?"

"The same wages as any other man who works for the company. Salary to increase on years of service and merit. In fact, I must tell you, from the beginning, it has been a disaster financially to hire men that we do not specifically need. There are more shipping companies now, and the fort is not as active as it once was."

Crow's face was twisted into a bitter expression. "I see…and so I was mistaken. But deliberately made so. I think that I must tell you…the indians employed in Detroit and in many of the other ports where Cross Shipping operates, they are not compensated fairly, and sometimes not at all. I believe that the men in the offices there are keeping this money."

Jacques pressed the heel of his hand to his forehead, his eyes skimming over the numbers on the ledgers on the desk. How far back did the treachery go? How much had he missed whilst mooning over his own sorrows?

Henri Crow exhaled and continued, "It is my belief that the men who were drowned, were murdered and mutilated because they knew of this plot, and were going to take their information to your father."

Jacques' head fell into his hands, and his thumbs came up to massage his temples. "This changes everything. It is more than our responsibility then, it is a stain on our name to have this blood on our hands."

Crow nodded, his eyes downcast, though he did not disagree with Jacques. "I am sorry for this burden. Raven told me that the men were close to your father."

If Jacques heard Crow speaking of his sister, it didn't register. He was thoroughly caught in the snares of the terrible information that was still pressing into him like stones on his chest. He worried he was going to have another episode, and the anxiety of the possibility turned it into a reality. His breathing became wheezing, and his attention turned from the throbbing pain in his leg to the constriction in his chest. He reached crazily for his top-button, ashamed of his frailty, but needing to undo it, to free up a little more space for air. Air, air. His breathing was harder and he could feel his face twist into fear. Crow lunged across the desk and grabbed his wrists, holding them, and speaking, though Jacques didn't know what he said. The words calmed him, a repetition, and he could feel his pulse slow. in the larger man's hands.

His breathing returned to almost normal, and he nodded thanks to Crow.

"My apologies, I am…inclined towards these episodes."

"Not at all. No apologies are needed. Just because you cannot so easily glimpse my weaknesses does not mean that mine do not exist."

Jacques puzzled, he supposed there was some truth to it. Not everyone wore their weaknesses on the outside, as he did. His mind went back to another day, another person who had seemed to understand his shame, instead of telling him it did not exist at all. But Crow was still speaking, and Jacques turned his attention back to the looming presence of the man across the desk who had only just rescued him from an episode.

"…and so when he arrives, he will know better whom to speak with in the tribal community, and to make clear who encourages this rebellion. But I fear he will not arrive in time…"

"I'm sorry, whom is it that you speak of?"

"My grandfather. He is the chief of a tribe of Hurons. He will not come until late summer."

They discussed for some minutes different ideas, the best way forward in such chaos was unclear to them.

Who was their enemy? How to know who they would harm next? What would happen if more indians were killed? And, what would happen if the rebellion began, now that the fort stood emptier than it ever had?

A rough plan was hatched, and as they sat discussing, ironing out details, Turtle crawled out from underneath Jacques' feet, stretching and yawning, and walked to the door, raising a paw to scratch it twice.

The door opened, and a young lady walked in. Her presence was not usual, she'd not been there many times before. But Crow and Jacques were equally shocked to see her in the doorway. And what's more… that perhaps she'd heard every word.

:21:

Peregrine

Her body shivered and then seized with an inhuman force. Sweat beaded on her brow, her china doll eyes moved wildly, seeing and unseeing, a cornered animal. Her breath was ragged in her throat, so much so that he feared it bled. The golden curls, that honey-wheat sunshine color that lit up every room, was diminished in the darkness of the chamber, and all was tinged with red.

Red for blood and anger and confusion—all swift partners on this stormy morning. Peregrine could not remember a morning of his entire life that was shrouded in so much darkness. What would have been expected, nay, natural, in the black smokiness of night was all the more frightening by the gleaming light of a new day. Day that had been expertly shut out of the room so that all inside existed in a sweaty hell. The heat of her body and of the other bodies in the room seemed to consume all of the air. He called out for a window to be opened—for the others to leave, and no one heeded him. Instead, all eyes rested, hypnotically, on the face of the woman on the bed. Her golden curls that had once bounced gleefully in the sunshine, sunshine that was just outside the window…and somehow far away. Those same eyes were dull and flat in the darkness—sparkling blue eyes that were now a lifeless grey. Her small rosebud mouth had lost its bloom, the lips forming words, nonsense words that neither had sound or meaning.

And the blood. So much blood. More blood than anyone could lose and live. Her blood covered the sheets, dyeing them a rich crimson. It was on his shirt and on the bed and on his hands. *Her blood was on his hands.* The blood stained his surgeon's hands, and it kept coming.

When he peered closer at the still moving lips, he read the words upon them, *"Murderer"*.

With a cry, he awoke. The early lights of dawn illuminating his room. The garnet ring on his finger seemed over-tight, and his belly was hollow, but not with hunger. He awoke from the dream that was not a dream, was instead a trip back in time. Perhaps the dream had some embellishments, but it was all true. It was precisely how Peregrine remembered it. But what had brought it on? Coralie's words? Perhaps.

In the events of the past few days, Peregrine had almost forgotten her. Gabrielle, his wife. He sat up in bed and looked at the clock in the wall, cursing himself aloud. Not only for the hour, which was very late, but for forgetting her. Her face hadn't come into his mind at all until the dream. He cursed himself——part of him had been relieved to be freed of the guilt of her, however temporarily. He blinked the bleary tears from his eyes, and ran a hand through his bed-mussed hair. He needed a swim. He knew a place, a lonely spot on the other side of the island where no one passed. Even at the lateness of this morning hour, he thought it would be a good place for private contemplation, and the good lord knew he needed time for thought.

He stretched his arms into a T, hearing a series of pops and snaps that relieved the tightness in his elbows.

A stray strand of golden sunlight caught the red of the garnet, and bringing his hand in slowly, he pulled the little ring tentatively from his pinky finger. Immediately images of Gabrielle flooded his mind, but happy ones, which somehow were more painful. The sound of her laugh, her arms holding her sister's new daughter, their little niece, a look of longing on her face as their eyes met. The dimple when she smiled, and the way her golden head had tucked just-so onto his shoulder when they were but children. The images kept coming, each one a stab in his chest, so that after after a few moments he felt as Jacques must feel, struggling for breath, unable to find the air he needed. He thought to throw the ring into a dark corner, or out the window or into the lake. But, instead, sighing, he replaced it on his finger. It reminded him of her, and as painful as that was, it was necessary. Penances for misdeeds shouldn't be pleasurable.

He rose and dressed hurriedly, shaving so quickly that he nicked his chin, the blood that dripped from the cut recalling him to Jacques and his bite, the drowned men, and the puzzle of Uncle Nicholas. All of which sent an entirely fresh feeling of guilt through his person. Why hadn't he seen his uncle's symptoms? Why did he not notice? He should have known as soon as he stitched the cut he'd offered to him the morning Nicholas had offered him the surgery, should have thought of the possibilities, the danger. But he'd been out of practice, out of his mind, out of his depth. And even now, there was precious little he could think to do. A low growl escaped his throat, further proof that he was the beast he thought himself to be.

"Is someone there?" A deep voice carried down the

path Peregrine was walking. Someone had heard the animal-like cry that had sounded involuntarily from his chest. The voice was almost familiar, like a voice from a memory in a dream. And rounding the bend in the path, he saw that it *was* known to him.

Henri Crow, the man whom Jacques could not stop talking about. Peregrine had known the man was there the night he was summoned to the Delacroix home to treat the boy's snake bite, but in a far-off hazy kind of way. The same way one knows one is breathing, the chest is rising and falling, but without true awareness. Such was the world when Peregrine was practicing medicine. His focus was single and absolute. His mind snapped back. Crow was eyeing him quizzically, and Peregrine realized he had offered no reply, though now it seemed unnecessary.

"Yes, it is I." He said, offering Crow a nod and an almost imperceptible bow by way of apology.

"Yes, that I can see!" Crow's voice was friendly, but his face was troubled. Peregrine looked closer at the other man, his mind running over the different possibilities for his obvious discomfort. Soon, he realized the complaint could only be of his mind or heart, two afflicted areas he had no business counseling in—excepting if the former were racing or the latter had been knocked against the skull in a brawl. The two men stood on the shore, silently regarding the other, and the water before them, unsure of what to say.

"I suppose we've never been properly introduced." Crow said quietly, extending a hand, "You're the surgeon, the fellow that's treating young Jacques."

"Correct", Peregrine replied, "And you are Henri Crow, the man who first found the boy. I am ashamed to say I know nothing more of your business on the island." Peregrine was surprised to see Crow blanch at his statement, the bright copper skin paling as white as the foam on the crests of the waves before them. It was almost a reaction of someone who was ashamed, or guilty of some nefarious deed. The expression unsettled Peregrine, though, at the moment, he could not quite identify why.

Instead of answering, Crow cleared his throat and began to take off his boots. Finely made and shined like a mirror, Peregrine thought the man was a study in opposites. Dark skin, light hair, the bearing of a chief and the tailoring of a dignified clergyman. A strange man, who defied classification.

"I'd come down here to bathe in the water. I assume you came for the same reason, and we're both concerned that we're too polite or grown-up to own to it." Crow's voice was full of smiles. Laughing, Peregrine nodded his agreement.

"True, I suppose after one leaves school it feels odd to have a swim. Unless, of course, one is a sailor or some such."

Peregrine had been about to say "a sailor or an indian", but had bitten his tongue in time. Silently the men undressed, their eyes fixed fast to the shimmering blue darkness of the water. Each item of clothing they removed seemed to shed years from their faces, until, stark naked, they jumped in, boys once again.

For some time, they swam about, kicking and splashing and diving to the bottom. But soon their ams and legs grew tired and they came nearer to the other, a brotherhood grown between them in the shared experience.

"Your accent, Dr. Rast, you are not from the island."
"No, to be sure. My family is in Devon, in England.

You too, sir, have a different manner of speech. Where do you call home?"

Crow laughed, a shaky thing like bones rattling, no humor in the sound. "Nowhere I suppose. My mother's tribe wanders with the seasons and I have spent many years with the Jesuits, and then earned a degree in law at University. I matriculated and discovered that I belong to nothing and no place. I suppose I am a drifter, traveling wherever I am needed."

He was staring off at the horizon, that line in the distance where lake meets sky. Peregrine's feeling of brotherhood deepened. He, too, felt like a man without a home, and envied this man his candor, his honesty. He could speak of feelings that Peregrine was nervous to admit to himself. *Isolation,* a word so like *Island,* was that why he had come here? To be alone?

Crow continued, almost speaking to himself and Peregrine began to feel like his companion's confessor.

"Here, too, I do not belong. You say you do not know my business here, and in truth, no longer do I. When I arrived, it was simply another stop on my tour for justice, the reasons, and the righteousness of my cause flew straight as an arrow in my mind. And now? Now obstacles have barred my way to the target. Or perhaps….perhaps I see more clearly that my aim was not true. I fear I have brought with me to this island a storm of sorrows."

His voice had gone raw, and Peregrine remained silent, splashing the cold lake water on his face, listening with fascination. The man's guilt coated every word, just as Peregrine felt his own guilt covering his every action. Their regrets were not the same, but the pain of them was crushing them both in the same way. Peregrine felt that to understand this man was perhaps the key to himself. If he could help this man, maybe his own sins would be easier to bear. Speaking quietly, he asked Crow to tell him of this enmity that he spoke of, and how he believed he caused it.

"Rebellion, Rast. I think I have brought the tremors of discord in my wake" His hand skimmed over the water, collecting it into a wall, until it broke and splashed down in ripples.

"Rebellion?! Of the tribes? You are jesting surely, or waxing dramatic." Peregrine was aghast.

"I'm afraid not. It is my doing, though, my intentions were pure. Or I believed them to be. But now…now I have lost all. I wish I had never come to this island." His voice spoke an opposite message to his words. His eyes took on a faraway look, one that Peregrine had grown used to seeing on the island. As if the inhabitants of this place were always seeming somewhere beyond. It was obvious to Peregrine that what Crow was seeing was a memory, replaying it in his mind, warming his features. All this, Peregrine noted, but his own mind was still full of rebellion and what that would do to the people, native and white alike, on this small island.

Peregrine could not help but think that Henri Crow was overly-dramatic, but he realized that Henri Crow wished to live his life so. But, even with his doubts, he acknowledged that whatever Crow had done had probably not helped whatever strife that had already existed. "If you brought the storm with you, and you wish now that you had not come, then why do you not leave? Surely you could steal back some of the angry wind, putting into the sails of the ship that would carry you away from here."

As Peregrine spoke, he watched Crow's face, and

when he mentioned leaving, he'd seen a shift, a wince, a mighty rebellion of the man's heart, raging on his face.

Peregrine continued softly,

"Ahh, I see. You cannot leave, because you are in love."

If there was anything that Peregrine understood, it was love. A pain in the chest, a tightening in the stomach, that spread warmth all over the body, and somehow attacked the mind, altering it forever. Killing reason, pushing aside caution. And there was no cure.

Peregrine could attest that it continued, in a fashion, even after death. He shuddered, Gabrielle when he kissed her, Gabrielle in that blue dress, the same color as these waves, the same dress they buried her in.

Crow did not speak, but turned his head, afraid that Peregrine would read even more of him from his features.

"Well, if you cannot leave, you must stay and dissuade the tribes from rebellion and violence."

Crow grit his teeth and splashed the cool water onto his face, and Peregrine was inspired to go on.

"I will tell you this, thought you may not wish to hear it. The right woman decides most of your happiness or sorrow. Everything else you strive for in this life will pale in comparison. The rest of your life will go grey without her. But, true love? The twin of your soul beside you, your burdens and missions will fall lighter on your shoulders, because they become burdens shared by two."

They were both quiet for a moment, perhaps feeling foolish to speak of such tender things. Neither met the other's eyes, and Peregrine was surprised by his own words. He would need to guard his secrets better around Crow. Though, he reflected, the image of this twin soul in his mind was not Gabrielle. She had been a golden apple, a goddess, never standing alongside him, but peering downward from her lofty perch. Where he had placed her, so far above him.

No, the woman he pictured in his mind was a vague blur, an idea of a woman. A hope that he'd had to have a partner in this life. All at once his own guilt for Gabrielle felt sharper to realize he'd worshipped her, but hadn't trusted her as he should. Who was he to give advice on love?

Crow nodded, not being privy to Peregrine's inner turmoil. "You speak as though you have experience. My grandfather would tell me to heed your advice. A truly wise man does not need to make every mistake himself to learn from it, but instead listens to the trials of another and uses them as a lesson for his own life."

Looking away, Peregrine thought his best course was to agree. "Your grandfather is right. I would not wish my sorrow on anyone. If you truly have sown seeds of discontent with the natives, you must reap the harvest of their unhappiness yourself, before it can hurt anyone else. I may not be an islander, but I worry for the tender balance of peace in this wild place. If you have tipped it, I beseech you to set it right again." Peregrine began walking toward the shore, turning his head back, without thinking, to call behind him, "And if you are in love, whomever she may be, I urge you to grasp it while you can. You never know how long you are destined for happiness. It is like these waves, boldly rolling in the sun one moment, dashed to nothing on the beach the next. Seize your time in the sun."

Peregrine tried to keep the pleading from his voice, but it crept in anyway.

"You must have been very taken by whatever lady that jilted you, sir. I am sorry for you." Crow spoke in earnest, but something within Peregrine snapped. How dare this man make such personal comments to him! The brotherly feeling he'd had before wilted. And if the man's melancholy and dramatic speeches were founded, then he'd probably started a war on the island. A war that Peregrine would no doubt be called upon to stitch back the bodies and staunch the blood of both sides if it was not reigned in. He gnashed his teeth and he hurriedly pulled his clothing back on, he had realized that he'd better hurry to alert his uncle and M. Delacroix to the situation.

"I was not jilted, sir. That would be nothing. My wife is dead. My wife was murdered, Mr. Crow. And you are looking at her murderer even now."

His hand came up to pull his shirt over his head, the noontime sun catching the garnet on his hand, flashing as deep and red as fresh spilled blood. And then they heard the war drums.

Crow ran into shore, scrambled into his trousers, and they ran together, Peregrine knew not where. He only knew he would need to be where Crow was if he was to help in any way.

Another glance at the shining gore of the stone, and he wondered how much violence would feed the gem this day.

:22:
Philippe

There is a barrier that exists between the living and the dead. A hard line that cannot be stepped over. What is a ghost, but a collection of memories wrapped in smoke and dressed in shade? What is death but a window into another room, a balcony that overlooks the happenings of a present and future that is closed to the dead?

As I visit the living and sing my songs, I trace back the ribbon of my memories, skimming over those that remind me that I was a fool. The memories that reveal my meanness, my coldness, my selfishness. I surround myself with the people I ought to have loved better before, and can no longer recall why I did not, when I had the chance.

I cannot experience the future sorrows that afflict them, nor can I understand the mechanisms that cause them pain. I am removed. I am a shade, a whisper of a thought of a memory.

But something of their panic does trespass that barrier. Pieces and shards of their emotions fall intermittently like a sunshower, just drips and drops and then nothing. I see chaos, and grief, but I can do nothing, having truthfully forgotten what can be done.

My spirit always finds its way back to Jean-Luc, my brother. I see him as he once was, golden-haired, tall and broad and shining. He seemed always to tower over me when we were boys. Running faster, climbing higher, with always the right words on his lips and kindness in his heart. Too good. He was always thus.

And I? *Quoi! Mon Dieu!* He was island, steady and sure...and me, Philippe, I was water. Slippery and cold, and looking for a victim to drown. Until finally, it was my own water that I drowned in. My own foolishness, my own vileness.

And now, when I remember this, it floats away like a wave on that same water. I turn my mind instead to following that golden head through the trails and up the trees, onto boats and into dark caves on the lake's edge. I was never afraid. What was there to fear if Jean-Luc was close to me?

But, we grew up. It is required. No one can stay young and trot about on boy's legs, seeing the world's from a boy's eyes for long. The boy becomes a man, and then he chooses which type of man to become.

Quelle sottise! I chose wrong.

The brothers Delacroix both loved the same woman, one loved her so callously that it terrified him, and he cast her off, like a thing dead. The other loved her so much, he brought her back to life.

I? Philippe Delacroix, former brigade leader of the Lake of the Woods, I am the one who found myself on the wrong end of a dagger to my heart. With Jean-Luc, beloved brother, on the other end.

The last and greatest gift he could have given me. Release.

:23:

Raven

Her father's face was strange, pinched and almost unrecognizable. He had something to tell her, but his words tripped and tumbled, so that Raven could not follow his meaning. One moment he was speaking of her mother, and the day that Raven was born. And the next he was speaking of the past, but in a far off tone, as if his words were being carried with the wind across the straits. Some inner turmoil roiled inside of him, demanding that he tell her something, even though it seemed as though he could not bring himself to do so.

They were on the path toward Waseya's cabin, but for what reason, she did not know. Raven had never seen her father go to Waseya without her mother present. If her father was not at work he was hurrying home to be near Cora and the rest of his family. Finally, the stream of his words slowed, and began to resemble something like normal conversation. She could feel her father calming, something about the woods always did this. He loved Cross Shipping, though, he was not a man to spend so much time near the water, for him solace was found only in the endless green of the forest, shaded and held closely by the leafy boughs.

"Have you heard the legend of Ayasha and Askook?" He asked, suddenly.
"I think I have heard all the the legends, Father, but, that cannot be what you needed to discuss…"

No matter what she said she could see he was set on telling her the tale, and so she quieted, allowing him to tell it.

"I don't think you have heard this one. It is a strange and special story. It is a tale very much like Romeo and Juliet. I would even think that perhaps Shakespeare had stolen it. Strange how the same stories are told the world over, with only the names changed." He grew silent, pausing his steps as if he heard something, or felt something change in the breeze. Shaking his head, he took her arm once more, tucking it into his, and continued.

"Ayasha was a young girl of the Wendat tribe. About the same age as you are now, though her legend is an old one. Her life was lived before a white man ever showed his face near these blue waters. *Elle était belle, mais oui.* Of course, she was beautiful, for if she was not, there would be no story. Ayasha, she fell in love with a brave called Askook, whom she saw paddling his canoe alone on the lake. The sun, it also loved Askook, and would reach its golden arms down, always covering the boy in light. Shining on the blackness of his hair, which gleamed in the caresses of the light. He was a warrior, and the son of the chief of his tribe. Askook had come to the island called Mackinac to watch Ayasha's tribe. To see how they lived, to see how many men were in their lodges, to see if they had land that his tribe, the Ojibwe, might want for themselves. But when Askook saw Ayasha, he thought no more of war. He thought no more of glory or of the blessings of the manitou. He thought only of Ayasha. And our *belle*, our Ayasha, she gave her heart to Askook on the first glance across the water. He paddled to the shore, and they swore their love."

"Father, what is this about?"

"Listen, *ma petit*, this is important. *Alors*, so, she went back to her father's lodge and told her father of her love for this brave, asking her father's permission to leave to join her life to Askook's. Her father did not say no, he only asked that Askook come to their tribe, because he was a lonely man, was her father, and with the death of her mother, was afraid to lose his daughter too. Askook had also returned to his father and declared his love for Ayasha. His father, a cunning Chief, declared they should be wed, and too, had suggested that Askook go to the tribe of his new bride. The day came, and Askook went to the island of Mackinac to live in a lodge with his beloved, Ayasha. But, when he put his foot on the path to the lodge, he felt the footsteps of others. He realized his error. His father had used him and his love for Ayasha to break into the defenseless village of the Wendat. To attack their lodges and take their women. To confuse the men following him, Askook drew a flint arrow head from the pouch slung on his hip, and he drew blood from his arms and in his chest, enough to scare the other men into thinking the Wendat were not as unprepared as they had thought. As they fled, the sun stayed, warming his body, shining on his form as it always did, keeping him in the embrace of light. This same brightness though, brought Ayasha, who did not know that Askook was only pretending to be mortally injured. Running wildly, she ran to the edge of the island and allowed her body to drop down to the waves so that she might join Askook on his walk to the path of souls."

"Father, this is a very sorrowful story, and I do not

understand what I am supposed to learn…"

"Shush, *mon cœur*. It is not yet finished. Where was I? *Oui*, yes, I remember. Askook lifted his head up to see his beloved running, and so followed her, plunging his body down the steep edge of the cliffs, joining his true love in death. Now, it is said that when the sun seems brighter in one spot, or a wave of warmth washes over you on the beach, that it is Ayasha and Askook, being embraced by the sun, strolling the beach of Mackinac, still deciding where to build their lodge."

Raven nodded, casting sidelong glances at her father, wondering what the purpose of the story had been. There was a strange heat in her chest, her breath felt shallower, and she wondered if he had found out about her and Henri Crow. Even though that was all over now, wasn't it? Even if it was all over, whispers may have reached his ears.

He smiled, and turned toward her, holding her palms in his, and looked over, as if seeing for the first time that she was no longer a small blackbird girl, but a grown woman. He sighed. "I suppose it wasn't entirely fitting, but I am a bit of a romantic, you know."

She thought of him and his hidden poetry, his Shakespeare and the way his violin sang passionate pleas that she did not quite understand. Yes, a romantic, for certain.

"I tell you this story to explain that sometimes it is right to disobey your parents. That sometimes, the goals and desires of your father or your community are not in tune with your own." He laughed, "Now, we will never raid another village or think it is okay to steal from anyone, but our vision for your future does not have to be yours. You are free to plunge off the side of the cliff— metaphorically only, *ma petit*. Or, if you would leave our lodge for another shore," His eyes twinkled slyly into hers, "that also is your choice. Mackinac will forever be your home, whether you fly off to another nest or not."

He bent down and kissed her cheek. "Your brother tells secrets in his sleep, *mon cœur*."

Ah, so it was Jacques, though how he knew she wished to leave, she did not know. She should have guessed though, he had a way of knowing all secrets. It was liberating, the permission, the blessing to leave. But where would she go, how would she make her way, a woman alone....?

She opened her mouth to ask, but her father paused again, turned his head. He cocked his jaw to the side, and they both heard it. The drums.

It is not enough to say that they ran. Their bodies shivered at the sound, and a deep, animal part of them was arrested by it. They did not move toward the drumming by choice, but by instinct. They did not draw nearer out of agreement to do so, but instead some ancient rumbling inside themselves propelled them forward toward the warning beat. Raven's legs moved rapidly, quicker, quicker, double time to the rhythm, pulling herself closer and closer to the sound. She did not know if the drums frightened her or thrilled her, but instead a heady mixture of both, taking over her senses, fogging her mind of thought and reason.

Raven flew over knotty roots and through tangled branches, the forest seeming to move aside for her as it did for her mother. She did not listen for the footsteps of her father, knowing instinctively that he was alongside of her, picking his own path through the brambles and bushes that barred the trail. Her lungs grew sore, but she did not feel them, beads of sweat formed on her forehead and down her back and in the bodice of her cotton gown, and still she ran—ran like Ayasha in the story, ran as if she would hurl her life from the cliffs.

The drumming grew louder and Raven knew they were nearly upon the gathering. She slowed, her feet picking carefully over logs and stones, she had kicked off her shoes somewhere in her race to arrive, though she knew not where or when she had done so. She stopped behind a large oak about 50 yards from the meeting of tribes, where she hid. Her father crept near where she stooped, putting an arm on her shoulder silencing her ragged breath.

Almost all of the tribes were represented, their faces painted and ready for war. Raven at first could not recognize any of the faces, drawn with deep lines of vengeful anger, but soon, she would notice an expression here, or a certain tilt of the head there. It was hard to accept that this menacing gathering, bent on destruction, was made up of those whom she sometimes had called friend. Those whose lodges she had visited, men whose wives had called on Waseya, and on her mother for cures their shaman could not supply. Some men wore the paint regally, as if every stroke they had disguised their faces with had transformed them into a formidable creature of the ancient world. The type of men that existed in a time separate from their own, something of legend. Others, looked awkward and uncomfortable. The paint sat heavily on their features and Raven fancied she could see their faces, unsure beneath it. When she tore her eyes away from the scene before her, she looked to her father. While the sight before her had upset and confused her, it had all but broken Jean-Luc. The sprightly and handsome man of her earliest memories had aged in those few moments. She realized that if the tribes rose, her family would lose everything. Not only their livelihood and perhaps their lives, but the peace and relative prosperity of the entire island. Right now, Mackinac was a part of Michigan and part of the United States, but being so far north, so removed from the mainland, it was difficult to feel as if the inhabitants existed under the same laws and rules. So Mackinac had largely made their own. They adhered to the law of the land, but they still thought of themselves as somehow out of time, out of the pace of the world that ebbed and flowed like the waves from the shores of the island. All of that would disappear, all gone, if the tribes rose against them.

Her eyes were drawn back to the scene before her, riveted by the faces of the men. One brave was speaking, rallying the others. He paced about the group, shouting and shaking his fist. He was pointing to their feathers, to their face paint, to the trees surrounding them and the waters of the straits beyond. Raven did not speak the language, but she understood the words. This man was reminding the tribes of their shared heritage. Of the promises broken and the indignities suffered by all red men, regardless of their totems. How the white men treated them like children, denied them respect, stole their lands—cheated them. Raven could feel the anger swell like the flames of a fire, roaring ever upward, all these words offered up like twigs to feed the ever-growing mouth of the fire.

Raven closed her green eye, the eye that saw the world as her father did, and opened only the blue. Her cold blue eye looked on the scene before her, and found only more horror. The men had ceased to be men at all, instead their characters woven tightly into one. A mob of anger and violence that had no other thoughts but the single vision that they shared. The retribution that they craved from the white men, any white men, regardless of guilt or innocence. Hatred was blind, and these men had willingly blinded themselves to all other realities but that of the man speaking, commanding them.

One by one she watched as the faces that had shifted uncomfortably under the paint, eyes that had darted about searching for a path back to their lodge and their children, she watched as these faces instead grew resolute, and angry. Even the men who had been less passionate grew red with hate and wrongs only newly remembered.

Her blue eye looked on and became clouded, fogged, the souls of the departed, Indian and white man alike had herded into the circle, as unsure of what to do as Raven was. How quickly the living turn to violence, an emotion only understood by those with hot blood in their veins. The dead then, could no longer understand what made these men's eyes wild, what caused their voices to raise in wrath, what force it was that cowed the more temperate men among them. Raven found herself shaking, manically, pulling on her hair and biting her lips until they bled. Powerless. Only a woman, and though black-haired and communing with the dead—a white woman. Small and frail and meaningless in this world of men. And then she saw him.

Her father gripped her shoulder as Henri Crow stepped into the middle of the fray. He, too, raised his voice, and his message was less clear. At first, she feared he was encouraging them. She was frightened that whatever plan he'd had in coming to Mackinac had been realized and this was the result. But soon she saw this was not his purpose. The men around him shouted still with hostility, but she saw it was not hurled *at* him, but to the words he was speaking. She had a feeling he was defending her father and the other merchants in town. Men the tribes felt had mistreated them. Murdered them.

His voice was deep, and Raven could see the two forms of his training merging into one. First, his upbringing as a member of a tribe, and second his years studying law and his belief in the power of the Christian God to bring peace. She knew he had settled disputes in other cities, seeking justice for the indian. But she was certain he had not been called to put down a boiling rebellion before, not with men so hot for violence as these. But he spoke loudly, and calmly, stating his case with reverence for the appointed leader of the tribes, and she could see he had already brought back some of those who had been unsure.

Something inside of him called out to her, made all the frailties she had felt before turn into strengths. She felt that he was communicating all that she wished to, but could not. From her frost covered eye, she saw the strength of the island spirits casting themselves about him, lifting up his words. If her father had been looking at her face as she looked at Henri Crow, he would know her secret. For pride flowed from every part of her body, the black coiled smoke of her aura floated toward him, bolstering his message.

"Father, do you understand anything he is saying?" She whispered, her voice was breathier than normal, but her father did not notice, his attention rapt.

"Only a little. I am not as fluent as I should be in Ojibwe. Jacques would know better, he understands all of the tribal tongues. From what I gather, he is telling them that there enemy is…hidden. That the Delacroix family is not to blame for their troubles, and that their is another enemy that must be found out."

"Does he say who this enemy is?" Raven asked, a trifle overloud.

"He does not. And I'll be damned if I have any idea. This is troubling. Who can he mean? Who is sullying my name?"

For a moment, Raven froze. She recalled the jeering taunt of a woman who had promised to drag the Delacroix name through the mud. This couldn't be Rose's doing? It wasn't possible, was it? It was a terrible coincidence though. Raven wished she had discussed the threats from the girl with her family, knew that she could not delay in telling Jacques that this girl would besmirch his name. Secrets kept protected no one. Raven realized that communication and honesty did more to strengthen ties than secrecy could. Not speaking up might save feelings from being hurt, but it would not do for the Delacroix family to shut each other out, not with a crisis such as this. She felt guilty, and distressed to think that this could have been caused by her own cowardice.

Then she realized, the full moon was a few days away. Rose would not have used her trump card before she was sure Raven was not going to rid her of the babe in her womb.

Raven was pulled from her thoughts by her father's whispers, translating the message of Henri Crow.

"He says that there is another force of men on this island that seek to turn the tribes against the men of the town. He is telling them that the Delacroix is their friend, and by God, he is reminding them that I hired them when the government had set them aside, stolen from them. *Mon Dieu!* But he is a talker, smooth as silk and tough as iron. I can't imagine who these men would be. Who would ruin us, *ma petit?*"

Raven shook her head in bewilderment. Who indeed? And why? Another figure was stealthily sneaking up, and at first she opened her mouth to scream, thinking is was an angry indian. But, she closed her mouth when she saw it was Peregrine. Her father nodded to him, not asking how he had come to be there, and continued translating in a whisper.

"He says he understands their anger, but begs them to wait for his grandfather, White Arrow..." Her father let out a low whistle. "Didn't know his grandfather is White Arrow, that is a stroke of pretty luck."

"Why, father?" Raven asked, Peregrine cocking his head to the side in curiosity as well.

"He's is a...*noblesse* to the tribes. Très, très important. He is a man, that when he speaks, all who are present listen."

"A brave warrior, then?" Peregrine whispered.

"*Oui*, but made for a different kind of battle, *mon ami.*"

Peregrine was about to ask what her father meant,

but Jean-Luc shushed them both.

"They have agreed to wash the paint of anger from their faces and from their hearts—for a time. They are turning to leave!"

Raven, Peregrine and Jean-Luc, clasped hands, watching the indians file away, heads high, marveling that Henri Crow had achieved this fragile peace without any violence or bloodshed. He was so fine to Raven's eyes, it was everything she could do not to tear herself from her cousin and father and throw her arms about him, covering his face with kisses, begging him to forgive her words.

Her father straightened to full height, and Raven and Peregrine did the same. They all made to walk to Henri in the center of the clearing where he still stood, watching the tribes depart.

Crow turned toward them, his eyes finding Raven's, the dark cloud of his character moving about him like a protective fog.

But not protective enough, for a moment later the arrow flew from amongst the trees. The arrow flew through true, straight into his back, his eyes opening wide, the word falling from his mouth as he fell to the ground.

"Raven", was all he whispered before he hit the earth.

And the world went dark for both of them.

:24:
Jacques

His lungs hadn't even the chance to realize they were tired until he finished running. But, by the time he came to the schoolhouse door, he had doubled over, unable to knock or grasp the door handle. His body crumpling in two, making itself smaller, in order to find the air it needed.

Jacques wasn't sure what brought him to the school room first, perhaps because it was close, or perhaps because he had every reason to think Raven would be there. But by the time he caught his breath, the door was already being opened by a girl with dark hair.

It was *not* Raven. It was one of the merchant's daughters, a hold-over from the fur company days who'd stayed on the island after Astor abandoned Mackinac. Her father had gone into business near his Uncle Nicholas. Though, instead of "women's flummery" as most of the island's men called the wares of his Uncle's shops, this man imported spirits. Liquors and cordials that he obviously did not encourage his sour-faced daughter to imbibe.

Jacques did not have time for pleasantries.

"Is Raven here? It's an emergency. Where is she? Is she…"

The vinegar-faced girl, turned her eyes skyward, as if asking heaven if it was witness to what she was being subjected. If her face hadn't been molded into such a nasty twist of irritation, she would have been quite pretty. Although Jacques preferred a fuller figure, and a fairer complexion, he would have been ready to admire her if she would have allowed it. As if responding to not only these thoughts but his hasty questions, she answered without lowering her face from the sky.

"*Raven*", she spat, "…did not come in to the school room at all today. Not only has she failed to come in, but she has been shamefully tardy or non-existent for the past few weeks."

Jacques rolled his eyes, but grabbed her arm. Was the girl stupid? Had she not heard the hubbub in the forest or in the town?

"Never mind that now, I'm here because the tribes are on the warpath, woman!"

"Warpath, indeed." She tossed her head, and shook off his offending arm. "And do not *touch me*. I've heard all about *you*, Jacques Delacroix."

She slammed the schoolroom door in his face, amidst the chatter and whispers of the children within.

Despite the fact that Jacques had recovered from the run, his face had grown rose-red again. What in the world was she referring to?

He walked slowly back home on the edge of town. The throb in his lungs hadn't totally abated, and he was sure that his running would neither prevent a threat, nor would it ensure, that anyone was on their guard. Worthless. A half man. A weakling. A dead man wearing the skin of one who was living. And who could blame her? That's what the girl at the schoolhouse had seen when she'd looked at him.

It wasn't only the news of the tribes' hostility, which he had heard in town, but he wasn't even sure he really believed it was serious. It was a common enough thing for the tribes to have quarrels, sometimes even wounding one another before the mayor arrived with a small contingent of soldiers from the fort and put the whole ruckus down without too much ado. His father would probably be there too, helping, because he was known to be friendly with the tribes.

But the main reason he had left the office so early this afternoon was because he had figured it out. He knew who was cheating his father, knew who was cheating Cross Shipping. She had come, but when she saw Crow in his office, she had bolted. But not before leaving the envelope on the desk of one of the junior clerks, who had handed it off to Jacques an hour ago. It didn't contain proof, not the kind he needed anyway, but the words within its message brought together all of the doubts and missing pieces he'd gathered from the ledgers and accounting books. He had thought he would find Raven, and together they would tell their father, after the tribes were settled. Perhaps father was already at home, having settled the tribes quickly.

The exertion of running to the schoolyard had tired him more than he realized and his leg throbbed painfully in his trousers. He scolded himself inwardly for not taking better care of himself, for neglecting his wound. What was the point of being healed if he was only going to re-injure himself? No one was at home, but, he told himself, he *was* early. No doubt his father had gone to see about the quarrel, and had stayed to talk to the other men, and his mother and sister were probably even now safely ensconced in Waseya's cozy cabin. He almost turned and took the path there himself, but shaking his head, he walked further down the hall into his room. He *was* tired. It was easy to forget how easily fatigued he became. Perhaps just a short nap. A small sleep until his father returned with news and his mother would make dinner, and then he could explain all, though he wasn't sure what action his father would take.

Hours later he awoke. His first thought was to be peeved his mother didn't wake him for dinner. It was dark outside, the moon winking through the clouds. Pulling a hand through his hair, he sat up and blearily came to the conclusion that it was not night, but the earliest hours of a new day outside his window. Even for such a time of morning, Jacques found too much silence. There was no sound of his mother's soft murmurings as she and his father sat and waited for the sun to rise at dawn, no click of Turtle's paws on the floorboards. Looking out his window, he saw no lingering pipe smoke rising from the corner of the porch, and found that sweet wail of the fiddle's strings had not played in his dreams. His family had never come home.

The house, too, seemed quieter, as if shadows had moved through it and silenced even the draperies in the windows, strangled the air from the place, leaving it lifeless. His first feeling was of fear. The tribes had taken them in their anger. Even now they may be dead...dear God, they may be dead inside the house, he had never looked through the other rooms in his haste to get to sleep.

Dressing quickly, he ran through the halls checking the rooms, and then he spun in a circle in front of his house, a house that seemed not at all like home. A house that used to be filled to bursting with love and joy, and now was a stark and dragging thing. His eyes searched for a sign, anything that would tell a different story than that which he feared.

A snap. So quiet as to be imagined. Just a faint breaking of a twig in the forest, almost ghostly in its gentleness. He took a few steps toward the wood, his heart hammering in his chest, a relentless tattoo that made him stagger despite his inner-urging to remain strong.

It was the color that stayed his steps. Even in the darkness he saw it. Her color. Jacques had been told that a woman with red hair should never wear yellow, and so it had caught him from the beginning. He had watched her walk from the Stephens' house day after day, watched her walk with the Mrs. Stephens to the market past his office window to the market, Mrs. Stephens always at her side. Her strawberry and honey colored hair always calling him to her like a beacon.

He had avoided her since it happened. Not because he wanted to, but because she seemed to prefer it. They'd only had the one encounter in the woods, all those months ago. They'd hardly spoken during, or ever before, to be honest. It had been…an almost animal thing. Her mouth on his, his hands sliding on her hips, pulling her skirts down and then off. It had been quick, and quiet and rough at first. But it had grown gentle, and when he released, he had realized that she was weeping. They had lain on the pine needle floor, softly fragrant in the moonlight and he had held her tightly, until she held him back.

His mother would ask what had made him tarry so long at work, and would scold his father for giving him too much to do at the office. Jacques had realized then that he did not know where or with whom Rose lived, only that her family had died of smallpox three winters ago. He had heard her described as slovenly, loose, and men at the docks called her a slut. But he had never thought of labels, himself being labeled no better as a weakling. He didn't know if what they said about her was true, and he found that he didn't care. They were two drowning people, and they had used one another as a life preserver in the simplest way imaginable.

Instead, he had found her warm, and her creamy skin had seemed to glow in the moonlight. He had traced his fingers over the gentle curve of her smooth belly, and kissed her neck, and for a few hours, had forgotten that he was anything but happy.

But, Turtle had found him. And she'd quickly gotten up and dressed herself, only kissing him quickly before bounding off into the forest like a sprite. He couldn't believe that it was to end, and so soon, but he was still a boy of 15. And no matter what the men on the island said, or what it would do to his reputation, if she'd have him, he would've married her. Because that night she had not looked at him with pity. She had not approached him cautiously as though he might break. Rose had reflected him back to himself, and the image had been of a man, and a man she lusted for.

Sometimes he had wondered if it all had been a dream. When he passed by her in town and her eyes did not meet his. Or when he had returned to the spot in the wood where they had lain, convinced that they might meet again, and he might tell her how he felt. Even though...he did not think he had the words for such a declaration. He hardly knew her, what could he possibly say?

But it was the yellow that gave her away. The flame red hair like a wildfire catching in the forest, showing by the light of a moon that ducked intermittently behind clouds. He took another step, raised a hand to hail her, and she turned. He should have asked her if she had seen his parents. If she knew where they were, but his voice was lost in his throat. It had been her that had appeared so suddenly in his office yesterday afternoon, though now that seemed like a lifetime ago. She had come in the door, and his heart had leapt. But then she saw Henri Crow, and then, letting out a small squeal, had closed the door and run off. Too quickly for him and his sore leg.

Now, in the wood near his house, so early that Jacques thought perhaps he was still dreaming, he had finally found her again. From the distance, he could barely make her out that the familiar yellow dress was different, appearing much larger somehow. And then he realized that it was not the dress that was larger, but the stomach beneath it. The same milky white skin he had caressed so lovingly with his hand on that night.

To see the roundness of her skirt, he knew it was his. The timing was right, and really, he didn't believe her to be what everyone said. And even if it wasn't his child, he wanted it to be. Even though he was only a boy, even though it would bring heartbreak to both of them. But he knew it was his child. She did not meet his eyes, and instead only pointed in the direction of the doctor's cottage.He wondered what she was doing out at this hour?

He called out, "Rose…stay, a moment. I must…"

But she shook her head and began to walk away. He shouted desperately after her.

"Rose! Please!" Jacques made to follow, but something in her walk held him back. She had wanted to see him, but she did not want to talk. There was a message, some knowledge she had that he didn't and she had come to give it, and now it was done. Perhaps there was nothing else to say. Only for now, he told himself. Later, he would seek her out. Tomorrow, he would make it right.

Jacques began to plod along the path she had indicated, the path to Perry's surgery. He knew he should be anxious about what he would find there. He knew something momentous had happened as he slept. Which member of his family had been injured in the melee he had missed? But his heart was gone out of him. Even as weak as it was, it now was beating inside of the little unborn chest of the babe beneath her yellow dress.

:25:

Peregrine

There was goodness here, in her hands. She worked so quietly, so uncomplainingly. Offering him the bandages and instruments before he called for them, never pausing in her work. She did not seem to observe the blood that had pooled on the front of her dress, or that had gotten into her hair, nor did she mind the crimson smudges she had wiped in her exhaustion onto her cheeks and forehead.

She looked wild and primitive and bold. God help him, he couldn't help but compare her to Gabrielle, and not for the first time…knew that in his mind, Gabrielle paled.

The realization had come on him like a thaw, slowly, slowly and then all at once, he was warm with the truth of it. She had not been a partner to him, or a help meet. A muse, an angel, beloved…but not an equal. Never someone he could confide in or work with. No one to help shoulder his sorrows and burdens. Gabrielle was the downiest baby bird, and to add any weight to her wings was to fell her. Is that how he killed her? Was that why he murdered his wife? How else could he watch the light of her eyes flicker and dull, and then deaden without wailing? A part of him had been relieved that she was gone.

No, no. That wasn't true. He had never been glad, only relieved her suffering was over. The suffering not only of her painful death, but of the difficult life he had given her since they had married. He worshipped her, always had, from the moment they had been introduced. But worship is not enough. Admiration could not be the cornerstone of a happy union. Especially...especially when it is one-sided.

He had exhaled hard, shaking his head, and Coralie had immediately leaned over to wipe his brow. She had asked if he needed water, and brought it swiftly before he answered. The wound on Mr. Crow was a severe one, difficult to treat. He would get the man sewed up, only for the stitches to break, and the blood to pour. Peregrine was concerned that it had pierced the lung... the arrow had penetrated deeply. M. Delacroix had left some time ago, hastening to bring Waseya, and also his wife, who Peregrine knew must have trained Coralie.

Peregrine sewed another stitch, pulling it tight, too tight. It tore the skin. Damn. His fingers felt more sure than they ever had, his hands steady, his thoughts clear, but each time he attempted to heal the man, something else would break inside of him. He would have to keep the wound clean, and simply wait for the women. They might see what he could not.

He sat back and took the man's hand. Crow had begun to feel almost like a friend to Peregrine, who had none this side of the Atlantic. Coralie came to sit near him, and Peregrine hadn't the time to stop himself before he leaned over and wiped her face with his handkerchief. She blushed, and nodded her head in gratitude before taking up Crow's other hand. Damn. Peregrine cursed himself. Why hadn't he seen before? A few moments ago he realized that Coralie Delacroix was his match, a partner for his work and his life—a woman he could love deeply. And now he saw that she had given her heart to Henri Crow. He was too late. Damn. Damn.

Did Crow return the feelings? He couldn't see how the man didn't. And yet—yet. There was a reserve to him. Something almost…religious in the man's manner. Peregrine watched as Crow turned his head toward Coralie, and then closed his eyes and slept. All the while, the wound on his back continued to bleed.

They were alone in silence. It was oddly intimate, but for the grievously injured man between them. Peregrine felt an odd longing in his breast, but for what, he couldn't quite grasp. Like the desire to hear a piece of music that one knows does not exist in the world. Or the necessity of glimpsing a work of art that has not yet been created. It was a longing for the future, but not so vague as that. The sadness that accompanies the beginning of something not quite tangible. The agony of epiphany of how great and far and all-encompassing the world is; and how small our own petty plans and worries are within it. Coralie made him feel these things. Not because she was devastatingly beautiful, though Peregrine thought her comely, or because of her fortune or social standing. Instead, to Peregrine, she seemed a complete person. Aware of herself and her place within the world she lived in, and still found utility for her skills and maintained a sense of wonder for the universe. She was comprised of so many things he wanted in himself. And he had never seen her like before.

Absently, he found he was dabbing Crow's wound with a clean piece of linen, a groan from the patient letting him know that he was applying too much pressure. He sat back, and surveyed the scene before him. Coralie, stoic, lost in her own thoughts no doubt. The surgery that had been given over to him from his uncle, and the herbs and plants each sitting within the various jars and canisters. The stark whiteness of the walls and the clear jars had come to symbolize a freshness that he could feel creeping into his life. Every patient he treated, every wound he wrapped, each malady he remedied, had fed the blood in the garnet, but if had also cleansed the bad blood from his veins. The ring, which he had worn as a penance, had somehow become a symbol of his strength. Of his returning health. Of the path he had taken from Hell after Gabrielle died, and each footstep that had brought him back into the light.

Because truly now, even when faced with the dark vision before him, he felt bathed in light. Her glossy-black, blood speckled hair, the cool calmness of the blue eye, the eye that seemed to look into his soul, and find nothing wanting, her grace when confronted with violence, panic and bloodshed. Gabrielle may have looked like an angel, but Coralie had a bit of heaven surrounding her.

It was still quiet, oddly so. He had expected Jean-Luc's return by now, with help. She did not seem panicked, though, and so he tried to match her composure. He hazarded a question to break the silence.

"I have heard some call you, 'Raven'?" His voice sounded strange to him, as if he were watching himself speak to her. She didn't meet his eyes, but answered his question quietly.

"It is a strange story. I was born blonde and fair

with green eyes like my father. But it was too soon, and the manitou—the spirit of Mackinac—wished to keep me for his own. But, Waseya, she refused him. She tore her hair and bloodied her chest, and marked me just here" She rolled up her sleeve to show him the arrow shaped scar on her arm, "… and she and my mother stole me back from the path of souls. But when I was returned, I was a creature of shadow. Hair like storm clouds, and one eye cursed to see into the souls of man, to see beyond. And so I am called, 'Raven', the creature that travels between worlds." She offered him an inscrutable look as she finished speaking.

Peregrine's eyes were wide. "Do you believe all of that?" He asked.

"Do *you?*" She tossed the question back at him, and raised an eyebrow, still speaking softly.

"I have heard stranger things. Babies are often born too soon, and die before they can live. It would be a comfort to know that death can be thwarted. So often, it seems that he bests me." Peregrine did not intend to sound pathetic, but he felt her hand on top of his for the briefest of moments.

"You saved Jacques." She said simply.

"Yes, but I had competent nurses to assist me." Peregrine and Coralie's gazes met momentarily. And she nodded in acknowledgement of the compliment.

He was seized by a desire. It was not something that could ever have been forced from him, but he wanted to give up the burden to her. Peregrine needed her to hear his confession, even if it meant she would despise him. She was not all goodness, by her own admission she dwelled in the dark, it was this balance, this equally weighted scale of justice that he needed.

"Coralie…do you mind if I call you Coralie? I do not care for Raven. It is pretty and mysterious, but I would not let any spirit steal your name and give you a new one. It is too much like making you its creature."

"Perhaps there is truth to that." Her forehead creased with lines again, and her eyes looked downward.

"Coralie…" Peregrine spoke, but his voice died away in his throat. She looked up again, her brow still furrowed.

"Peregrine?"

He swallowed, and knew it was time.

"I…Can I tell you a story?" He noticed she was still clasping Crow's hand, a sight that made his heart jump in his chest, but he had resolved. He would continue.

"Please do. If I haven't something to think on I believe I shall go mad." One corner of her mouth moved upward a fraction, but Peregrine was certain the anxiety of the moment was pressing onto her, as it was him. There had been much blood loss from the arrow and the fall, and though he had tried two more times to stitch, he continued finding other wounds in the skin from the rocks he had fallen on and new bruising in worrisome places.

"I too knew a woman, a fairy creature, who was trapped by death." A dramatic start. Pathetic. Peregrine never had the words he needed.

"This woman…this was your wife?"
"Yes, my wife. Gabrielle. I…I killed her."

The door opened and four sets of eyes looked into

the surgery, followed by a flurry of activity. They were carefully flipping Crow over, then they were stitching here, and Waseya was laying hands there. She spoke strange words to Crow, not words of a different language, but words that Peregrine did not understand nonetheless. Mutterings about taking leaps, and ignoring the manitou. She scolded him, told him that he was living another's destiny, and had gotten caught into a web not made for him. A mix-up, a mistake, she cried as she prepared a paste from herbs to help stop up the great slash that the arrow had made into his body. It had flown in at a strange angle, lodging itself deeply into a lung. It was the final proof to Peregrine, the shallow breathing, the coughing, blue lips, and the crackling as Crow's chest rose and fell. He had seen it before, his friend, Henry Ffoulkes, had found himself on the sad end of a pistol duel. The same creaking breath, the confusion, and the rapid breathing. He had expired there, the green grass running red with his blood. His opponent had run off, leaving Peregrine with the blood. Alone with the blood.

He had tried to keep it from Henry's sister, his little wife, Gabrielle. Had tried so desperately to keep her from reading the papers, didn't allow friends to call. They had been orphans, she and Henry, and so very close to one another. He was the only family she had, and Peregrine hadn't known how to tell her that she was wrong. That Peregrine was her family too. But, he'd never been good with people that were well. Never had the words, and still didn't. And so when Gabrielle learned of Henry's death, dear Henry, she had given up. Hardly eating, barely sleeping, only weeping and crying. And Peregrine had allowed it. He had let her continue because he had no idea how to comfort her. Blamed himself for Henry, blamed himself for her pain. And when the baby came, a month later, he had killed her.

Waseya was still laboring over Crow, wiping the blood that came from his mouth, and speaking to Crow in languages Peregrine did not know, in words he would never understand. Peregrine, Coralie and her mother obeyed Waseya's every command, fetching and carrying and bandaging and stitching, applying pressure and blankets and then removing both when told to. Peregrine could imagine the small woman fighting the same fight the day that Coralie was born. Struggling against the evil as one would an fast approaching army. The same sweat, the same intrepidness, the same attitude of battle. She was the chief, the general…and if there truly was a spirit of the island, Peregrine could not see how it would not cower before this tiny warrior.

Peregrine found himself taking over from the woman as her eyes grew farther away, as if her efforts were stealing some of her life force from her. His hands became her hands, as she directed him, or pointed to an area of flesh that she judged to be hurt. He realized that a piece of the arrowhead was still inside Crow, and if it was inside the lung, the man was already dead.

His ring, taken off while he cleaned his hands earlier, caught his eye on the washstand. Peregrine knew then, that all was lost. It did not gleam, nor did it shine with the healthiness of lifeblood. It was dull and dead. The man on the table knew it too. Waseya shook her head and retreated into a chair in the corner, her physical presence diminishing like a snuffed candle, and she folded into herself. Cora, too, nodded, and took Peregrine's hand leading him to the corner, leaving only

Coralie with Crow.

The scene before him was private and Peregrine knew he should not watch, but he could not keep his eyes from it. Coralie did not wail or whimper, but she took Crow's hand and kissed it, and leaned down to his mouth so that he might speak to her. Though he was ashamed and angry with himself for listening, Peregrine found that he was straining every fiber of his being to hear. Some terrible part of him was possessed with the need to know every word. Despite all of his straining, he heard only the words, "Go. Do not bind yourself. Go."

There was an intake of breath, that same horrible creaking, crackling from his lungs, and silence.

He looked up to see Coralie closing Crow's eyes tenderly, tears running unchecked down her face. She bent to kiss him, once, on the mouth, and then swept his chestnut hair from his forehead, and walked toward the corner of the room, where everyone waited.

She nodded at her mother and at Waseya, who walked past her to the body, which they both began to pray over. Cora in a mix of Latin and English prayer, psalms in both languages that seemed more beautiful to Peregrine's ears when mixed. And Waseya began a low chant, almost a whisper, so that Cora's prayers seemed like song to the rhythm of her own strange words. Coralie and Peregrine were left together, in the corner. Coralie, silenced by grief, and Peregrine silenced by failure.

He looked over to find her eyes on him, and realizing his last words to her, he felt an even greater desire to explain and confess. But her eyes trapped him, kept him silent, until finally she spoke.

"Sometimes, the path of souls is the straightest way a man might tread."

"Some are too good for the land of the living" Peregrine replied, unsure why he said it, except to hope that it would ease her grief.

She nodded, and began to walk toward her mother, but turned her head briefly and whispered, "Yes, and some are too wicked."

:26:
Sarah

News blows quickly over a small island. The wind whips it from one house to the next, from cabin to shack on the beach, down chimneys and through the cracks under doors. From tavern to hearth, around tree trunks and down trails. The wind doesn't always whisper the truth, though. Or, some folks do not always hear it correctly, as the words twist and garble as they rush from mouth to ear.

So it was that the knock came at the door, the insistent desperate knock that brought Mason and Sarah from bed so early in the morning.

The world was still streaked with the dark grey of night, fading away into the frozen silvery dawn. The coldest time of day, when it is not quite sunrise, and the night is still shuffling on slow feet from the sky, the sun not quite ready to awaken from slumber and begin the new day.

Sarah heard the knock first. Sometimes she thought it was because she never really slept anymore. Perhaps she was not really fully alive anymore. Hovering, like that same dawn, in a space between life and death. She heard the knocking, but she did not wake Mason, even when the knocks grew louder and more frantic. Anyone coming round at such an early hour to the house of the mayor cannot have good news. It is only tragedy that would bring a man from his bed at that hour.

Mason finally slipped back into the present from his dreams, smiling at Sarah before realizing that something was amiss. She watched him pull on his trousers, quickly, motioning for her to stay in bed, which she did not do. If he would move so rapidly into the day and the terrors that lay outside their bedroom door—he would do it with her by his side.

His hand was in his pocket, worrying at his handkerchief, trying to keep himself from patting his pockets thrice, or wiping his brow in three spots. She knew he was constantly vigilant over his eccentricities —and usually unsuccessful. He reached for the door, Sarah at his heels, and exhaled, patted her on the back tenderly—three times—and then opened up to the news of the day.

On the other side of the door, was a man from Cross Shipping, Josiah Watkins. She recognized him, a shifty man. It was rumored he beat his wife and his children. It was said his dog wasn't safe from him when he'd been in the drink. He was looked down upon on the island. He had never been promoted at Cross Shipping, as M. Jean-Luc didn't advance men but for service and merit, of which Mr. Watkins was known to have neither. And though at the moment his face was filled with emotion, Sarah felt he was concealing something. She had seen his face around town for some years and believed she should know it better than she did now. She was struck at the time by the effect his visage had on her, how discordant it rang with the morning, but she couldn't reason out the why of it.

He was breathing hard, and his speech was nonsensical. Sarah found herself leaning forward to watch his lips as they moved, not understanding, or perhaps not wanting to understand what he was saying.

"Dead. Boy's dead." He wheezed between gasps.

"Dead?" Mason replied, startled. "Another indian?

Dead? Good gracious, where will it end? Who is it that is killing my islanders? Uncivilized. And not civil."

"No." The man was staring at Mason, the expression on his face hiding his true thoughts. "No, not an indian. Jacques Delacroix. Dead of an arrow shot by one of the natives. Tribe's rebelling, mayor. The militia will have to be called in. Apparently the Delacroix's incited the whole thing."

Sarah pulled her head back, and knit her brows. Nonsense. If she had her voice she'd shout the word at the man. Absolute nonsense. The Delacroix family, inciting violence? Ridiculous. And then it hit her.

Jacques Delacroix, dead. The boy she'd swore she wouldn't let die.

She'd begged God. Begged the powers of heaven, and of fairytale, deities real and imagined, beings of legend and folklore to protect the boy who'd been bitten. Not him. It couldn't be. She wouldn't believe it. She'd only sent his father the envelope yesterday. She wondered what had happened, could it really have been an accident? Or was this retribution? Had Jean-Luc acted on the information she'd sent? Had Jacques somehow been caught in it all?

Mason was asking Josiah some questions about the riot, questions Josiah didn't know the answers to— though it seemed he concealed this by making them up when it suited him. Sarah grabbed Mason's hand, trying to communicate that Josiah was not being honest. Mason squeezed back three times. He knew.

He left Josiah Watkins at the door, and pulled Sarah

back to the bedroom, whispering all the way down the narrow hall.

"Something is afoot, my girl. Mark my words, there is something afoot, indeed. I smell a rat. A bigger rat than even that raggedy Josiah Watkins, if you can believe there is one. Of course you can, you always were the brains of this partnership, weren't you Sarah my dear? Yes, you always have been. My better half you know. Even without your voice you're wiser than I am. Most wise."

He kissed her on top of her head, and looked into her eyes.

"Don't you cry, darling girl. Just a goose of a girl, you always were, you look just precisely how you did the night we met. I always think so, you know. I'm sure you do know. But, ahh, no, please stop up those tears, I can't bear it. I haven't any left, you know. Of course you know, so wise."

He kissed her again, and she couldn't help but smile at his foolish speeches and silly words. He was a strange man, but she loved him very much. He always had known her mind and knew when her smiles were for show. Mason pulled on his coat and put on his spectacles, folding his arms around his belly, before toddling off to see about the calamities on his island. At the doorway he looked back and blew her a kiss, just as if they were 16 all over again, and the world wasn't falling apart around them.

She waited until his footsteps could no longer be heard on the path to allow the tears to fall silently down her face, though no wailing could break from her chest. She had no more sorrowful sounds left within her body.

Hours passed. At first she did not mark the time. Moments had a way of standing still and then rushing forward with a jolt, and so Sarah thought of time differently than she once did. Mary, their cook showed up at her expected time in the afternoon, if she'd heard the bad news she did not discuss it with Sarah. People often didn't, thinking her too strange or too frail to hear tales of the misfortunes of others.

But it was the arrival of Mary that pulled Sarah her determined state of melancholy. Rose had not come.

Rose, who was thick with child. Rose who would not confess whom the father had been. Rose...who had been sent to deliver the envelope to M. Delacroix the day before.

Rose, who might have only thought of one M. Delacroix, the handsome boy who was her own age, and mistakenly delivered the envelope to his hands.

And for the second time that summer, the barren throat of Sarah Stephens filled with sound. The scream was a release, like the turn of a key in a lock. She followed her feet into the wood, without thinking of destination, following the sound of her own fears, the vibrations of her heart breaking.

She prayed she was not too late.

:27:

Raven

A few steps out of the door of Peregrine's surgery she was met with the soothing turquoise-blue glow that could only come from Jacques. But it had no power to calm her emotions. It was still night—but barely, and the moon hid in sorrow behind the clouds. The day was creeping in on slow feet, and Raven hid in the shadows, not wanting to be seen.

She walked in the other direction from his coming steps. She did so without speaking, she willed herself silent and she was certain she was almost invisible. To speak to anyone, even one who would give her solace, was unbearable. Raven could think only of being alone.

It was not yet time for weeping and wailing, though she knew that time would come. It was the confusion and anger that turned in her gut like a screw. He had died for nothing. Accomplishing nothing, besides making her family a modicum safer. Which should count—did count. But not enough to give his life for.

It was the rage that twisted her, the fury in realizing that it was what he wanted. In her heart, she wondered if that was what his life was about. Finding something to die for. To throw himself off the cliff of life, in order to give himself meaning.

She walked farther and farther into the woods, but the more she tried to hide herself into the darkness of the retreating night, the lighter the skies became. First the cloudy grey of dawn, and then the first brave strokes of rose colored sun streaking across the heavens. She was weeping now, but she wasn't sure why. Raven did not feel sadness, but instead broken. Aimless. Had it been love? Did it matter?

The tears fell intermittently, like sudden summer rain, and the nature of the unexpected proof of her inner turmoil made her more angry. Why had he deceived her in the first place? Why did he come at all?

But Raven knew, because had she been a man, she might have done the same. He, like her, had no place. Did not really belong anywhere. Although his was a divide of self because of the divide of his cultures, hers was a split based only on a feeling. A melody that called to her from distant shores, begging her to take her place. Sights that called to her eyes to be seen and sounds to be heard. Memories that were not yet made, but whistled to her nonetheless, calling her to her future.

Henri Crow had not been a member of a tribe, nor a man held to a place by blood and industry. He had not the devotion of a priest, nor was he called to family life. His existence had made sense to her, a man wandering. She understood because she would have gladly wandered alongside of him.

But something pulled on her heart. Something tugged it down into her stomach so that she felt that she might open her mouth and expel her own heart from her body. It was now that she *knew* the torment of his soul and the desires of his mind. But she did not share his passions or his mission. She never would. She believed in other things. In helping with her hands and with her skills. In lending aid to any individual that needed it. Her's was not a life spent in ideas and concepts, in justice or hope. But instead, her life had been about love. And giving the love away to others by watching their hearts, seeing the color of their characters, and by giving whatever words of succor or assistance that she could. She was the daughter of Cora Delacroix, and could not abandon the power of her gifts, even if she did not use them in the service of the manitou of the island.

Raven had made her way to Sugar Loaf, and was now crying in earnest. She wept for the kisses that she and Henri Crow had exchanged, the feelings of passion she had for the idea of the man whom she had shared tender moments with. She wept knowing that those beautiful, too-short moments were gone forever. Her heart ached to know that he would never grow old, would never see his purpose through, would never accomplish his missions. Raven shed her tears for a man she hadn't had the time to fully understand, and for the knowledge that no one else would ever truly know what had been between them. The burden of her sorrow for this lost love would haunt her always.

Or, she hoped it would. Because she could not yet let go of the darkness of him, darkness that had become a beacon to her eyes.

A rustling of last year's leaves that stubbornly refused to bury themselves into the dirt of the forest floor caught her attention. Someone was watching her. Raven wiped her eyes on the hem of her dress and pulled all of her heavy hair over her shoulder. She didn't much care what she looked like, but she didn't want to be found weeping like a scolded child. To give away the depth of her pain was to give away part of herself.

Looking around, she searched the trees bordering the clearing looking for a familiar light or color that would give away her pursuer's identity. She knew it was not a ghost, for the only sounds a ghost made were those they wanted someone to hear, and this person was clearly trying to remain hidden.

"Who is there? I can hear you…" Before she finished she found the spot, almost hidden in the morning sunshine. There was a spot that was brighter than the others in the early shadows of the trees. A spot of sunlight that reminded her of her father's story of Askook, and how he had been a man beloved by the sun.

"Peregrine…I can see you." Her voice was low, and she was not as angry that he was spying on her as she thought she would be.

He stepped out from the tree he had been standing behind, his face red under his copper hair. He was studying her face and her body, but not in a way that made her uncomfortable, but in a way that she knew was natural for him. He looked at her with his physician's eyes, searching for her reaction and looking for symptoms, though they both knew there was no cure for what was afflicting her besides time. Which made the wound in her heart rip all the further.

"I'm frightfully sorry, Coralie. I was concerned about you." His voice was even quieter than hers had been. He shuffled closer to her, and then sat down a few yards away on a rock. Peregrine no longer looked at her, but instead was intently studying the rocks and pine-needles beneath his leather soles.

"I hardly knew him." She found the words escaping

from her mouth before she thought of speaking them.

"It hardly matters, I think. Hearts need less time than minds do." He replied, still looking down. They sat in silence for some time, though Coralie did not know if it was minutes or an hour. She heard the song of a robin and the chirp of some chickadees, and the sorrowful call of the whippoorwill. No other step traversed this spot on the path, and Raven began to wonder about her mother, father and Jacques. Were they worried about her? She guessed that they would be, but she had not the energy to return yet. Before she could think further, Peregrine's quiet voice crept into her thoughts.

"You probably want to be alone, and if that is so, I will leave you. I came into the woods this morning to seek you out, because after my wife's death, I too, wanted only to be alone. And then I was alone for so long, that I forgot what it was to be in the company of others. I forgot what it was to find joy in sharing my gifts in the service of those who required them. I became guarded over my private thoughts, and isolated myself from all who cared for me. And worst of all, I blinded myself to the beauty that was left in the world. And to the opportunities for happiness that still exist for me, even though this is still difficult to imagine."

He grew silent, and Raven wished that he would continue. She did not feel that he was seeking sympathy or that he was intruding, but instead she saw a fellow sufferer. He did not say he was sorry for her, and he did not pry into her pain. His voice was low though, and his accent was just lilting enough to sound the tiniest bit like a melody. It lulled her like the sway of the trees in the wind, and covered the rawest part of her heart's wound like a bandage. He exhaled and continued.

"I told you that I had murdered my wife, and I will believe so until my dying day. You say that you hardly knew Henri Crow, well, I did not know Gabrielle Ffoulkes at all. I had loved her since I was a boy. I had placed her on the highest shelf, like my mother did her best china, and like my mother, I put her behind the glass of that cabinet and locked it in place. I never wondered what her passions were, or if she had any. I never discussed my work with her, I doubt that she would have wanted to know anything about it. I loved her like one loves the sun. Something warm and bright and far away. Do you understand?"

Coralie nodded her head, though neither of them were looking at the other. She had a picture in her mind of a china doll, delicate and painted and perfect, and then in the same moment, realized how easily such a doll would shatter.

"We married young, and I thought I could never be happier. But I know now that I knew no joy. Instead, I thought of nothing but of protecting her, and allowing her to stay a girl forever. The housekeeper managed the home, I handled the finances, and Gabrielle had friends to tea and went shopping in town or spent months away at country houses being petted and cooed over. My own fault, you see. I didn't want to know her. I wanted only the idea of her. The promise of her beauty and her innocence. But when she became pregnant after being away at one of these country parties, I knew it wasn't my child that she carried. I knew. And she? She batted her eyes and cooed right back at me. Teasing me and cajoling me, those perfect blue eyes and that shining golden hair, and I gave in. The illusion was broken. She wasn't an angel, she was my wife. She was my wife that I never bothered to know, that I never really looked at, and so someone else had."

Raven sensed that he was weeping now, but silently. She could just detect the sunlight that surrounded him growing dimmer. He straightened his back and continued.

"It was her brother that had finally challenged her seducer. 'For her honor', he had said. It should have been me, but I couldn't bear it. I didn't want to challenge him, because if I did, then everyone would know. Everyone would see what a pathetic wastrel I was. To challenge him was to admit that it had happened. And so Henry met him on that meadow in the morning. And Henry died by the man's hand. And Gabrielle, when she finally found out, went into labor —too soon. Too soon. And..." He offered Coralie a very small smile, "...there was no Waseya there to bargain with the spirits. And I...I...I was an imbecile. I didn't call the midwife at all. But instead chose to deliver the babe myself. Thinking ridiculous thoughts. Thoughts in the vein of....a midwife would come and see from the darkness of the hair or the color of the eyes that it was not mine. That I would have to face the fruit of my wife's adultery, confront my own shame in the presence of a woman whom I did not know. And so I delivered myself. But, it was too soon. Too soon."

Coralie was staring at him now, watching his anguish bubble like a boiling pot, about to run over into madness. She listened, but she did not speak, but she saw now what holding sorrow in did to a person, and knew that she could not live with a ghost in her heart all of her days. It would kill her.

"The baby, a little girl, red and twisted, never inhaled a breath of life in this world. She was born with her face distorted into a wail, a cry that never rang out. And my delicate doll wife, broke then into a million little pieces. Her eyes became glass and her rosebud mouth grew even rosier with blood. In death she became porcelain, a painted imitation of the warmth of life. My hands, my surgeon's hands had ripped the life from her with my own arrogance, my own shame. I let my fear of judgement kill her. Though, if I am being honest, the love between us was as dead as the child I pulled from her womb. It had never really lived. I didn't know her at all."

He did not speak again for some time. Raven did not either. She was caught up in the traps that people lay for one another. Expectations that cannot be lived up to, love that only exists in the mind and ideas about duty and destiny and every other force that preys on a body. Even if she reminded him of how often women died in childbed, especially women who had received a shock, women who were small in stature, this would not ease his mind. Just as if he were to remind her that men who seek out confrontation, that use their body and their lives as an instrument of causes greater than themselves, these men are willingly entering into danger. These men are willing to die for their beliefs. Knowing that Henri died in the midst of one of his own missions did not make her mind easier. There is no reason in grief.

The sun climbed higher in the sky, and still they sat.

And though they both were silent, Coralie felt a shift inside herself. She was on the edge of something. And then he spoke again.

"I have recently found a way to wash my sins away, even if it is only temporary. As you said to me in your speech the other night, *I am of use here.* I have helped. My hands, though sometimes the sight of them and the memory of the horrors they have committed and the deaths they have been unable to prevent makes me ill, these hands are skilled. These hands, *my* careful surgeon's hands have done much good. I have lived in England and here on this island, and no matter where I sail to, or where my feet take me, my hands know their purpose. It is my gift, and my calling. And I have decided to use it."

For the first time since he had begun speaking, Raven spoke in return.

"What will you do?"

"I will leave." He spoke the words simply but she felt as if a nail had pierced her side.

"Leave?" She asked, her voice a bit more shrill than she would have expected.

"Yes. I will spend summers here, when the tribes come. And then I will travel around Michigan, learning what I can from healers like Waseya, and consulting with medical minds in Detroit and maybe as far down as Cincinnati. There is so much I could do with these hands. So much good."

He turned shining eyes on her, and it was this, this moment that brought down the cascades of her tears. His overwhelming belief in his own redemption, and the hope he had of realizing a destiny of his own making. A surge of hope filled Raven. She brimmed with a chaos of sorrow and ambition and possibilities for transcending the present into something so beautiful her mind couldn't even conjure it. She wished she could leap into his dream and live there, could see the future through Peregrine's eyes.

"I wish I could go with you…" She said, her eyes turned toward the water and the places that lay beyond.

He opened his mouth to speak, but Jacques burst into the clearing and promptly, collapsed.

:28:
Jacques

It had all begun when he was certain he'd seen a phantom in the dark. Just a fluttering of breath and the smoothest rustle of fabric in the early morning, the darkness still so thick that it formed a cloak around him. He would not have been surprised to find that it was a ghost, after all, anywhere his mother was, his uncle seemed to find her. But this presence was alive, it just hadn't wanted to be seen.

Stepping into the surgery door, he almost ran into Peregrine, who appeared to be hurrying out. The young doctor looked pale, and the room behind him seemed indecently quiet. Peregrine clasped Jacques by the shoulder and squeezed, and then walked past him out the door, shutting it softly, following whomever Jacques had seen earlier, no doubt.

He stepped into the little space, and his eyes could not believe the tableau before him. His mother and Waseya were washing a man's body while his father spoke quietly. It could not be Coralie on the table, for the figure was much too large to be his sister. Because he could not see whose body it was, he took a step closer.

It was to be his last step, for this next sight brought him to his knees. The broad chest, the athletic frame, they belonged to Henri Crow. The man who had saved him, who had only yesterday sat in Jacques' office, making plans for a future that he would never see. Jacques wept, unashamedly, reaching toward Crow, arms outstretched unable to think for some moments, only feel. Sorrow, deep and painful, tore through him. Until, a word formed in his throat and traveled up and out of his mouth, "Why?" he asked the room. "Who has done this?" he begged, a little louder, before crashing into sobs anew.

His mother turned around, and instead of motioning for Jacques to stand up, she kneeled beside him, and put her arms around his shoulders.

"Shhh, shhh, my boy. He is gone…"

"*Oui*, and you will tell me it is to a better place, no doubt." Jacques replied, his voice sounding petulant to his own ears.

Hearing this, his father paused in whatever poem he had been reciting over the body to look sadly at his son. "*Non*, I am certain your mother would say no such thing. Not a better place, but perhaps, a different one, *mon fils?* I do not know what that place is like, or what the path after this one is, but I am confident that M. Henri Crow will find greater peace there than he felt in this life."

Jacques saw that Henri's death had deeply affected his father and mother also. He sighed, and searched for a stronger voice to ask again, "How did this come to pass? Why?"

Pulling him close, his mother quietly whispered the story of Crow's death, told how he had died bravely, and with honor in an attempt to prevent violence. Jacques could not keep the tears from sliding down his cheeks, nor did he wish to stay their progress.

Waseya was singing now, a Menominee song for the dead, but Jacques did not know what the words meant.

"He was Huron." He said quietly.

Waseya nodded, still singing, washing his body tenderly as if he were own child, which was how she treated any who came near to her hearth.

"You speak the truth. He was truly the grandson of White Arrow, though they shared no blood, their hearts beat as one. Both men lived to suffer for their people, both of their bodies breaking for it."

No one spoke, because there was nothing to say. The loss was too fresh. No one had known him well—in many ways he was still a mystery, and now would remain so. Jacques did not know this man that Waseya spoke of that she called Crow's grandfather, but if she spoke with such reverence, Jacques knew he was someone worthy of great respect. Like Crow.

There is much to do when preparing a body for burial, and Waseya and Jacques' mother spoke in low tones about whether he should be buried as a white man or an indian.

"He was a man of faith", said Cora, "I had heard him speak many times of his strong belief and reliance on the Christian God. He had been raised in a seminary."

"Yes, he was dressed in the trappings of the white man, but in his heart he was Huron. His blood was the blood of his people, and it was for them that he gave his life. His mission was for them." Waseya insisted.

Jacques spoke then, before the words could fully form into his mind.

"He was both. Give his heart to the tribes, give his body to the Christian church. He was divided in life, and should remain so in death, it is the only way he will rest in peace. His grandfather will come soon, he said near the end of summer, which is now upon us. We can give the heart to him and tell him of Crow's bravery."

"This is wisdom." Waseya said, and continued singing.

The women were busy, and Jacques was reminded of the news he had for his father, news that now seemed hollow in the circumstances. But nevertheless, the treachery had lain undisclosed for far too long. Even if Jacques did not yet fully understand how the crimes were committed, or who the man's confederates on the island were, the truth he had discovered could not be delayed. It was time the men responsible for the deaths of the indians, the thefts of Delacroix money, and now, the incident that led to Henri Crow's death, were unmasked.

Jacques asked his father to step outside, his voice so low that Jean-Luc did not hear him at first. Slowly he stood up, unfolding himself from the chair, his knees and elbows issuing forth a series of pops and cracks that sounded like wood in a fire. They stepped out of the close confines of the cabin and into the air of the pinewood forest surrounding them.

"What is it, *mon fils?* Your heart is heavy I am sure."
"Yes, Papa. But, there is more. So much more that I do not have the words."

"Do your best." His father's face had grown lined

and for a moment, Jacques had a glimpse of his own face, speaking to his future child when he was his father's age. The child that Rose carried in her belly would one day come to Jacques the way he was speaking to his father now. He hoped that he would meet the conversation with as much calm and openness as his father.

"I have spoken to you before, Papa, about Cross Shipping. You remember what I told you about the ledgers and the accounts?"

His father's face was even more confused, but he nodded his head, his chin cocked to the side.

"*Oui*, you have said they will not balance and that the story within the numbers is not the true one."

"Yes, exactly. I believe that I now know why."

His father's eyes grew wide, and he placed an arm around Jacques, pulling him in more confidentially.

Jacques began, "Cross has never been for sale, but there are those who have offered to buy her, and her ships and her accounts. When that did not work, they offered to pay to requisition and refashion the ships for their own use. But you did not like these offers, or the man that made them. *Maman* said he was a demon surrounded by disaster and Raven said she could not see his soul at all, and doubted he had one."

"M. Wells." Jean-Luc said, his hand coming up to cover his mouth. "*Merde.*" Jacques could just hear under his father's breath.

"Yes, Mr. George Wells, who would like to ravage our isle for her lumber. Who could easily do so if he could buy us out."

"Merde!" Jean-Luc's face had grown tight and his hands had balled into fists. Jacques could see his father shaking, could feel the rage within him surge, the flames of it fanning higher and higher.

"A murderer…but how?"

Jacques' own angry expression grew puzzled, and he extended the envelope and the letter within to his father, so that he might read for himself the information that had been sent to him. He was on the verge of explaining whom had sent the epistle, when Mayor Stephens arrived, and swooned.

Jacques cried out, bringing his mother and Waseya running from the cabin. The man who had arrived with the mayor stared, kept staring at Jacques. He was a Cross Shipping man, though he was only still given the work because Jean-Luc pitied the man's family. He stayed employed on sufferance, and he did not look pleased to see Jacques now. The look the man gave him made Jacques feel cold, as if the man was looking at him and seeing a ghost.

Waseya patted the mayor's belly, and sat him up gently, his white hair a match for the puffy clouds in the morning sky above them.

"Gave me a fright. Never one to believe in the beyond, you understand. I love the Lord and his good book as much as the next man, but I don't put much credence towards spooks and spirits. But I thought I saw…I thought…" He looked toward Jacques again and his face grew pale, his eyes rolling back into his head. Waseya promptly slapped him, which brought his eyes back to Jacques.

"My goodness. Gracious. Are you alive then? It's been a mistake? Thank the Lord."

Jean-Luc extended a hand toward the mayor, pulling him up. "My son, Jacques, is unharmed, Mason. But, another man, Henri Crow, has been felled with an arrow. He was a stranger to our shores, but a great friend and protector of the tribes."

Mason stood, shakily, and reached up to scratch his head, uncertainly. "Josiah, here, he came to the house this morning, he said…" The mayor had been motioning over to the place Josiah Watkins had been standing, only to find him disappeared. The man had slithered away upon finding it was not Jacques who was dead.

Jacques stepped toward the mayor, "Sir, I think you should see this letter I received from your wife yesterday, perhaps everything will be more clear."

Mayor Stephens sputtered, "My wife? Why would she? What in the world?"

Jean-Luc passed over the envelope and letter to Mason, and dipping his chin to his chest, he read the writing he knew so well.

M. Delacroix,

I am sorry to write you so mysteriously, but I hope you will not misunderstand my intentions. I have reason to believe that one of my husband's business associates is a nefarious man, and that he means harm to your family.

I have not acquainted my husband with these suspicions yet, because they are colleagues, and I confess I am concerned he would think my worries unfounded, or motivated by personal concerns. You may think the same.

The man known to you as George Wells has supped in my

household and has been a frequent guest over the course of his business dealings with my husband. Mason is the type of man that tries to see the goodness in all men, though, I am unsure what he could see that was not darkness in the heart of George Wells.

One night, before our maid left for the night, I saw him making unwanted advances toward her. I am not a prim woman, M. Delacroix, and I am acquainted with the act of flattery and flirting, and no young lady has ever been safe from a man sloppy in his cups. This was not the case. I fear what would have happened if I had not walked into the room and given my maid means of escape.

As you well know, I have no voice. I cannot speak for myself. But I can be silent no longer. I have observed this man's deeds in a myriad of ways, but he revealed himself to be the rogue and murderer I had feared on his last visit. He spoke these words,

"Mayor Idiot is terrified. But Delacroix won't budge. How many more of these redskin chugs you reckon we should kill until Delacroix turns coward too?"

I tore my mind in two trying to find a different way to interpret those words. To find a mistake in my own mind. But I cannot. I know what I heard. If that is not an admission of guilt, I do not know what else it could be.

I hope you are convinced by the written word of a mute woman. And once you have formed your opinions, I beg that you relate the information within to my husband. I hope the good men of Mackinac can expose and punish the wickedness of Mr. Wells.

Sarah Stevens

"Oh, my wise girl. My beautiful, wonderful woman. I've never deserved you. There can be no doubt of what she says. No doubt at all." Mayor Stevens was overcome. He looked around at the group around him, daring them to disagree. When no one did, he exhaled forming his mouth into an O, as if he gather his breath and blow all the evil from the island.

Jacques was relieved that the news had been so easily accepted, though they were no closer to understanding how Mr. Wells had effected these events. He had worked out the means of his treachery, but not how he had turned honest men against his father. Even as his mind whirred, his eyes kept traveling back to the door of the surgery. Back inside, to the table where Crow's cold body lay, now clean and prepared, but Dr. Rast, would still need to remove his heart.

So many things were happening at once, so many secrets bursting open. He knew his duty was now to assisting Mayor Stevens and his father. He was ashamed to find that he suddenly did not feel ready to take on this conversation of what was to be done with George Wells. Where was his place in this?

The questions in his mind were soon answered by the appearance of Sarah Stevens, who had silently appeared at her husband's elbow. She was an unusual woman, almost a ghost herself. She was now breathing hard from exertion, but no sound escaped her, as if she were a player acting out weariness on a stage.

She was tugging on her husband's sleeve and mouthing words, her face filled with desperation. He began by thanking her, trying to explain that he had seen her letter, but she seemed to have forgotten writing it at all. Mayor Stevens shook his head, and the rest of the party assembled grew quiet, unsure how to to help, or how to determine the content of her message. Mason shook his head again, and drew his face closer to her lips, not comprehending the message his wife was silently shouting.

Jacques watched, carefully, almost floating out of himself, as everything fell away. The morning sun, the cheerful chirping of the birds who did not know they should be silent on this day, and he *saw*. He really saw Sarah Stevens, and realized how hidden away she truly was. Jacques had always been gifted at reading faces, seeing the desires and thoughts there that others did not. To him, it had always seemed as though the words they held back were spoken aloud, and that anyone could hear them, if they only knew how to listen.

And her words were so clear now, now that he focused, that her screams of terror blared in his ears.

"Rose?!" He said, running up and grabbing her hand from Mayor Stevens' arm. "Take me to her!" She gestured at the door, indicating she needed a doctor, but Jacques shook his head, and ran. She pointed to a place, a place he knew too well. He knew where Rose was, exactly where he had searched for her as often as he was able since their stolen night, hoping to steal another with her.

They were running together now, and Jacques was surprised to see how quickly the older woman moved. She ran as if death was behind her, and perhaps it was, chasing her, following her to Rose.

"I will fetch the doctor, and meet you there." She nodded her head and squeezed his hand, before splitting off to find Rose.

It's too soon, Jacques thought. Too soon. Too early for birth, like me, like Coralie. There will be three souls born too soon on this island and the baby will be tainted and weak like me.

He hardened his features at the thought. No child of his was tainted. No child of his would be marred or broken, or too soon— not to his eyes. This child was perfect no matter its abilities. His feet followed some strange rhythm he didn't know, didn't hear, only followed, knowing it took him to Peregrine somehow.

He burst in upon the clearing near Sugar Loaf, and catching sight of his sister and Peregrine, his lungs gave out and he collapsed.

:29:
Peregrine

He hadn't thought of leaving the island until the moment Raven asked of his plans. The sound of her voice and the stillness of the wood, crystallized the decision in his mind. He knew he had to work toward a future the moment he realized he hoped for something.

And that something was the love of this girl, sitting on a rock, her heart twisted with grief for a man he could not save.

She had spoken the words, though. Beautiful words that sounded like poetry and added a spoonful of hope to him. Hope that she might grow to admire him, maybe love him. See him the way he was finally seeing her, though he had been blind for so long.

I wish that I could go with you, she had said.

And now Jacques, fallen in a heap near where they had been sitting. Peregrine had leapt to his feet upon seeing him, and was even now feeling for his pulse. He laid him on his back so that his lungs might slow from the speed his legs had been carrying him.

A few seconds later, his eyes opened, and Coralie exhaled with relief. She cradled his head, and gripped his hand tightly in her own.

Jacques' eyes fluttered open, and determination took over his features. He forced himself to sitting, over the protestations of both Peregrine and Coralie.

"Peace, Jacques! You are not well." Coralie could not disguise the fear from her voice.

"I haven't time. We haven't time. Peregrine you are needed!"

Peregrine took the boy's hand and held it, "Jack, my friend, Crow is dead. I am sorry, there is nothing more I can do..." But the sentiments were abruptly curtailed. Jacques waved a hand in a motion of frustration.

"I already know. I have been to the surgery myself this morning. This is about Rose, she is giving birth, in the forest. Come now! There is no time!"

Peregrine felt all the blood leave his face. He looked down to the little garnet on his baby finger, and the brilliance of the red glistened in the sunlight. There was a lump of fear in his throat too thick to swallow. Not again. Jacques was pulling on his arm, but he was frozen to the spot.

"Come on, Perry! We must go now!" Jacques' eyes were frantic, the green within the same green of the forest around them, and suddenly all the color hurt. The red of the stone, the green of the trees, the limestone seemed too bright.

And then her hand slipped into his, and he looked up. All he could see was the darkness of her hair and of her presence, and something in that blackness was calming. Like falling asleep or jumping into a deep pool of water. She was pulling him up, from the spot he had been crouched in, pulling him up for air, pulling him back into himself. And they were running. Peregrine did not ask where, and instead only followed, his mind considering what could be done. His thoughts running over what had gone wrong before, what could go wrong now.

"How far along is she?" He called to Jacques.

The younger man turned his head around to answer, "She is near her time, but not quite. It happened 8 months ago."

Coralie slowed, "How do you know this?" She demanded, her voice raw.

"Because it is my child!" Jacques shouted back.

Peregrine watched as she slowed even more, and he called to her, "Go back to the surgery, bring Waseya and fresh water. Also bandages and wrappings. Hurry!"

He wasn't quite lost in the part of his mind where only surgery lived. He hadn't escaped there quite yet. He knew how deeply confused she was to hear that the child was her brother's. And so he sent her off to be useful, something Peregrine understood. When thinking itself is a kind of torture, it is better to keep the mind and the hands occupied until one has time to reason.

But soon, following Jacques, he considered the size of the unborn infant. The mother, Rose O'Malley, he had seen in the market with Sarah Stevens over the past months. He had noticed her condition but had not wondered if she had a husband or if she appeared ashamed of it. Truth be told, Peregrine had really not thought about anything besides himself and his troubles. He was certain that everyone had known she was with child, and perhaps had assumed because of her status on the island that the father could have been any sailor or villager that showed her affection. It didn't matter though, not now, not to Peregrine. His duty was to deliver the baby, alive.

He would be more confident of success when Waseya was near. She was a proper midwife, having a lot of experience delivering babies, especially delivering those that came too soon. Peregrine was no midwife, child birthing was normally a woman's business. But today, it was his.

He had no medicine to dull the girl's agonizing pain, and he knew 1 in 8 women died in childbirth, a statistic he had read in a medical journal before he left England. A statistic that was all too real for Peregrine.

He also knew from a lecture he'd attended that in the last few months of pregnancy anything could go wrong. Women have less energy, and they are susceptible to all manner of diseases. During childbirth itself, they can fall victim to childbed fever, or hemorrhaging like Gabrielle. With all of the calamities that could befall a woman giving birth, it was a wonder that they agreed to do so at all, and also a marvel when both mother and child emerged from the experience healthy and glowing.

Screams cut that air, and Peregrine knew they had found the spot. Sarah Stevens was holding onto the girl as if she were drowning, and the sounds escaping Rose's mouth were so harrowing that Peregrine could not believe her lungs had not collapsed. Jacques sank to his knees, and Peregrine noted that his breath was ragged, but his eyes were bright as his hand sought out Rose's white knuckles.

"How long?" He asked Sarah, knowing the response would be silent. She mouthed something to him, thrusting her throat forward as if greater effort would set her words free. Jacques peeled his eyes from Rose and looked at Sarah, watching her lips before reporting to Peregrine.

"Sarah says she thinks she has been in labor for some time. Maybe a few hours." Jacques paused. "Oh God, *Mon Dieu!* It must have begun just before dawn, right after I glimpsed her this morning." His face was agony, and he looked at Rose, who was whimpering and wailing, her strength failing her. "Is this why you stayed away? Is this why you avoided me? Why? Why? I would have done anything. Everything. Why?"

Peregrine was feeling for her pulse, and together with Sarah was pulling the girl up, forcing her to walk, hoping the movement would bring the baby out of the already flagging mother. But as soon as they had settled her onto her feet, she crumpled, and Peregrine caught her, laying her back on the forest floor. Peregrine took off his linen shirt, uncaring about the indecency, and instructed Jacques to rip it into strips. Jacques removed his coat and placed it carefully under her head, though Rose barely seemed to notice the act such was her torture. The pleasing fleshiness of her hips and bust belied the smallness of her frame, and Peregrine paled, thinking there was no way this baby would not kill her. Or if it did not, it would tear her apart. She was too small, it was too soon.

Sarah had spread her shawl underneath the girl, and the screams had subsided, the scene had become too silent. Once again the sunlight glanced off the trees, but this time the ring did not flash with fiery red. He could hear the birdsong and the trees in the wind. Where was Coralie? Where was the water and bandages?

The thought disappeared from his mind when Coralie crested the hill, with her father and mother behind her. They were carrying supplies, water, linen bandages and herbs. Cora ran to the girl and began pressing some type of ointment to her womb, and forced an elixir to her lips. To Peregrine, she said only, "for the pain". Their eyes exchanged a silent message of understanding. This was a bad birth, the blood had begun, and so far it had only continued, without a baby to be born. Day passed into night, and lantern light gave an eerie and terrifying glow to the scene. They talked of moving her, but Peregrine said it would do more harm than good.

They worked together now, massaging, pushing, kneading, encouraging. Rose would fall back, her eyes closed, face too ghastly grey, and then someone would shake her back up, scold her. As though the sheer force of their collected wills could produce the baby. And it did.

A little girl, a head full of black curls so like Cora's that she began weeping at the sight, finally slipped from Rose's womb, and into Peregrine's waiting hands. The moment her first lusty cry filled the moonlit forest, Jacques' own wail matched it. Rose lay dead on the pine-needled floor, her strawberry hair swirling around her like a halo. The grey had faded back to her normal glowing pink and white complexion, so that she looked as though she slept. Jacques laid his head on her breast, the tears coming strong and fast. The final push had loosed too much blood. And so with her death, she had given her daughter life.

Waseya cleaned the little girl, and handed her back to Peregrine. Creamy skin and hair like midnight, she was a bonny baby, Peregrine thought, as he placed her in Jacques' arms, he handed her over.

"This little beauty needs her father." He said simply, and Jacques reached for her, the tears still flowing, though now from both loss and joy.

"Father?" Cora and Jean-Luc said together, and then peering into the little face, they wept again, to see the truth of it.

"She is perfect." Jacques said, and looked at Peregrine for confirmation.

"A trifle small, but yes, she is perfect." Peregrine smiled and edged closer to Coralie, whose face was a strange mix of happiness and woe.

"But...she did not want the baby." She whispered. Before Peregrine could answer, Sarah Stevens pulled a dirty envelope from her dress, and extended it toward Jacques. Who was still holding Rose's cold hand, the baby in his lap.

Sorrow was etched on Sarah's face, and Peregrine guessed that losing Rose was another of a string of tragedies that had plagued this good woman's life. She had written on the outer envelope, but indicated there was a different message inside. Coralie held the lantern aloft, and squinting his eyes, Jacques looked to the outer flap, which read:

I believe that the letters were mixed up yesterday. Rose left this on my desk, and delivered the letter meant for your father to you. I have read the words within. Forgive me, I did not know they were private.

Jacques nodded, and holding his daughter in one arm, he opened the envelope and took out the dusty page. He cleared his throat and read aloud. It might have been private, but all who were gathered in the clearing were tired of secrets.

Jacques,
I am writing you this letter to explain myself. I stayed away

from you at first because my feelings afeared me so. And I knew a fine man like you would not be allowed to court me proper. And then when I knew that I carried a babe in my belly, I put myself further from you.

I must confess. For a time, for a long time, I was uncertain if it were yours. You see, a man used to come and stay at the Stevens'. And though Mrs. Sarah did try to protect me, he was poison. He found me and did violence to me.

I wanted the baby to be yours, but I weren't sure. So I asked your mother and your sister to rid my belly of it, both of them not knowing that you could be the father. They both refused me.

I see now that they were right. I think my time is coming soon, and although I have no proof, I believe that the child within me is your own, and I am heartily glad that I did not destroy it. I will not force you to love this baby, nor can I make you claim her —nor me. But if you want to be a father, you are welcome in our lives, no matter what the gossips say of me.

Your Rose.

Jacques cried and kissed his little daughter's head, walking her over to show her to his mother and father, to Waseya who offered her a blessing in her native tongue and then to Sarah, whose eyes filled fresh, but only with love.

A low voice near Peregrine spoke, and he realized that he had been holding Coralie's hand all the while, the coolness of her palms and the heat of his creating a comfort and harmony of togetherness that felt natural to him.

"What will you call her?" Coralie asked.

Jacques looked about him, and then tilted his head looking at the little girl in his arms. He came back next to Rose's body and looked down on her fondly, tears coming afresh, before he answered.

"Cordelia, for her grandmother and aunt. Rosalie

for her mother, and Saragrine, for her godparents."

Waseya harrumphed, but then smiled.

"A good name" Jean-Luc began, "if a little odd. Now, help me with her poor *Maman.*"

The group bent over Rose's form, Waseya cleaning the blood from the girl and covering her chastely. Peregrine and Jean-Luc agreed to carry her to the church. Such a mixture of grief and gladness, rejoicing and torment. Someone would smile one moment, and shed tears the next, the whole way through the forest, to the church, but not another word was spoken. It was not until they laid Rose's body out and had also sent for Henri Crow's that they roused Father Santelli from his midnight devotions at St. Anne's. A few hours later, as it dawned on another morning, he dispatched Mason Stevens to find the women of the town to prepare both bodies for burial.

From the moment they left the church, Peregrine had not let go of Coralie, beneath her palm his fingers had traced the arrow shaped scar on her arm, and the mark gave him comfort. They all had such scars, and hers at least, pointed toward her heart. And although there was no promise of anything to be found in that hand or in that scar, it still held hope.

Hope was what he was living for now.

:30:
Sarah

After three days of tragedies, one right after the other, time began to move a little slower around the island.

Yes, three days. Isn't that how sadness always moves? In triples, three shots to the heart, and if one is still moving forward, one survives.

For Mason, it ushered in a new period of his life as mayor. Sarah wouldn't say he was not still ridiculous, he was. But his odd mannerisms were more a means of momentum, a way of pushing him from one responsibility to the next. His head was held higher, his speech more sure. She had always seen the best in him, and now that best was realized.

The days grew shorter in length as autumn rolled in and Sarah found that she was no longer a mere observer, as she had been before. She was visited almost daily by Jacques and his little Cordelia, and Mason had asked her to write a letter to the governor of Michigan, sharing her account of what she had heard. He had bundled her letter along with testimony from Josiah Watkins that there had existed a conspiracy against Cross Shipping. A conspiracy to allow Mr. George Wells to run the Delacroix family out of town, by any means necessary. The arrow that killed Henri Crow was meant for Jacques, as one of the indians in Mr. Wells' employ had mistook the white man who spoke their language to be the son of the owner of Cross Shipping. A young man who was known to speak many tongues. A small coincidence, Sarah thought, but one that had impacted the whole island. It was not better that Crow had died, and Jacques had lived, no man should die for such a thing. But, it meant that Cordelia had not been born an orphan. A fact for which Sarah gave thanks to God, whom she still was not certain she believed in, but was beginning to see his mysteries.

It had not mattered, in the end, that Mason had sent such evidences to the governor. It would take many days by lake to reach him. The day after the dispatch had been sent, word arrived that George Wells had been found dead, killed by a fellow timber baron that he had been plotting against. And then all silent tongues began speaking—save Sarah's.

At dusk, one day, a lanky indian named Ogima knocked on Sarah Stevens' door, and asked to speak with her husband. It seemed that a Chief named Grey Wolf had orchestrated the murder of the three indians at the behest of Mr. Wells. Mason had asked the young man a few more questions, speaking to him kindly, but sternly, and listening to his broken English replies.

A few soldiers from the fort were sent to Grey Wolf's lodge, but he was gone, disappeared into the straits. If he was half as intelligent as he was evil, Sarah knew he would never return to Mackinac.

Finally, the officials came from downstate, and Mason was closeted in his office with them for many day. They discussed the government, the events of the summer, and the industries on the island. Sometimes Jean-Luc Delacroix would meet with them, being the largest business owner on Mackinac. And while the men discussed these things, the island swelled. Every day more tribes and families came to Mackinac, the

Great Turtle, as she was called, in readiness to collect the payments from the government.

As the wife of the mayor, Sarah would sit beside Mason as payments were divvied among families and individuals according to their tribe. Three days before these payments were made, she headed to Mr. Nicholas Rast's shop to procure a new hat. She wanted Mason to be proud to have such a wife. But when she arrived, she found it closed. Mr. Rast was such a kind man, an excellent and jovial salesman, Sarah could not imagine why he should close up shop just as the natives were arriving. This was the high season for Mackinac merchants, the tribes would spend much of their coin before they climbed back into their canoes. Most of the money never left Mackinac.

The old Sarah would have silently shuffled back home. But she was concerned. There had been so much death already, she still could not hear a girl's laughter without thinking perhaps it was Rose.

She followed her feet to the Rast house, which showed nothing from the outside, but a kind of buzzing energy seemed to hum from the place anyway. She knocked, and the door was opened, revealing a small red-haired girl, the image of her father.

"Mrs. Stevens, can I help you?"

Sarah very slowly mouthed, "Papa" at the girl, who smiled and brought Sarah into the parlor, which looked empty. A few moments later, Isabel Rast came sailing in, grabbing Sarah's hand in friendship and directed her toward a chair.

"Mrs. Stevens, I am guessing you went by Nicholas'

shop and found it closed?"

Sarah nodded, glad that her errand was understood.

"Do not fret. Everyone here is well. Mostly well. Our good nephew, Peregrine, Dr. Rast you know, has been reading over his medical texts, and thinks perhaps it is wise for us to move to a warmer climate. And so, Nicholas and I, and the girls of course, are going to North Carolina to stay with some relatives on his mother's side."

She was smiling, but Sarah could see the stress beneath the surface of her straining lips.

"Yes, I can see you are not easily fooled. It will be a great trial, but a much greater trial to lose my dear Nicholas. Perry has not promised us anything, but we have every reason to believe he will improve. It will be an adventure, if nothing else."

Now her smile was genuine, and Sarah returned it. She made a motion indicating she knew the household was busy. But, standing up, realized she had one more question.

She carefully mouthed, "Shop", and Isabel, thinking for a moment, nodded in understanding.

"Yes, the shop! We are looking to sell of course, including the materials. A few other merchants have expressed interest, but Nicholas will only sell to someone who will leave it as a Tailor's, Dressmaker's and Haberdashery." She paused, "As for the house, Nicholas has given it over to Peregrine. He says, that it's a Rast house, and it should stay in the family."

Sarah nodded, she liked Peregrine, and hoped that the young doctor would stay. Even if his family left, Sarah thought she knew one reason he would be drawn to the island. One black-haired, unusual-eyed, good-hearted reason for the doctor to make Mackinac his home.

Isabel walked Sarah to the door, inquiring after her health and her husband's, accepting quick nods of her head as a reply.

She put one foot on the front stoop, and spun around, causing Isabel to take a step back in surprise. Sarah had made up her mind. She would have a new adventure too.

And for the third time that summer, she spoke.

"The shop....I'll buy it!"

:31:
Raven

When Henri Crow's grandfather arrived on the island, Jacques was there to greet him. Waseya had told them White Arrow was known as a great and wise chief, a great orator, well-loved by his people and feared by his enemies. Coralie at first did not understand the reason; he was not fierce nor intimidating, or even able to defend himself from an attack, for White Arrow had no use of his legs. They lay withered beneath him, and he was carried lovingly by strong men in his tribe.

Coralie saw it was a fierceness of spirit, a strength of mind. No one could meet him and doubt his status as chief.

This was another gift Crow had given to Jacques. Meeting a man, a chief, known to be weak in body, and yet revered for his strength of mind.

Many who had known Crow remarked on the resemblance between them, though, it was whispered they did not share blood. Coralie did not see it. Instead, she saw Crow reflected back in his mother, a small, quiet woman who walked straight-backed and carried herself like a queen. This woman who was curious, who had a smile for every child and was clearly devoted to White Arrow. It was this resemblance, that kept her heart from healing in those last weeks of summer. She tried to appear cheerful and kind during the daylight hours, but each night she would crumple at her bedside, surrendering to despair. Grief and tears weighed down her body like an anchor, and she might have been little Cordelia, a newborn, unable to speak or stand.

But then the morning would come, and some days, extra sunlight came pouring into the Delacroix house. Extra light in the form of Peregrine Rast.

He had every reason to come. Peregrine would check Jacques' leg, his lungs and heart, and then move on to baby Cordelia, who was thriving on the milk of her wet-nurse, Tilda. Uncle Nicholas and his family had left for the Carolinas on the last boat bound east, and she smiled, knowing that Peregrine had saved him too. He was alone in the Rast house now, and so it made perfect sense that he came so often to the Delacroix house for breakfast, for dinners and to sit on the porch and read Shakespeare aloud with her father. Peregrine was an Oxford man, and her father and he would discuss literature for hours. They would debate the talents poets and playwrights until it could only be settled by Jean-Luc taking down his fiddle to play.

Yes, he had every reason to come, but Coralie knew when her eyes met his, over dinner or as they sat around Cordelia's cradle, Jacques' beaming face between them, that he came for her.

She found that she looked forward to his coming. She wished for it. The black swirls around her had lightened too, she was trailed now by wisps of smoke and sparks, as though she were walking through a candle that had only just been lit. He was handsome, and good, and everything she could want. But her heart was still torn.

She did not think it could shred any further until the day he announced to her family over dinner that he would be leaving for the season. Coralie was stunned, she did not believe he would still go, not with the house, and the bud of what was growing between them. Perhaps she had mistaken his kindness for something else. All at once, her head was bent over her mother's white fish, the steam mixing with the tears that were threatening to stream from her eyes. She could not imagine her days without him coming into the house, bringing the dawn with him, sunshine surrounding him. She would miss the way he spun the garnet ring on his finger when he was thinking, or the sound of his laugh on the porch when he spoke to her father.

She thought back to the day she had decided her life had become one of her father's Shakespearean plays, but could not now decide if it was a comedy or a tragedy. Would it end in a wedding? Or would it end in yet more death?

After dinner that night, she had taken pains to make certain she had a few moments alone on the porch in the twilight with Peregrine. His whole person seemed different. He had come to the island a folded up and broken man, his mind dark with pain and guilt. And now he was healing, soldered back into shape, stronger in all the places he had been torn. A light came from him that warmed her from fingertips to toes, and she found that she could not but smile when in his presence.

He was watching her, out of one eye as he whistled, a small smile pulling at the side of his lip, his quicksilver eyes flashing in the coming moonlight.

"You are leaving?" She whispered, not trusting her voice any louder.

He nodded, "Yes. As I told you I would. But I will return in the spring."

She considered for a moment, and bit her lip before speaking. "I would that I could go with you."

He grew very still, and he turned both eyes to look into hers, he studied her for a moment and sighed. "I would like that very much. It will be…painful to be away from you. But I cannot take you. A woman cannot travel with a man who is not her husband or her family."

"We are relations." She said, and a lightness swelled her chest.

"Only distantly, and not by blood. If I were to take you with me, to explore the forests and lakes of this place, it would be as my wife, and my companion…." He heard her gasp for breath, but continued on, "… But your heart is still full of another. I would not ask you to cast him aside so soon."

She sighed again, and willed the tears to stay in place. What he said was right, if she left the island now, neither of them would know if it was because she was running away from the memories of Crow, or if it was because she was ready to love Peregrine. She leaned forward and kissed his cheek, and saw silver tears in his eyes, tears that he did not wipe away.

"I will see you in the spring." She said, and it was more than a sentiment, it was a promise.

"I will write." Peregrine told her, his voice a shadow of a whisper.

That night, Coralie found herself crumpled up next to the bed again, so weighed down and drained by grief that she could not get into the bed. Tears fell like rain, without thought or sound. It wasn't until long past midnight, when she finally summoned the strength to pull herself onto the mattress, that she realized that all of the tears had been for Peregrine.

:32:

Philippe

Not every man who dies stays to haunt this island. Some, take their last step in the land of the living, and then their next footfall is on the path of souls. Some have completed whatever share of life they were called to, and upon death, move on into the land of the spirits.

We are very few, those that cannot choose the light. It blinds us, you see. When we die, we shout at the chaos, "It is too soon! I am leaving them behind! I must stay!" And the light dims around us, and we become observers of the living.

Time is meaningless. It ebbs and flows and moves about us, and we can only press a ghostly finger into a moment, and sometimes it will slow, allowing us to peer in.

Spirits come and go, when their purpose is fulfilled they step onto the path. But mine is not yet finished. I take no part in the tragedies of those whom I love, I can only give faint warnings or make them aware that I am still here, somewhere, with them when they have need of a presence.

The island itself has become a stranger to me. I do not recognize the changes, and they happen so quickly that it is frightening to me. The women look different, the speech and words, and the names of the tribes also come and go. The voyageurs do not dip their paddles into the water of the straits as they used to, only a brigade here and there still exists, and so I am diminished. The aspects of my life that gave solidity to my existence evaporate, vanish, into the sky and are buried in the soil of this island. Covered by the earth alongside my bones.

But my purpose is not yet fulfilled. For when my brother pierced my heart, he released me from the pain of an agonizing death. I had been betrayed by a man, a man that I do not even remember now. And he had tried to take my life, left me to watch myself bleed into the alley. And Jean-Luc, the kind. Jean-Luc the good, he found me. And even though I had taken everything he loved and thrown it aside, including Cora, he still gave me the gift of release—with tears in his eyes, and love in his heart.

And so I wait. I will wait for him and for Cora. I will wait until it is their time to walk the path of souls, and I will escort them to it, making sure neither of them put their foot to that path without love beside them. This is my purpose, and for this I will wait.

God willing, it is a long wait ahead of me.

Until then, I will gambol, and watch, and sing my songs.

"If you will come and dance with me, if you will come and dance with me,

A red kerchief I'll give to thee, a red kerchief I'll give to thee.

Come, my love, a dancing, so far into the night.
Our feet will trip so lightly! We'll forget that time's a flight.

EPILOGUE

Her eyes looked to the water. But for the first time, Coralie wasn't straining to look for the land on the other side, to see her way to the shore beyond the blue. Instead, she was searching for the sight of a ship, the *Starlight*, her father's favorite. The ship that carried the first passengers from the harbor in Detroit every spring.

The winter had been an exceptionally cold one. But only in temperature. Memories of Henri Crow would chill her, his mournful coal-black eyes appearing in her mind. But those moments were few, and she had little time for them. The house was warm and fuller than it ever had been, and little Cordelia was the delight of everyone's eyes, especially Jacques, who was a doting father.

It seemed that every day as the baby grew stronger, so too did Jacques. Her giggling laughter healed him, the sight of her fleshy baby-fat legs crawling across the floor, and the way her perfect green eyes followed him gave him purpose and strength. Cora and Jean-Luc would dandle her on their knees and coo at her, and she was so much sunshine that the family could almost forget it was winter.

But not Coralie.

Because it was so frigidly cold, the sleighs laden with mail from the mainland had no trouble flying over the icy lake. Every time they came, there was a letter— sometimes 3 or more— for Coralie.

His letters were friendly and conversational, written so that she could hear his accent and see his wonder.

She could picture all of the new procedures he described, and the treatments he learned from other doctors or native healers. Some he described sounded so ridiculous she laughed out loud, only to grow silent when she thought she could hear his laughter, faintly, as he had written the words.

Peregrine's letters conjured the man, and she would trace the whorls and swoops with her finger, feeling foolish. But also hoping somehow that he who had written them had put a little of himself into that writing. That by reading and feeling the words he was close to her again.

The feelings terrified her and made her stomach leap and clench, alternately. She hadn't been certain that she wanted him to return. Perhaps the paper man was more real to her than the flesh and blood one had been. Mayhap she was fooling herself. She surmised it would be easier to love someone for their thoughts and ideas than it is to love them to their face. And she wasn't sure that she should love anyone.

But she had hardly been able to sleep that night. Her father had come back from the office saying that the *Starlight* should arrive at the dock the next day, noon. At dawn she had jumped from the bed, and her feet found their way to Waseya, whom she had helped make corn cakes, and then she had listened to a story before she was shooed out into the brightness of day. Turtle had found her in the wood, and together they had walked to Sugar Loaf. Coralie had not been back since the day she had come to mourn for Crow. The night that Cordelia had been born in the moonlight. She supposed she was bidding a kind of farewell, though if it was to Henri

Crow or a different version of herself, she didn't know. Perhaps it didn't matter.

Then Beshkno, the little indian ghost, had appeared right back in the tree, hand extended toward the water, and grinned at her. This time she hadn't had to wonder what his message from beyond the grave was. He was coming. Peregrine was flying on swift falcon's wings to her.

Standing on the dock, she watched the *Starlight* glide gracefully into the harbor, and for some reason she was seized by the eerie feeling that this had all happened before.

She strained to catch a glimpse of him, her fingers worrying the fabric of her skirt so roughly she was afraid it would tear. The wind picked up, blowing her black hair over her eyes, so that it fell from its bun and blew around her face like a storm. She closed the green eye and looked only with the milky blue, trying to find the sunshine spot of light that would be Peregrine.

"Coralie!" An undignified voice shouted, and she found him, straining at the front of the ship as if he might pull the whole *Starlight* into the harbor by the force of his will alone.

Before the anchor had even been lowered, he leapt onto the dock, falling on all fours, before running to her, uncaring as to who was watching or what people might think.

Coralie flew, her hair trailing behind her like blackbirds, into Peregrine's arms. Never again would he leave the island without her by his side. Never again would they ever face the world alone.

"You're finally home." Coralie said as she wrapped

her arms even tighter around him, breathing him in, running small fingers through his blazing copper hair.

"I never really left…" He whispered, "…you've always had my heart, here, in Mackinac."

FURTHER READING & NOTES

It should be understood that the overwhelming majority of my characters are fictitious. They sprang, fully formed, from my own imagination, and any resemblance to actual historical humans is serendipitous. The exception to this rule is Father Santelli, who really was the Priest at the lovely church of St. Anne's on Mackinac, though, he is largely unimportant to the story.

The detachment from major historical events is deliberate. I find that the little people, for whom we usually do not have much in the way of historical records, are far more fascinating.

Finally, I wholeheartedly encourage anyone to visit Michigan. Lover's Leap, Sugar Loaf, Arch Rock, Devil's Kitchen, the Fort at Mackinac and cottages and houses dating from the period in this story still exist, as does the unparalleled beauty of the forests and the straits.

For my own research, (and for your own further reading) the following books provided the knowledge and inspiration, which led to the events and characters of the story.

Bibliography:

Gringhuis, Dirk. *Lore of the Great Turtle; Indian Legends of Mackinac Retold*. Mackinac Island, MI: Mackinac Island State Park Commission, 1970. Print.

Johnson, Ida Amanda. *The Michigan Fur Trade*. Lansing: Michigan Historical Commission, 1919. Print.

Massie, Larry B. *The Allure of Michigan's past*. Allegan Forest, MI: Priscilla, 2008. Print.

Porter, Phil, and Thomas Kachadurian. *Mackinac: An Island Famous in These Regions*. Mackinac Island, MI: Mackinac State Historic Parks, 1998.PrinWilliams, Meade C. Early Mackinac: A Sketch, Historical and Descriptive. St. Louis, MO: Buschart, 1901. Print.

ABOUT THE AUTHOR

ALEXANDRIA V. NOLAN was born and raised in Michigan's second motor city, Flint. She attended the University of Michigan, earning a Bachelor of Arts in English and History, with a specialization in Shakespearean Literature.

Alexandria is a frequent travel contributor to various online and print publications. She loves to read, travel, and read about traveling.

She reluctantly resides in Houston, Texas, with her extremely attractive husband and three unbelievably spoiled pets.

AlexandriaNolan.com